ROCK CON ROLL

Sage Ardman

Fame series #2

R.L. Ranch Press

Portola Valley, California

Books by Sage Ardman

The Westerley Series:

#1: *Executive Sweet*

#2: *I'll Get You My Pretty*

#3: *Seductive Synchronicity*

The Fame Series:

#1: *The Fiery Boys*

#2: *Rock Con Roll*

Rock Con Roll

Copyright © 2017, R.L. Ranch Press
A division of RuLabinsky Enterprises

Print ISBN: 978-09914205-44
EBook ISBN: 978-09914205-51

Book layout by: Steve Rubin
Cover art by: Diogo Landô

Disclaimer: This is a work of fiction. Any resemblance of characters to actual persons, living or dead, is purely coincidental.

Warning: This is an erotic story and should not be read to little children before bedtime.

Acknowledgments

This book was shaped significantly by Amy Lansky, my publisher, editor, collaborator, close friend, and so much more.

My other editor, Jena Roach, continues to push me to do better. She takes my unpolished ideas and makes them sparkle. Thanks also to Mark Manasse and Izaak Rubin who gave the book a final cleanup.

Diogo Landô did a great job on the cover art.

Finally, thanks to Gilda Garretón for helping me craft a Chilean hero.

Table of Contents

Rules for Con Artists

- Don't call attention to yourself.
- Before the con, study the mark.
- During the con, listen carefully and observe the mark.
- Never look bored, but don't appear too eager, either.
- Never let them see you sweat.
- Offer them something for nothing while actually giving them nothing for something.
- Never fall for the mark.

Rock Con Roll

One

Ugh, Los Angeles! The city held too many bad memories for me, and this police station threatened to become another disturbing experience. The police were not my friends when I was a kid, and I'd never completely gotten over that feeling. So even entering the building made me uncomfortable, and after wandering down narrow stairways and poorly lit hallways full of locked steel doors, I felt truly lost. Ironic, because I was looking for the lost-and-found department.

Most people wouldn't get so anxious about going to the lost and found. But I had a reason for being nervous: I was pretty sure I was about to commit a crime. Normally, there's no crime in making a claim. I should be able to go in there and ask for the big stuffed panda I lost in the park last week, without getting arrested. But since I'd just landed here in Los Angeles and hadn't been near that park in years, my claim was a lie.

But worse than the lie, I worried there was something unusual about that panda. This had to be more sinister than a missing plush toy, because the person who wanted me to make the claim was Bea Kirkland, my foster mother since age two, and an accomplished con artist. If Bea wanted me to do this, then it was no ordinary panda.

I hadn't returned to Los Angeles to see Bea. In fact, I'd left here seven years ago, because of her. When we were young, my brother, sister, and I were taught to cheat and steal. A fun thing to do, back then, but when the cruelty and danger of such a life became apparent, I had to get out. So I ran away to New York City—rather abruptly—and hid from my foster mother.

In New York, I made an honest life for myself and didn't do any cons. I thought—no, I *hoped*—that I'd never see Bea again. But she called me yesterday in a panic because my Uncle Carl had been arrested. He needed my help to save him from a long prison term, so I had to come back.

Carl meant the world to me—he had taught me to paint, which was my livelihood now. Of course, a skilled painter can also be a skilled forger, so Carl and I had done quite a bit of that, too. With him in jail, I was his only hope. He'd been caught with explosives, and unless he could furnish a proper federal license for it, he'd be in trouble. Bea also pointed out that Carl had been in the middle of another con when he got busted. Something about a lost panda. Which is why I was here, looking for the lost and found.

I finally located the department in an abandoned corner of the station. The small room was decorated in Modern American dungeon, with flickering fluorescent lights that gave the scuffed, off-white walls a subterranean pallor. On the other side of the room was a small window where I could make my claim. And between the door and the window was a single piece of furniture: a tired-looking bench with a sign over it proclaiming, "Wait Here." But there was nobody in the room—evidently not peak hour at the lost and found.

As I started to walk to the claim window, I felt a full-body shudder ripple through me, forcing me to a halt. My old phobia again: the dread of bad cons. A deep fear of the repercussions that happen when everything falls apart, when the game blows up, or as Bea would say, when the con curdles. I'd seen one go seriously bad when I was a kid, which filled me with dread and drove me to leave L.A. Now here it was again, reminding me that this was dangerous and just plain wrong. I shouldn't be here.

I needed a moment to process my fears, so I sat down on the bench, leaned back, and closed my eyes. To cover this awkward moment, I brought my phone up and pretended to be in a conversation. Then I let out my breath slowly and tried to relax.

In the dark silence, I noticed faint elevator music attempting to lighten the mood. It took a few seconds before I recognized an old Alejandro song. The juxtaposition of this upbeat, familiar rhythm with the austere little room almost made me laugh.

I shouldn't have been so surprised to hear Alejandro's music—the man was universally popular. His music topped charts all over the world, and he kept pumping out the hits, year after year. Besides writing songs, singing them, and playing guitar, he also happened to be the hottest man on the planet, with a stunning body and a face that melted my heart in every video of his I watched.

Yeah, I was a hard-core fan. I had all of his music and had been to as many of his concerts as I could. But I'd never heard this version of "My Year of Loving You." The song's pounding beat and jangling guitars had been re-recorded in a more mellow style, suitable for police use. I wondered if it was a Los Angeles thing.

After the song finished, I opened my eyes, ready to play my part in this little con game. Even small doses of Alejandro could cheer me up, so I walked to the claim window full of renewed enthusiasm. With any luck, I could get that panda just like a regular person would.

Although I hadn't done any trickery in years, I knew what to do. I'd pulled off plenty of more complicated cons. But I also reminded myself that anything could go wrong—I'd been taught that since I got out of diapers. So to make sure everything went smoothly, I made use of every trick I knew. I had dressed modestly, in skinny jeans, a cream knit top, and a gold blazer. I had pulled my baseball cap down low so the visor would hide my eyes from the surveillance cameras. The cap also covered my spiky bleached hair so I'd look more normal. I was ready to pretend.

On the other side of the window, a lonesome policeman sat at his desk. I went through the basic steps of preparing him to be my mark: making him smile and complimenting him so he'd feel superior. If he felt good about himself, he'd be less likely to challenge me.

I started with a sweet, shy smile—all girl-from-back-home innocence. The officer looked up at me and raised an appraising eyebrow. I'm decent looking, especially when I smile. My small nose and mouth aren't Hollywood quality, but I get no complaints. I caught the quick scan of his eyes as he took me in. His lip curled ever so slightly, and his eyes widened. Yes—his churning brain was telling him—I want to talk to her. A good start.

I then used a helpless-girl routine to make him more pliable. "Oh. Um. I'm looking for the lost and found. . ." An easy request, considering I was already there.

The officer was happy to assist. "You found it, babe. What'ja lose?" His crooked grin assured me that he was on my side and wouldn't be asking too many questions.

Next, I added a layer of sadness to my innocent and helpless act. Something to make it real and get me into the part. This might have been an excessive level of manipulation, but I needed to finish this job smoothly and get out of here. So I dredged up some unhappy memories to make the emotion real.

I thought about a hungry little five-year-old girl. Her foster mother was off somewhere, working a con and hadn't been seen in days. The only food in the house was a partial bag of potato chips and a nearly empty box of cereal. When that was gone, the girl went outside and climbed through a few garbage bins, returning with a stale loaf of bread and a half-full jar of mayonnaise. But that didn't last, either, so her older brother broke into mother's precious chocolate bars and handed them out. The little girl was worried. "Mother will be angry," she warned him, but he insisted it was okay. So she ate the chocolate, then hid under the covers of her bed, less hungry but more afraid of what would happen when mother returned.

Stop, stop! I had my sadness. Now I could tie it in with the role Bea wanted me to play. The missing panda had been my most treasured possession for years. I loved it and had been a wreck since I lost it. If I didn't find it here in the city's lost and found, I'd be devastated.

Interestingly, the lost panda story also made me sad, even though it was a lie. One quick dig of my nails into my palm, and the tears started to flow. I gave the officer a little sniffle and began my sorrowful tale.

"My panda! I lost it last week. Do you have it?" I curved my arms wide as if hugging a tree trunk. "It's big."

Now some people might ask why a full-grown woman was pining for a stuffed animal. But I figured I could still have a lovey, even at age 24. So what if it was a little immature? And if Officer Lost-And-Found asked about it, I had a story all worked out.

But he didn't care. "Yeah, we have it." He flashed a smile and started to type into his computer.

I knew he had the panda. It had been there for a week, ever since Carl and his grandson had brought in. But the officer's quick recollection of the panda made me pause. Either he knew about it because big stuffed pandas are hard to ignore—which would be good—or they'd discovered something unusual about it and were waiting for it to be claimed. And that would be bad, possibly prison-time bad.

I started to sweat from the con tension. Funny how this never happened to me when I was young. But there it was again, wrapped around my spine like a serpent. I remembered how the fear was worse when guns were involved, when the people I was conning were dangerous or powerful. When, for example, I was pulling a con in a building full of armed police.

I had to step carefully. If the officer gave any indication that he thought this was an unusual claim, I needed to leave. But for now, I continued to play my part. "That's wonderful!" I clasped my hands together with a relieved sigh. "But are you sure it's *my* panda?" If I got any bad signs about this, I'd simply say it wasn't mine.

"We have *someone's* panda. Could be yours. Let's see. . ." He consulted the screen. "When did you see it last?"

"Tuesday, in the park." I gave him the long story so I could watch him more closely and sense for trouble. "I know I shouldn't take it outside like that, but I'd just broken up with my boyfriend, so my sister suggested that we celebrate." I gave him a light laugh. "She never liked him."

I was cooking now, and the officer was following attentively, so I finished the story. "Anyway, she knows how much I love my panda, so she suggested that I bring it. We had a picnic lunch and took a walk. But when I got back, it was gone!" I rubbed my eye to wipe away another tear.

The officer let his gaze linger on me for a few seconds, then he turned to his screen and read the report. "Yeah, some kid and his grandpa brought it in. The kid took it, but gramps busted him and made him bring it here. I'll go get it."

That was a relief. My story fit with his, and he didn't ask any difficult questions. This meant that I'd soon have the panda and be on my way. I could relax.

Unfortunately, it wasn't over yet, and waiting gave me more time to worry. My palms got clammy, my breath grew short, and I had to swallow an involuntary cry that bubbled up from somewhere deep. I plainly wasn't suited to this kind of work anymore. Who ever heard of a con artist who was afraid to con?

Two minutes later, the officer came back with a big stuffed panda in his arms and set it on his desk. I waited a little longer, still gauging whether or not he knew that it was more than a toy. But all he did was mutter, "Recovered," click his computer, and hand me a form to fill out. I exhaled slowly and let my worries fade.

Naturally, when I filled out the form, I lied. I listed my name as "Daisy McTavish" and gave a fake address in Glendale. I even had a phony driver's license that supported this lie, if he asked for it. One of five fake licenses I'd had back in the day, all of them now expired. Yeah, I'd done some bad things when I was a kid, and I still seemed to be doing them. Just last night, while packing to come out here, I'd touched-up Daisy's license to make it current.

But my fake identity had one sliver of truth in it. One thing that was always true. My first name does start with the letter "D." I'm Dee Kirkland. And believe it or not, I was intentionally named Dee, a name that sounds like a single letter, so I could play con games more easily.

My foster mother, whose real name is Beatrix, thought it up when she was young, and she used it herself, shortening her name to Bea. She reasoned that if her real name sounded like a single letter, then she could choose any fake name that started with that letter when doing a con. As Bea, she could call herself Betty, Bonnie, or Barbara. Then, if she accidentally ran into someone who called her "Bea," she could explain it as a nickname, and the mark wouldn't suspect a thing. This wasn't a problem when we ran into other con artists, because we had signals we could give to tell them to stay away from our game. But Bea's naming concept gave us extra protection from our school friends and from other acquaintances who didn't know who we were.

So when we were brought into her care, Bea changed our names to sound like single letters. As Dee, I'd done cons as Darlene, Della, and Dominique. My younger sister, Elle, could do cons as Linda, Laurie, or LuAnn. And my older brother Jay could call himself John, Jason, or Jeff. No, we weren't your typical family.

I handed in the form and was given the huge stuffed animal. Relief washed over me when I finally got it to my car and drove off to see Bea. One more illegal act of forgery and Carl would be safe. Then I could stop this conning and go back to New York.

As I drove, I took a peek at the panda. The doll was pretty nice—I wished I'd had something like that when I was a kid. Maybe when this was over, Bea would let me keep it. If there was anything left of it, that is. You never knew with her.

Two

The mere sight of Bea's home sent a mix of emotions through me. This was the woman I'd lived with until I was seventeen, so I felt a brief sentimental twinge. But she was also the woman who'd raised me to be a thief and a con artist—to pick pockets and locks, plan elaborate stings, and forge everything from documents to famous paintings. So I felt shame, too. She always used us for her own gain, never seeming to care about anything else, so I felt anger as well. Missing panda, indeed! I couldn't wait to see what that was about.

The small house looked like all the others on this suburban street, east of Los Angeles. Bea made sure it was as good as the rest of them, never shabby but never too fancy, either. Her intention was to make sure the house didn't stand out in any way. "Hiding in plain sight," she liked to call it. The taupe and white trim matched the house next door and three others on the block. I remember once coming back home after a con and trying to enter a neighbor's house instead. That's how forgettable our home always was.

But I didn't forget anything today. I parked and quickly walked to the house, carrying a big black plastic bag with the panda inside. Whatever it was about that thing, Bea didn't want to draw any attention to it, so she insisted that I bag it once I'd claimed it. I walked around the side of the house and grabbed the key from its hiding place. Then I went to the back door and let myself in.

Bea and I didn't part on the best of terms, so I was on delicate footing here. I'm told she was incredibly angry when I left, which is why I hid from her. But she wasn't at all angry with me when she called yesterday, so perhaps seven years had wiped that slate clean. I hoped so, anyway.

If I could return to New York without having to hide anymore, life would certainly be better. All I needed to do was make peace with Bea. I didn't expect to become friends with her—that would be pushing things. But since I was here, I could try to understand her better and get a new perspective on my childhood. Was she really always on the lookout for a scam? Did she care about anyone but herself? I wanted to know whether these images I had of her were true. How bad was it, really? Because the scared girl who ran away from this home thought it was incredibly bad.

On the positive side, Bea seemed very concerned about Uncle Carl. And she obviously knew where I was in New York, but had left me alone until now. So perhaps she *had* changed. Or perhaps she was such a good con artist that she could even con me into doing something for her. I was about to find out.

The house was just as I remembered it, and the rush of nostalgia temporarily immobilized me. After a few seconds, I made my way to the kitchen to find Bea. Seeing her sitting at the table in the exact same place and posture as all those years ago sent an even stronger burst of nostalgia through me. It felt like I'd gone back in time.

Bea looked very much the way I remembered, her pinched face long and weathered. Her short blonde hair had more streaks of gray now, and I noticed a few more lines etched around her mouth. Other than that, she looked just the same.

I was amused to see her surrounded by bags of her favorite chocolate bars. Although the candy company currently made over a dozen different varieties, she used to buy only two of them, and a quick look at the bags on the table told me that she still did. Her favorite chocolate bar, Nuts to You, was loaded with almonds and covered with dark chocolate. But when she needed a change, perhaps something sweeter, she'd reach for a Low-Hanging Fruit bar. Personally, I hated them both because they reminded me of my life with her. A life where these treasured candies were given to us only when we pulled successful cons. When we picked a pocket or tricked someone. When we came home with cash.

Bea regarded the lawn bag with a half grin, then smacked her hand on the table. "About time you got here." She jumped to her feet and headed to the stairs. "Bring that along, and let's have a look."

Yep, that's about as warm as she ever got—no hug, no kiss, no mention of how I'd changed over the past seven years. I'd have gotten more love if I spent the night at the police station.

I chuckled sadly to myself over Bea's lack of warmth. Perhaps she truly was a harsh, conniving woman. At least she didn't offer me a candy bar for having scored the panda. I'm not sure I'd have been able to control my anger over that.

I stopped her halfway up the stairs and broke the silence. "Nice to see you again, *Beatrix*." I emphasized her real name to prod her, to get some sort of a conversation going beyond her joy over the panda. When we were kids, she'd get pretty annoyed if we ever used her full name, often smacking us in the mouth. As we got older and could defend ourselves, we used it when we were feeling brave and defiant. Right now, I was merely trying to tell her that I wasn't interested in picking up where we left off. I was here to help Uncle Carl, not her.

She turned to give me her most withering glower. "Don't you dare start with that again!"

"Whatever." I followed the rest of the way quietly. She clearly cared only for the panda, and by this point, I did, too. Forget about understanding her; just get me out of here.

The upstairs room had all the windows covered to keep out prying eyes, so she turned on the lights and closed the door. I handed her the lawn bag and she practically dove into it to retrieve the panda. With a big grin, she hugged it to her chest, squeezing it all over. "All right! Good work."

"What's the deal with this thing?"

She gave me her first real smile, and I could tell that it was more for the panda than for me. Nice to know where I stood here. She pulled out a chair and sat down, so I did the same.

"This. . ." She gestured to the panda. "Is one of my cleverest cons. I met a guy at a bar a few weeks ago, and he turned out to be a cop. Works inside the evidence room. We had a good time, and he told me all about his job. Even invited me to see his workplace. And guess what?" She paused, proudly building up to a big finish. "The lost-and-found department keeps their stuff in the evidence room!" She chuckled and gave me a wink, so very impressed with her cleverness.

"Wait a minute. I thought I was helping Uncle Carl. But now you're telling me that this is just another one of your cons."

"It *is* my con, but Carl is involved. I needed you to finish this up to keep things from getting any worse for him."

I was growing more and more suspicious over this. She could have asked anyone to claim the panda. Why me? I pushed away my annoyance and motioned with my hand for her to continue.

Bea nodded and let a huge grin spread across her face. "You see, nobody gets in or out of the evidence room with anything of value. Even my cop buddy and I had to be searched when we left. But I figured a way around that. Well. . ." She offered a modest grin. "I saw them do this on an episode of *Hustle*, but it's still a great idea." She stood up straight and pointed to the panda. "I carved a pouch inside it and had Carl and his grandson take it to the lost and found. Then, a few nights ago, I invited myself back to the guy's workplace. While we were sitting there in the evidence room, I slipped Ipecac into his coffee to make his gut churn. That sent him to the bathroom, which gave me a chance to wander the place and stuff the panda with juicy evidence." Her eyes sparkled as she concluded the con. "Then I had you claim it, and here it is." She waved her arms over the panda, like a magician conjuring the impossible.

Bea then proceeded to pull out a huge knife and run it up the panda's back, splitting it wide open. She held up the knife with a grin. "I've always wanted to do that." Yeah, I knew I wouldn't be able to keep that cuddly panda.

Still not finished with her carnage, she ripped the panda apart, flinging its contents across the table. I watched as sealed bags of cash tumbled onto the floor, along with two bags filled with something white. The woman was incorrigible. I reached down to retrieve the two white bags, and sure enough they were filled with powder. "Drugs? Are you serious? You never cared about that stuff."

"It's cocaine. I'm not snorting it, but you never know when shit like that will be useful. And check this out. . ."

She cut open the evidence bags and thumbed through the cash. "Looks like two hundred grand, at least." She tossed a bundle to me, probably ten thousand dollars. "That's your cut."

Furious rage swirled around in my head. She'd tricked me into playing a con game for her, and I began to doubt this had anything to do with Uncle Carl or my forging skills. At least I'd progressed to the point where I earned a cut of the take instead of a chocolate bar. That was good. But now I was back to being her con artist partner, and that was definitely bad. I had the sudden urge to slap some sense into her, which would take an awful lot of slapping.

"Is that all we are, after so many years? Partners in crime? I didn't fly across the country for a cut of this deal, and I don't happen to need any money right now." I tossed the cash back to her.

"I came to help Uncle Carl, Bea. But I figured that since I was here, we'd catch up, reconnect. Maybe even repair our old wounds. But you're acting like you don't even care." I blew out a breath. "Talk to me. What's been going on since I left? And what happened to Carl?"

Bea gave me a sheepish grin. "Nothing. He's fine."

I could feel my brow twisting into an angry knot. "He's not in jail?" I suspected I'd been dragged across the country on a lie, but I still couldn't believe it was all for this stupid panda. Something bigger was going on. "Why am I even here?"

She shrugged. "I also wanted to see you again. Reconnect, as you say. You left L.A. in an awful hurry."

"I was running away from you and from conning. So I'm certainly not here to start up again. I only did this panda swindle to help Uncle Carl."

"I understand, Dee." She gave me a sympathetic smile, but I knew all her facial expressions, so I didn't buy it. "I'm sorry about tricking you. And I *do* want to talk, just not today. I've got to get rid of this stuff and take it to my locker. Can you come by tomorrow evening? We can catch up then."

Something was definitely going on beneath the surface here. But I was willing to come back tomorrow and find out. Why not? I was already here, and Bea didn't seem too mad with me. Tomorrow we'd be able to talk and—hopefully— I'd get to know her better. Also, I had a small twinge of nostalgia for my old friends and my former haunts, so I didn't mind a day out here to wander around.

"Okay, see you tomorrow." Before leaving, I checked my watch and the contents of my purse to be sure she hadn't stolen anything. Some mother!

Three

Since I was back in Los Angeles, I decided to drive around my old neighborhood. Could any of my friends still be there? Would they be at the same places? I went out to find the remnants of my childhood.

I got into my rented brown sedan and cruised the streets. The car was painfully ugly, but it looked like every other car out there, so it accomplished Bea's cardinal rule of not drawing attention. As I drove, I called Elle. Unlike my manipulative foster mother who I'd avoided for years, I did keep in touch with my sister, the only remaining member of my family after Jay had died. She was still a con artist, running a crew of grifters up in Oregon. Of course, Elle never told Bea we were in touch—she knew I wanted to keep my whereabouts a secret.

Elle had left town a few years after I did, but unlike my departure, hers was an amicable separation. After the splash I'd made on my way out, Bea didn't want any more trouble, so she let Elle go without a fight. They even kept in touch with occasional phone calls.

I should have called my sister last night before I left, but everything had happened so quickly that I didn't think to do it. Now I regretted that oversight. Elle knew Bea much better than I did, and I needed some of her wisdom if I expected to make it through this visit. My foster mother certainly had something brewing.

Elle picked up quickly. "Hey, sis. What's up?"

"You're not going to believe this, but I'm back in L.A. Just saw Bea."

"What! Do you have a death wish? That woman still hates you for running off. God! No wonder we called you 'Dummy' when we were kids."

"Hey, Loser. . ." I threw back her childhood nickname, just for fun. Then I let out a long breath. "Actually, you may be right. She called me last night with some lie about Uncle Carl being in trouble, so I came out today. Even did a small job for her which I thought would help him. Anyway, I'm here now, and she's not screaming at me like I thought she would. In fact, she seems happy to see me."

Bea was happy to see me? As soon as I said that, I knew it was wrong. Even Elle laughed at my preposterous statement. Bea's happiness wasn't about me, it was about the panda. The only thing that ever made her happy was a successful con job. But it never lasted because the next job was always waiting.

Elle finished her laugh with a snort. "You did a job for her? I thought you got out of the game."

"I did, but she tricked me, told me it was for Uncle Carl. Anyway, that's over. I don't have to do any more cons. Now I'm just curious to reconnect after being gone for so long."

"Look, if it's family you want, forget her. Go find your birth parents."

Not that again! Elle found her birth parents years ago, when she left Los Angeles. I had yet to even feel the yearning. The way I saw it, they abandoned me, so I didn't have to parade myself in front of them for hugs and kisses. Elle and I even had a fight over this at one point, after which the subject of my birth parents was declared off-limits. "Hey," I protested. "I thought you agreed to stop bothering me about that."

"Yeah, but you're the one who's waxing nostalgic down there in L.A. I figured maybe you're ready again."

"Not even close. I don't care about my birth parents any more than they cared about me."

"You'd be surprised. All parents care about their children. My birth parents were too young and poor to raise me, but they were delighted when I found them. Let me tell you, it was amazing—gave me new perspective on the F.M."

I chuckled at her reference to our foster mother. "Hey, I'd love to get a new perspective on the F.M. To talk to her and ask her some questions. Try to understand her. The last thing I need is *three* parents to figure out."

"That's ridiculous. I'm sure your parents are interesting. They made you. Hell, *I'd* like to meet them." She sucked in a quick breath. "You know what? I'll make you a deal. You let me find them for you, and I'll never bother you about them again. I promise I won't even ask if you contacted them. But you *have* to let me find them for you. I'll get the hacker on my crew to do it. Okay?"

Silence filled the phone line for a few seconds. She was right about the nostalgia. Even though I should be getting on a plane and leaving here, I remained in town, looking for answers. Maybe I did need to meet my birth parents—one of these days. In a rare moment, I caved. "Okay."

"Excellent!" Elle whooped. "You'll thank me for it. And please get your ass out of L.A. as fast as possible. You and Bea in the same city? That worries me."

I laughed. "Don't worry. I'm nearly done with her. I'll go over again tomorrow, then that'll be enough. By the weekend, I'll be home. I'm curious to get to know her better, and she isn't screaming or yelling at me, so that's a good start."

Elle blew out a long groan. "Girl, you've been conned. That woman will never make peace with you. Trust me, she wants payback. Don't forget who Bea is."

"I know! But she sounded so desperate when she called me that I couldn't refuse. And now that I'm here and done with her tricks, I figure I can get to know her better. Get some closure."

"You want closure? Go meet your birth parents. And in the meantime, please watch your ass around the F.M." We said our goodbyes and I resolved to be careful when I went back to see Bea tomorrow. Then I got back on the road to continue the tour of my former neighborhood.

I rounded a corner and realized I was at the old pizza place. When we were teenagers, we spent many hours there. At the time, there were six of us in the crew: Bea's three foster kids, plus Hale, Scott, and Yuki, friends from school who also did con games. The old pizza place was our hangout.

The first time we went there was after a good day playing card tricks. Back then, Bea would search us when we got back from swindling, so whatever we had on us got confiscated. But since we'd scored some money that day, and Bea didn't know exactly how much, we could spend it before we got home, and she wouldn't notice. We couldn't buy things for ourselves because then she'd see the new items. But pizza worked perfectly. Soon we were meeting there all the time.

The old pizza place was a significant landmark on my tour of Los Angeles, so I parked and got out of my car. Still there and open for business, it looked smaller than I remembered it.

Years ago, we always sat at the booth in the back corner. The middle seat was the power seat because you had the best view of the table and anyone coming our way. Hale sat there because he was the oldest, although my brother Jay was only a month younger.

I always liked Hale. He and his friends were poor kids who went to school with us. We took it upon ourselves to teach them the tricks we'd learned at home, which they picked up quickly. Although they started as helpers in our cons, they soon ran their own games.

As much as my old grifting life made me sad, I still longed for the days when we would sit around and eat pizza. Those were good times, proud moments when a band of teenagers owned the world. I wondered if Hale or Scott or Yuki could still be there, if any of them would be around after so many years.

I stared at the pizza place for a while, then I walked up and down the street, taking in the area. Most of the buildings were the same, but I noticed that the gas station at the corner was boarded up. Business wasn't exactly booming.

The door to the pizza place opened, and a man stepped out who reminded me of Hale. He had the same gait that Hale used to have, but he had a more solid body, muscular and perhaps a bit taller. Could it be Hale Drummond, all grown up? If it was, then he looked pretty good.

As the man approached, I watched carefully, trying not to stare too hard. When he got closer, I could tell it was him —I saw that familiar face, aged seven years, with a hint of mature ruggedness. Good old Hale! I was amazed to see him still hanging out at the pizza place, and I wondered if he'd recognize me. I was older, too, and my hair, which used to be dyed brown and shoulder length, was now shorter, spikier, and bleached white, falling about my head unpredictably. He was going to have something to say about that.

Hale stopped at the sidewalk and paused to talk on his phone. I wanted to run up to him and say hello, but he seemed busy, so I waited. When he hung up and turned to walk my way, I smiled and started to speak.

Then I spotted it. Something was wrong—he wasn't looking at me.

In a flash, I understood what was going on: Hale hadn't recognized me. And worse, he was about to rob me—I knew it. The way he'd paused on the street with his back to me, pretending to be on the phone, was an obvious ploy that all of us had used. And the way I'd walked aimlessly up and down the street when I first got here loudly proclaimed that I was lost and confused. An easy mark. I found it strangely amusing that after seven years of clean living, my former friends were now targeting me.

I played along, looking away as he came closer. Then, as expected, he tripped when he came near me and fell against my side. One hand went to my shoulder, ostensibly to steady himself, but in reality to distract me from his other hand, which was now in my purse. I kept my eye on the correct hand and watched him remove my wallet. Now more steady, he pushed away from my shoulder and offered a mumbled apology for his clumsiness.

"It's quite all right," I assured him. Then I clamped my hands around his wrist and brought it up behind his back. He twisted away from me, his hand still holding my wallet. "Smooth move, Hale," I whispered in his ear.

He froze for a beat when I spoke his name, then continued his struggle to get free. But I held him tight while I retrieved my wallet and dropped it back in my purse. I also took the opportunity to relieve him of his wallet and wristwatch, just for old time's sake. Then I let him go, and he stumbled away.

Hale looked up at me, obviously trying to figure out where he'd gone wrong. Was I an undercover cop or just a savvy target who'd gotten the best of him? "Sorry, lady. I meant no harm."

I laughed. "Don't you remember me, Hale?" I stood there with a smile on my face, waiting for him to figure it out.

At the sound of my voice, his mask of fear and confusion slipped away, and a huge smile spread across his face. "Dee! I didn't recognize you. God, how you've changed!" He laughed and gave me a hug. "It's really great to see you. Come on in, let's talk."

The pizza shop was nearly deserted, even though it was dinner time. Other than Hale, there was just an older couple up front. We went to our booth, and he gave *me* the honor of sitting in the power seat. I dropped into it with a flourish.

He slid in next to me. "So, what brings you home?"

"I just came to see the old gang, especially Bea. But I've stopped grifting."

"Oh, yeah?" He grinned. "Then how come you took my watch?"

I laughed and gave it back to him. "I took more than that." I gave him his wallet, too.

He shook his head with an admiring smile. "You still have the touch, Dee. You were the best pickpocket of us all, and such a good artist that everyone came to you when they needed something forged. Hell," he chuckled. "You could copy an old masterpiece, down to the brushstrokes. Too bad you're out of the game."

"So where are the others? Scott, Yuki?"

"Believe it or not, they got hitched. Moved to Reno where they claim to be doing fabulously well, ripping off out-of-town rubes."

"And they left you all alone to pick pockets by yourself."

"Hey, I'm much more than that. After you blew out of town, I decided to go to school. Studied business so I could learn how to rip off the fat cats. Minored in computers, too, because you can't get far without that these days. Then, three years ago, I joined a long-con team. The short cons were getting boring—I was tired of proposition bets in bars and card tricks on the sidewalk. The long cons are much more elaborate and exciting. I'm the team's electronics guy —spy cameras, tracking devices, network hacks." He let a shy grin slide onto his face. "I only pick pockets when a mark begs for it, like you did, standing there on the street looking so confused."

He suddenly got excited and pulled out his phone. "Hey, never mind the con chat. Have you seen Alejandro's latest video?" He started to play it for me.

I'd seen that video, at least ten times already, even though it had just come out. Hale and I always kept up with Alejandro, years ago, playing his music on the jukebox at the pizza place and dancing with abandon. I was happy to see that he was still just as devoted.

Alejandro was irresistible. His muscular build made my heart pound, often long into the night. His black wavy hair framed piercing, slate-gray eyes, a dark shadow of a beard, and incredible lips with a little bow on top that I longed to kiss. And talk about talented! Where others had good and bad years, Alejandro's career continued to top music charts all the time—he was prolific. *No Moss* magazine had dubbed him "The Lord of Rock and Roll," and he still ruled.

Even my New York friends were huge fans. Wanda, my neighbor and business partner, bonded with me over his music as soon as we met. We went to every concert he gave, and we spent way too much time watching his videos.

Even my so-called boyfriend, Roman, had liked Alejandro at one point, although he never really loved the music, and now he claimed to hate it. In fact, Roman rarely loved anything or anyone, including me. A hipster, who worked in a coffee shop when he felt like it and refused to commit to anything, he shunned labels like "boyfriend." But since he didn't ask too many questions, he was perfect for a woman trying to hide from her foster mother in the thick of New York City.

I'd had other boyfriends who cared more. After I fled to New York, I dated a few others. They were decent lovers, but they kept getting serious about me, asking questions about my family and my life. I told one or two of them the truth, but that made them uncomfortable around me, as if they were afraid I'd steal their wallets. I tried the silent treatment with a few guys, refusing to talk about my past. Unfortunately, it made them feel shut out and hurt. I even tried lying to one man, making up a fictitious childhood, with aunts and uncles and cousins and such. But it was too much trouble to maintain a lie that big, with so many details. One evening, I slipped up on something, and he caught it. The lie was quickly exposed, and the relationship didn't last much longer.

So Roman's disinterest in my life made him perfect—he never asked me questions. And for the past five years, we made it work. He spent his time being critical of the world and suspicious of everything in it. The only things he cared about were his reefer, his unstylish hats, and his ever-changing facial hair. Way too cool for someone as popular as Alejandro, who he accused of selling out.

But I didn't care if Alejandro was popular. His lyrics were edgy, and his rocking techno beats were wonderfully danceable. I also loved that he played guitar and sang his songs with a smooth and seductive voice. In his shows, he'd expand each song and make it into an elaborate spectacle. The stage would be filled with backup musicians and dancers, lights and videos, but Alejandro always stood out, the center of attention. Whenever he came to New York City, I found a way to see him. And when we were kids, Elle, Jay, and the rest of us would sneak into every show we could.

His latest video was one of my favorites because the music was so exotic. In the video, a shirtless Alejandro danced on the streets of Los Angeles. The song was a delight to hear, and even more of a delight to watch. Ridiculously handsome, he was one of my guilty pleasures, so I indulged myself and let the video play to the end.

Hale stared at me for a few seconds after the video was over. "You've seen this already, haven't you?"

I nodded. "Lots of times."

"Don't tell me you still have a crush on him. Seriously, Dee, you need a man."

I laughed. "Got one. But he's no Alejandro." I smirked. "What about you?"

"Nah. Nothing at the moment." Hale's eyes suddenly zeroed in on me. "So what happened to you? One day we were eating pizza, and the next day you'd left town. Heard you live in New York now."

"I had to get out. After Jay got killed, I was numb, totally whacked. I didn't want to cheat anymore, and the fear made it hard to con. So I held it together for a while, then I had to split. Sorry I never got a chance to say goodbye, but you know how it is in this business."

"So you *are* still in the business."

"No. I told you. I'm straight now."

"Why don't I believe you?" He squinted at me for a second, then shrugged it off. "Anyway, how long are you around?"

"Not long." I shook my head. "Bea tricked me into coming back here, so I figured it was just her way of trying to reconnect. Unfortunately, I can already tell we're not going to be friends—hell, we never were. So I probably won't stay much past the weekend. Sorry."

"It's okay. I'm glad I got to see you again. Glad, too, that you've still got the touch."

We talked for a few more hours, then I drove off. Thank goodness I had a friend here in Los Angeles.

Four

I got a room in a local motel, because I didn't have anywhere else to go, and I'd rather chew broken glass than stay at Bea's place. Frankly, I just didn't trust her not to rob me in the middle of the night.

Interestingly, the motel I chose was the same one we'd used as a safe place, years ago. Bea and her fellow grifters had an arrangement with the owner to set one room aside, for emergencies. The motel was perfect because it was right in the middle of the neighborhood, walking distance from most of our homes and businesses. In Los Angeles, that was significant. Every one of us carried keys to the motel safe room back then. So it seemed like the perfect place for me to stay.

I woke up late and decided to visit another of my favorite places, the library. It brought back memories from long ago. The library was my second home, a place I could go to when I didn't want to go home or couldn't. I had my own little corner, way in the back, where I liked to read. The great thing about my corner was that it had a loose panel near the floor, which opened up to a small space under an adjoining stack. The space was dusty and dark, but safe. And when I brought in an inflatable mattress, a flashlight, and some blankets, I had a secret home away from home that was even secure against the library guards. So secure, in fact, that all of my items were still there, seven years later.

After visiting the library, I played tourist and did some things I'd never done in Los Angeles. Museums and coffee shops and just walking down streets—I found it all nicely relaxing. Not pressed for time, I had all day to fill before I'd see Bea again.

She was in a much better mood that second evening. I brought takeout Thai food, and we ate at the dining room table like some sort of normal family. But it wasn't until we were done with dinner and she unwrapped a Nuts to You bar that we really started to talk.

She exhaled slowly after the first bite. Chocolate truly was her drug of choice. Then she looked up at me and shook her head. "I was pretty pissed off when you ran away."

Good, we were talking. This was what I'd hoped to accomplish yesterday. "I'm sorry, but I couldn't help it. I had to get away. I was scared, and I couldn't do cons anymore— the tension was making me a wreck. Don't forget I saw Jay get killed. That changed everything."

"What?" She darkened. "You never got over that? Get real! People die all the time, especially in this business. Jay was unlucky. But you survived, which proves *you're* lucky. And it made you a better grifter."

As if I wanted to be a better grifter. She never understood that I'd grown to hate that life. Sure, when we were young, energetic, and misinformed, we stole with glee. It had been fun back then, especially when the cons went well. But once Jay was gone, none of it was fun anymore. Our lifestyle, combined with a terrible mistake on my part, killed my brother. I never really got over it.

"I learned to be more careful, but I also learned that I wanted to get out."

"So you robbed me? Ran off with all the money from that last con? That was pretty low—didn't I teach anything?"

"Oh, you mean honor among thieves?" I laughed. "I thought there wasn't any."

"Damn straight!" She grinned. "We take what we can get in this business. And you. . ." She regarded me with what seemed like pride. "You actually swindled me. I was impressed."

A compliment! From my own foster mother. She was smiling at me as if I'd just earned an entire bag of chocolate bars. Perhaps she was having a bad day yesterday, but my presence and the panda's bounty had somehow mellowed her out. In any case, this was turning out to be a pretty good visit, after all. I basked in the warmth of my foster mother's pride.

Until I felt the burn. Her smile hardened, and the shine disappeared from her eyes. "So, you're helping me with my next con." I guess this shouldn't have surprised me. My memories *were* correct: she never took any breaks between jobs. Here she was, ready to launch into the next one.

"Now look, *Beatrix*. . ." She flinched at the name, then glared harder. "I agreed to come here because I wanted to help Uncle Carl. Maybe even get to know you better. I didn't do it to help you with your panda swindle. And there's no way that I'm going to start conning again. I've got a legitimate business in New York, and I'm doing fine."

"Legitimate?" She coughed up a laugh. "You've got to be kidding. Your business is the biggest con ever. Painting cheap hunks of pottery and pretending they're art." She blew out another laugh from a twisted mouth. "I've been watching you, little girl, and it seems to me that you've become a bigger grifter than ever. So don't give me any crap about being too good to work with me. That's all about to change."

So she did know about me—I'd wondered about that. Bea wasn't easy to fool. And she didn't care at all about reconnecting with me. All that mattered was the con. Nothing had changed.

When Jay died, she told me that I had to get back in the game and prove that I could still do it. It was the only way I'd ever get over my fears. But without him around, everything was different. I did my part and gritted my teeth through the cons, but I kept my eye on a different goal: getting out.

Then, four years later, I saw my opportunity. Bea, Elle, and I did a con that netted a big pile of money. As usual, Bea was going to stash it all in her locker, but I beat her to it. I took it all and ran, sending some of it to Elle. I was done with Bea, done with my cheating life, and done with all the lies.

Flush with cash from that con, I moved to New York City and found a place in Chelsea where I hid out for months, waiting to be found. But nobody came looking, because I knew how to stay off the radar. The first thing I'd done when I got to New York was change my hair to make it short and white, a total reaction to the years spent hiding my looks to please Bea. Then I forged new documents for myself, and Dee Kirkland ceased to exist. Now I was Dee Frank, just another jobless kid on the streets of New York.

I became friends with the woman living across the hall from me: Wanda Petrillo, the hat-lady of Manhattan. Wanda had so many hats that she could have kept every New York City milliner in business.

So with Wanda and a few other friends, I made a new life for myself. We floated through the New York scene without ever looking forward or back. The present moment was all we cared about. My new family might not have been as together as some, but we were way better than a family of con artists.

Everything was going well until Wanda discovered I could paint. We went to one of those pottery places where you do your own painting, and I decided to do something fancy. Everyone else just got drunk and slopped on the paint. But I hadn't done any art in a while, so I had some fun and really put in the effort.

Wanda went nuts over it—she wouldn't stop telling me how impressed she was. She kept it up until I finally quieted her down by giving her the pot. Then, much to my dismay, she showed it around and got people to order more of my work, offering me an embarrassing amount of money for each one. And that was the beginning of my strange ride. Wanda made me into a New York art sensation before I could stop her.

So although I'd never thought of it that way, perhaps Bea was right: I had accidentally perpetrated my biggest con yet. I had managed to convince people to like my art, and I'd become moderately popular. Did that mean I was still a con artist? I hoped not.

In any case, I wasn't about to admit that Bea had a valid point. "You're just jealous because I found a legitimate way to support myself." The idea of earning an honest living was always a big joke when I was little. None of Bea's friends thought much of the idea. So I had to force myself not to smile—she needed to know I was serious.

As expected, she laughed at my way of life. "I'm not jealous of your stupid legitimacy. I'm jealous of your grifting skills. You've got to help me. Besides, you owe me for that last con."

"How about I pay you back and call it even?"

"That's no fun! I've got a great con planned, and you're going to help me do it."

I folded my arms. "No."

"No? Are you sure?" She stood up and leaned close to me, beady eyes drilling deep. "I heard that two bags of cocaine got taken from the police evidence room recently, and someone's fingerprints are all over them. If they suddenly turned up in your car or hotel room, what do you think the police would say?" A shadow of a smile crossed her face.

Her tiny smile punched a hole straight through me. I had picked up those bags of drugs from the floor yesterday and put them on the table. I'd wondered why she threw the contents of the panda so haphazardly all over the room, and now I understood. She was tricking me into touching the bags so she could blackmail me into the game again.

Stupid me—I *had* been conned, just as Elle said. I needed to be more careful. And that started right now. I'd come here to make peace, but Bea wanted war. So war it was. I returned her little smile. "I'm listening. . ."

Bea sat back in her chair. "We're going to con Alejandro. The man collects guitars like a fiend, and he's made of money. I've got a plan to get some of it."

She had to be kidding. She wanted me to con the most famous, talented, and sexy musician ever? A man whose love songs helped conceive an entire generation? Wrong! I would never con him. Besides, even if I tried, I couldn't pull it off. I doubted I could even be in the same room with Alejandro without becoming incoherent.

I shook my head. "Oh no, no, no." Just thinking about the mega hot rocker made me weak. How would I react when faced with his long black hair and luminous gray eyes? What if he took off his shirt, like in his videos where his chest gleams with sweat as he makes love to the camera? Oh my God, the mere mention of his name was getting me excited. There was no way I could possibly con this man.

But Bea disagreed. "Oh yes, yes, yes. You don't have any choice, my dear."

"But," I stammered. "Why me? You could play this game with anyone else! Why pick someone who's a huge fan of his music, hasn't conned anyone in years, and hates doing it?"

She drew in a long hissing breath. "Because even though you hate it, you're good at it. And you owe me. So suck it up and do what I tell you."

Damn. I should have known I'd never fully escape my former life. Now I was being forced to swindle Alejandro, no doubt a mortal sin. I knew I'd never be able to forgive myself for what I was about to do.

I took a deep breath and settled back, waiting for Bea to unveil her plan. In the meantime, my brain quietly churned at top speed, hoping to find a way out of this mess.

Bea got comfortable and started to explain. "Since Alejandro collects rare guitars, we're going to sell him one. I understand he owns over fifty already."

I groaned. "So that's where Uncle Carl fits into this." Carl and his wife, Franny, were old grifting friends of Bea's. They owned a music shop where other con artists liked to gather. When I was young, Elle, Jay, and I spent hours in the shop while Carl and Franny planned cons with Bea and all of the other grifters.

Carl spent much of his time in the music shop's back room, where he did instrument repairs and built custom guitars. Known for his beautiful work and detailed craftsmanship, the man could talk endlessly about musical instruments. He lived for his guitars, his art, and his con games. So I knew that the con would involve selling one of Carl's fake guitars to Alejandro.

Bea grinned at me. "See? We make a good team. You already know my plan. Yes, Carl's going to make a guitar for us. And I've got our stories, too. I'm your old mother, moving to a nursing home. You're my daughter, selling my house and getting rid of all my stuff. I had an old friend who was a roadie for some famous bands, and he stashed stuff in my attic before he died. Now that I'm moving, we've discovered all sorts of rare gems up there. We can sell him dozens of fakes."

"But surely you don't think he buys guitars without checking them out. I bet he has a team of experts. What makes you think you can fool them?"

"Poor confused girl," she condescended. "Carl's the best. He can do this in his sleep."

Her plan still seemed incomplete, so I probed further. "And how do we cool out the mark?" The cool out phase was an important part of a con that would make sure the mark didn't come after us if he figured out he'd been swindled. "Alejandro has enough money to find us, you know."

Bea waved her hand dismissively. "He wouldn't even think about doing that. He's bought dozens of rare guitars over the years, and I've never seen a story about him being cheated." She squinted at me as if I'd just landed here from outer space. "Don't you get it? I'm sure Alejandro's been swindled, but he'll never admit it. That's our cool out— coming after us would be bad publicity for him. And that's why we're going for someone so famous. A less well-known person might be willing to fight back. So don't worry."

She leaned close to me and tugged on my hair. "But I'll only tell you this once. Get that wild mop of hair under control. Dye it, or cover it. We don't make spectacles of ourselves when we're conning people—we act normally. And for this con, you have to be a conservative woman, not some fucking New York weirdo."

I felt ill. A familiar sensation washed over me, like I'd been kicked in the stomach. Con tension started to rise up again, just from thinking about all the deception. It washed over me, leaving me fatigued and afraid. I was fifteen again, setting up a con and feeling it in my gut. I didn't want to do it then, and I certainly didn't want to be doing it now. And worse, the mark was Alejandro, which made my chance of success impossibly low.

But I was stuck, so I had to follow orders, at least for now. I nodded toward the nearly-empty bag of Low-Hanging Fruit bars. "Can I have one of those?" My body could tell I was conning again, and it traitorously wanted me to eat one of those vile snacks.

Bea smiled and tossed the last bar across the table. That never would have happened when we were kids—she would have withheld the candy until the con was over. Some things had definitely changed.

I hadn't had one of these chocolate bars in years, so I was surprised at how much I loathed it. But I'd asked for it, so I choked it down quickly, just like I used to. Back then, I was hungry. Now I just needed something in my gut besides the feeling of doom. When I finished the bar, I continued to play the child and dutifully fetched a garbage can to clean up the wrappers and empty bags.

I had reverted to Bea's little girl again, eating candy, planning scams, and cleaning up after a mother whose notions about parenting lacked many basic concepts.

The Setup

Five

I plunged into the deep end of the nostalgia pool by going with Bea to the music shop. This was where I had spent so much time as a kid, kicking around, listening to customers play instruments, and waiting for Bea to take us home. Now we were here again, preparing for another big con.

We passed by Aunt Franny, who was sitting up front by the register, reading a magazine. Her swept-back white hair, thin face, and bright red lips gave her a fabulously edgy look, as always. Today she wore jeans and a denim blouse that she accessorized with turquoise rings, a turquoise necklace, and big, round, turquoise glasses. The woman had a style all her own.

Next to the register was one of my favorite parts of the shop: the pick bowl. The big glass bowl held a huge collection of guitar picks, with a sign that read, "Take a pick, leave a pick." Customers could have one if they needed one, and others could contribute to the supply. Those who contributed usually had very nice-looking picks: often brightly colored and decorated with ads for some music service or another. Endlessly entertaining, I used to spend hours rummaging through the pick bowl when I was a kid.

But today I didn't have time to admire picks. Before Franny and I could have even the briefest welcome conversation, Bea whisked me down the narrow back corridor to our destination: the workshop of the old guitar forger, Uncle Carl.

Carl and Franny Geiger weren't really my uncle and aunt. They weren't even related to Bea—just fellow grifters. But I spent so much time with them when I was young that they became the best aunt and uncle anyone could have. Certainly better relatives than my so-called mother. Franny taught me the finer aspects of conning as they pertained to the human body, including self-defense, the light touch needed to pick a pocket, and how to cold-read people from their facial expressions and body language. But an even better skill was taught to me by Carl, my dear sweet uncle. In addition to being a master woodworker who repaired broken guitars and built copies of rare ones, he also taught me to paint and to forge.

Little had changed in Carl's workshop. Every wall— floor to ceiling—was still covered with guitars. Instruments were piled everywhere along with scraps of wood, metal, and other materials. The dusty old display case on the side was so covered with grime that the glass was nearly opaque. I remembered when it was cleaner, and I could still make out the jumble of strings, frets, capos, and musical detritus, piled everywhere and impossible to properly appreciate. When I was young, I spent plenty of time trying to figure out everything in that display case. Almost as much time as I spent staring at the pick bowl.

In the middle of this messy workshop, hunched over a table cluttered with guitar pieces, was Uncle Carl. With a pink shirt, dark tie, and maroon suspenders, his white hair gave him an air of authority. No wonder he dressed as Santa each year when I was a kid. All he needed was a herd of reindeer.

Carl never budged from his worktable when I was young, so it was comforting to see him still there. I started to say something, but Bea called out first. "Carl! Look who's here."

"Hold on a minute," he barked. "Be right with you." He didn't even look up from his work.

But Bea wouldn't give him, or anyone else, a minute. She pushed her way through the clutter and made it to the table. "Oh, for God sakes," Carl muttered as he set down his screwdriver. "I said I'd only. . ."

When his eyes landed on me, he immediately halted. Slowly, he pulled off his wire-rimmed glasses and blinked a few times. "My God, it's you, Dee!"

"Hi, Uncle Carl." I ran around the table to give him a big hug. "Good to see you."

"What brought you out of hiding? Wait, let me guess. . ." He pulled away and stared at us for a few seconds. "You're helping Bea with her guitar swindle." He leaned back in his chair with the barest of smiles. "Looks like we'll get to work together. So what can I do for you ladies? You said you needed a guitar, but you didn't say anything else. Who are you selling it to?"

Bea stood straight, proud of her cleverness. "Alejandro."

Carl whistled as he slowly shook his head. "Big collector. And he's hard to fool. Uses one of the best authentication specialists."

Bea waved away his concerns. "How much and how quick?"

Carl shrugged. "That depends on what you want. Alejandro tends to favor guitars that were owned by famous rockers. They say that his manager, George Rawson, collects stolen guitars, but I don't know if I believe it. Rawson's collection's never been seen."

"Screw Rawson." Bea got right to the point. "We're targeting Alejandro. What do you recommend?"

Carl leaned back and stroked his chin. "Stevie Ray Vaughan had an old '65 Fender Stratocaster that nobody's seen since he died in the 90s. I've studied that guitar quite a bit, and I even made one a few years back, just for kicks." He got up and rummaged through a pile in the corner, finally pulling out a guitar case and setting it on the table. Inside was a dark wood electric guitar with the letters "SRV" on it, big and sparkling. "I've heard people offering six hundred grand for this particular guitar." He paused and laughed. "Well, for the real one, that is. Anyway, you should be able to get a half million for this, once you get it past his expert. Just don't let him take it away for more advanced tests, because then he'll notice the flaws."

That seemed like a problem. "How do we get him to accept the initial examination and not take it for further tests?"

"Oh, I wouldn't worry about that. Alejandro's authenticator is a smarmy son-of-a-bitch who thinks he can spot fakes instantly. He would never take it for further tests because then he'd have to admit he couldn't do the job by himself. No. . ." He shook his head. "This will fool that guy. Just give me a day to clean it up and get it ready."

Bea leaned closer. "How much do you want for it?"

Carl laughed. "You don't mess around much, Bea. No small talk about how you suddenly found your lost daughter?"

"Life's short, Carl."

He sighed. "Okay. I'll take ten percent. Fifty grand and it's yours."

Bea grunted. "I'll give you ten grand. Take it, or else."

Or else? Was Bea blackmailing Carl, too? I wouldn't put it past her.

Carl rolled his eyes and grimaced. "Fine."

Bea pulled a wad of cash from her purse. She counted out a fat handful and dropped it on the table. "Here's half." She stared at me but kept talking to Carl. "Dee will come to pick it up tomorrow, and she'll pay you the other half." My nod was both an acceptance of Bea's demand and an assurance to Carl. We had a deal.

Bea and I slipped out the back door of the music shop and returned to her house. She wanted to talk about the next step, but I needed air. I was suffocating, pulled in by the quicksand world of grifting. The game-playing, the tension, and the gut-wrenching fear of bad outcomes had me spinning out of control. I desperately needed to recover that blackmail evidence.

Back at her home, Bea seemed to be wound tighter than a rubber-band airplane. I felt the pressure of the con oozing from her, the excitement she got from tricking people. Aunt Franny called this "con energy," and she could always spot it in people. I could certainly see it in Bea—it practically radiated from her. She lectured me about my role, the backup strategies, and whatever else she could think of. This went on for hours, only stopping when my attention started to fade and I pleaded exhaustion.

One difference of opinion we had was how we would handle Alejandro. Could we admit to knowing who he was, or would we have to pretend to be mostly ignorant? I argued that ignorance would be foolish, because everybody knew Alejandro. Bea insisted that we play it cooler, allowing ourselves to be aware of him but pretending to be indifferent. She argued that if we came across as rabid fans, it would be harder for him to take us seriously. My problem was that I was already a rabid fan, so I couldn't imagine pretending otherwise.

I felt like an idiot, getting stuck in Los Angeles. Who knew how long it would take to rope-in Alejandro and con him out of his money? My brief visit was about to be greatly extended.

I left Bea's place and stumbled back to the motel, falling onto my bed in a stupor. To try to distract myself, I turned on the television—some mindless entertainment to make me forget my problems. Ironically, the first thing I saw was a puff-piece about Alejandro. The smitten female reporter talked about his latest album and rehashed news about him from the past few years. They showed him with Quinn Freeling, the Hollywood starlet who dated him briefly. Other pictures showed him at nightclubs, out on the street, or in the middle of interviews. In each, he was surrounded by beautiful smiling women, all of them staring at him with the same longing that I always felt. These women wanted his body. What kind of a fool was I to think I could take his money?

After the segment ended, I turned off the television. Then I called Wanda. I needed to talk to someone normal, someone without criminal intent. Wanda had lectured me about finishing this visit quickly and getting back to New York. She was wary of Bea, even though the two of them had never met. Unfortunately, Wanda was right—she had an intuition about these things. She was certainly more of a mother than Bea had ever been.

"Dee! How's it going?" I smiled just from hearing her voice. Typical of Wanda, she didn't give me a chance to answer and went on at double speed. "The shop is selling your pottery like gangbusters. We've sold six pieces since you've left. I ordered another palette for you yesterday. And on Sunday. . ."

Wanda loved to talk more than anyone I knew. Under normal circumstances, I'd be happy to let her go on for a while. But today, I had to deliver some bad news. "Hold on, Wanda. Things aren't going so well out here. It looks like I'll be staying for a few weeks."

She groaned. "And just what do you mean by 'a few,' my dear? You realize that you're the lynchpin of this business. At the rate things are going, we'll be completely out of stock in three weeks, so you need to get back here sooner."

"It's okay, Wanda."

"Okay? You told me when you left that you'd only be gone for a few days. But now it's a month." She grumbled. "This is Bea, right? Do I have to fly out there to fix things? Because I will. I'll give her a piece of my mind that she'll never forget."

"Whoa, Wanda. Chill. It's complicated, but I've got it under control."

I had to force myself not to laugh out loud at that statement. *I've got it under control*, indeed. I didn't have *anything* under control. But Wanda needed assurances, and this was the best I could do.

"Are you sure, Dee? We need you. Let me tell you a little something that happened this morning. . ." I settled in for what I knew would be more than a *little* something. "Some guy came in and asked if you did commissions. He's building a fancy home and wants you to make two huge urns to flank the entranceway. It would be *so* cool to do work on that scale, and I know you're intrigued by the idea. I mean, how amazing would it be to paint monster urns that filled your studio? They'd probably need a crane to deliver them through the skylights." She let out a short giggle, clearly taken by the thrill of it all. "Anyway, I got his card and promised you'd get back to him, but if you aren't going to be able to do this, you have to tell me so he can make other arrangements." She stopped and took a breath. "Tell the truth. Do you really have it under control?"

Oops, busted. I gave her an appreciative chuckle. Wanda could wear anyone down with talk; it was one of her skills. I'd even seen her make things up on the fly, spinning tall tales like a true con artist. That might be the reason we'd become such close friends—fellow tricksters.

"Yes, Wanda. It's all under control. I'll be back as soon as I can. Sorry, girl. At least Roman won't be upset."

"Roman won't even notice you're gone." She shot out a brief laugh, then fell into a long, exaggerated breath. "But I do. Looks like I'm in mourning now. I'm going to have to wear a dark veil tomorrow." Wanda liked to express herself with hats, so tomorrow's veil would be her secret way of telling everyone that I was temporarily lost to her. She always posted her hat of the day online, and I couldn't wait to see this one.

"Thanks, Wanda. You're the best." She really was. And Bea was the worst, without a doubt.

Six

Wanda's call energized me—few could resist her upbeat attitude. So I decided to go see Hale at the pizza place. He might be able to help me track down that cocaine. I also needed to get some cash so I could pay Uncle Carl for his guitar.

As I walked through the motel parking lot to get to my car, my eyes were drawn to another vehicle, a few spaces down from mine. The first unusual thing about it was that it was parked backwards, facing out. Also, there was someone sitting in it. But the thing that really caught my eye was the fact that this person was reading a newspaper, holding it up so high that the paper filled the front and side windows of the car, blocking all view.

I walked past the car a bit more slowly and kept it in the corner of my eye. Everything about the car screamed surveillance—bad surveillance. Whoever was behind that newspaper was watching, prepared to move quickly. But this person was being too obvious—no one could fail to notice.

So imagine my surprise when I got in my car, pulled out onto the road, then saw *that car* pull out behind me. *I* was the one being followed! The driver was disguised with a hat pulled down to his eyes and big wrap-around sunglasses.

Who had hired him? The only person I could think of was Bea, but I doubted she'd hire someone so incompetent. Unless she *wanted* me to know I was being followed. That would be like her.

I also wondered if this was mere coincidence. Had I left the motel just as this person's real target was departing? I decided to experiment, making random turns as I drove. I even did a full circle of four right turns around a block. Unfortunately, the car followed me everywhere I went.

I had intended to go visit Hale, but I definitely didn't need to bring this tailer with me, so I called him up. "Hale, I need your advice. I'm on the road now, and someone's following me."

"Can you get me a license plate? I've got access to the DMV." That was easy. Mr. Bad Surveillance was keeping way too close, affording me a perfect view. A few minutes later, Hale started to laugh.

"What's so funny? Am I being tailed by a circus clown?"

"Just about. It's that idiot, Victory Vance." He laughed some more.

I groaned. Vance was Carl and Franny's son, who used to sit around playing video games at his parent's music shop. I heard from Elle that he was married now and had a kid, Roger, who was an aspiring grifter. It was Roger who, along with his grandpa Carl, had brought that panda into the lost-and-found department.

Vance had been a skinny kid, and I could see he hadn't grown much. Five years older than me, he never socialized with any of us when we were young. All he did was camp out in his corner and play games, offering a sneering frown to anyone who bothered him. We used to call him "Victory Vance" because whenever he won a game, he'd throw his arms in the air and yell, "Victory!"

Naturally, Vance did some cons too, but stories of his screw-ups were legendary. Back when I lived in L.A., Carl and Franny used to give him simple tasks: drive a car, get supplies, load gear. Occasionally, they'd let him appear in a con when they needed someone who looked tough. Vance might have been skinny, but he knew how to scowl.

Everyone liked to tease Vance back then, but I always had a soft spot for him. Underneath that nasty exterior was a sweet kid who just wanted approval. Way, *way* back, when I was seven years old and Vance was twelve, we played video games together a few times. And although nobody else knew this, Vance was my first kiss. Nothing ever came of it, but I was never afraid of him after that, no matter how mean he pretended to be.

So why was Vance following me? I doubted his parents had sent him out to do it. And Bea used to complain about him all the time, refusing to work with him at all. That made me doubt she had hired him. But I couldn't deny that many things had changed in the last seven years. Maybe, now that she didn't have any foster children under her influence, she'd taken on Vance.

When I got to the bank, I waited for Vance to park his car. Then I walked over to him before he could get his newspaper shield up in place. Yep, even with the dark glasses and seven more years of age, this was Vance.

I knocked on the glass, and he gave me his usual scowl. Then he rolled down the window. "What do you want?"

"Hi, Vance. Nice to see you. I was just wondering why you're following me."

"I'm. . . not. . ." Vance sputtered his reply, but finally slumped in his seat with a big exhale. "How you doing, Dee?" He reached out a hand, and we shook.

"I'm good. Who wants me followed?"

He folded his arms. "Can't say." Yeah, probably Bea.

"That's okay." I patted his shoulder. "See you around." I got the money I needed, then I drove back to the motel. Vance followed dutifully.

I still wanted to talk to Hale so I could enlist him in the search for Bea's locker and those fingerprinted drugs. But the last thing I needed was Vance reporting all of this to her, so I had to lose him. Good thing Vance wasn't the sharpest pencil in the box.

One of the features of this motel that made it a useful hideout was that it had a back exit. The bathrooms had windows large enough to climb through, leading to a fire escape. That led to a strip mall around the corner and from there, to freedom.

Because Vance was parked outside the door to my room, I climbed out of the bathroom window, hailed a cab at the strip mall, and rented a different car. My plain, brown sedan was easy to ignore, but I needed something completely different. I needed a car that could hide me both physically and conceptually. It had to be so outlandish that nobody would suspect I was driving it. I chose a big, black SUV with tinted windows. The car screamed for attention while remaining anonymous—just what I needed. Now I could sneak around town in relative safety.

For the duration of this con, whenever I went to see Bea or someone related to the swindle, I'd drive the brown sedan. But when I was visiting Hale or someone unrelated, I'd turn on the television and sneak out the bathroom window to my SUV parked at the strip mall, returning the same way.

Safely in my SUV, I drove to the pizza place to see Hale. Since he'd been able to hack into the license plate database, I asked him to invade Bea's finances for me, too. If I could find a payment for the rental of a storage locker, I'd know where it was and could get my incriminating evidence back. Hale agreed to look.

Next, to make Bea happier about my wild, white hair, I bought some hats. They made me feel like I was channeling my inner Wanda. Now I was no longer calling attention to myself, at least not with my white hair. I also bought a few proper outfits so that when we ran the con, I'd look like an appropriately serious daughter.

Finally, I parked the SUV in the strip mall and returned to my room. When I got back, I peeked through the front curtains to check on Vance. Still there—he hadn't noticed I'd left. Good. Mission accomplished.

The next day, I went to the music shop to pick up the guitar, sneaking in the back door so I wouldn't have to deal with any of the shop's customers. Carl was proud of his work, and wished me luck.

Now we had the guitar—that was the easy part. But next came the hard part: selling this fake instrument to the most famous rocker on the planet. And doing it without trying to kiss him madly. Good luck!

Seven

That night, Bea and I sat in an upscale restaurant, pretending to finish our dinner. She was dressed in conservative clothes, a brown wool pantsuit over a black turtleneck sweater. Demure and elderly, she even wore a gray wig so she'd look older.

I was playing the part of her daughter, which wasn't a complete lie. But today, I was a dutiful, doting daughter, looking after the welfare of her helpless mother. That was definitely a stretch.

To appear more proper, I wore a vintage black fitted suit over a sky blue scoop-neck blouse, with dark stockings and black pumps. The modest pencil skirt went below my knees. I even added a stylish blue hat, to cover my wild mop of hair.

One of Bea's rules for a con was to know the mark—to study the person ahead of time. But I didn't need to study Alejandro at all: I'd been doing that for ten years. Of course, Bea was not a fan, so she'd had to do her homework. And her research told her that George Rawson, Alejandro's manager, would be the man to approach. He arranged all of Alejandro's rare guitar purchases, and he knew quite a bit about the instruments. If Uncle Carl's rumors were true, he even had his own collection of guitars, separate from Alejandro's. Bea's sources also told her that Rawson would be dining at this restaurant today, so he'd be our point of entry. That was good—I could more easily deal with him than his famous rocker boss.

Bea faced the door, one eye on the restaurant entrance. I just picked at the remains of my meal, moving food around and occasionally taking a bite. It might have tasted like something, but I was on stage, about to do a con, so flavor was irrelevant. I just chewed and swallowed, then I continued to play with my food.

I was about to fork up another mouthful when Bea nodded at me. Rawson was in the restaurant. According to her research, he always sat at the same table. The unoccupied table next to ours. He'd be sitting there soon.

We started to focus more on our meal, and our conversation became more animated. We spoke about the good old days and those crazy aunts and uncles who mooched off of us. My fictitious mother didn't want to sell her house, but it was getting to be too much work. So she would soon be moving to a residential care facility, with easy access to a dining room and people to keep her life running smoothly.

Staying in character, I didn't even glance at Rawson as he walked past me and sat down. Instead, I kept up the charade. Bea and I had whole stories made up, which we delivered effortlessly, with smiles and sighs and soothing pats. We did a pretty good imitation of a mother and daughter who loved each other—surely the most easy-going conversation we'd ever had. Proof that I truly *was* a con artist.

Finally, Rawson placed his dinner order, which meant it was time to cast our line into the waters and try to land this big fish. Bea dropped her fork on the floor, with a loud, clattering sound. "Oh, dear me."

I got up to retrieve the utensil and managed to brush against Rawson, just in case he wasn't paying attention. I even apologized to him for the intrusion and smiled briefly. This gave me my first real look at our mark.

George Rawson was well dressed, with a black suit and a white dress shirt casually unbuttoned at the top. Clean-shaven, but with a heavy beard shadow already present, his short dark hair was lightly graying on the sides. He seemed like a serious man, someone who wouldn't tolerate fluff. To make this work, I would need to appeal to his skeptical side.

I returned Bea's fork, and we started our routine. "You see, Mom. This is why you need to move to the new place. You'll have people there to help you. And you won't have to climb stairs anymore."

Bea sighed like the helpless older woman she was pretending to be. "Don't be silly, dear. I can still walk up a flight of stairs. Why just yesterday I was in the attic, looking over everything your Uncle Norman left behind. You could set a stage with all that stuff: lights and speakers and musical instruments. Did I ever tell you he was a roadie for some famous bands?" Neither of us turned to see whether our fish was sniffing at the bait. Besides, we were just getting started.

I let out an annoyed laugh at this tale of my stupid but non-existent uncle. Then I leaned closer to Bea. "Screw Uncle Norman. All he ever did was mooch off you for months at a time, then leave his crap in your attic and disappear." I couldn't tell whether Rawson was listening, but I didn't hear anything coming from his direction, which was a good sign.

Bea twisted her mouth. "Well, he's been dead for years, so he won't be mooching anymore. Anyway, I thought I'd take a last look at his pile. Some real pretty guitars. One of them has a note in it—says it's a gift from some famous musician. I've heard of his name. Steven. . ." She wiggled her fingers and pretended to be concentrating. "No, *Stevie*. Stevie Ray. . ." She continued to struggle, then gave a shrug of surrender. "Stevie Ray something-or-another. I can't remember."

"Stevie Ray Vaughan?"

"That's it. Fancy guitar."

"Don't be ridiculous, Mom. Why would someone that famous give Uncle Norman his guitar? Maybe Norman stole it—that would be more like him." Since Rawson supposedly collected stolen guitars, I threw in this line to make sure he was listening. Then I collapsed slightly and shook my head with frustration. "Norman was a drunk who couldn't even support himself. Anything he left in your attic is garbage, Mom. And when we sell the place, I'm getting rid of it all."

"But I know this one is special. It even has the man's initials on it in big sparkling letters." Bea and I made brief eye contact when we noticed a rustling from the next table, but we kept up the act.

I leaned closer to her. "Look, I don't want to hear. . ." But that was as far as I needed to go—the hook was set, and the fish was tugging on the line.

"Excuse me," Rawson interrupted us, leaning closer from his table. "I couldn't help but overhear that you found a rare guitar. I happen to collect guitars, and I might be interested in taking this one off your hands."

I kept up the routine. "You see, Mom? Now you've got everyone thinking that the crap in your attic is valuable." I turned to Rawson. "I'm sorry to bother you—I'm sure it's nothing. My mother is always finding things that she thinks are gems. And my uncle was a complete loser, so whatever he left up there is worthless, believe me."

Bea got excited. "No it's not. I even took a picture of it." She fumbled in her purse and pulled out her phone. "Norman told me once that he had treasure up there."

She worked her phone in a fumbly old-lady fashion while I turned to Rawson with a sympathetic smile. "Uncle Norman wouldn't have known treasure if it fell on him."

Bea continued to stretch out the moment, pretending to have difficulty with modern technology. When Rawson started to fidget, she nodded. "Aha, here it is." She held out her phone with a grin.

Rawson's eyes widened slightly, and he let out a barely audible gasp. I could tell he was trying to stay calm over this rare guitar, but he was doing a poor job of it.

I helped him hide his enthusiasm. "See, I told you. Just another piece of junk from my mother's attic. Sorry."

Rawson rose to Bea's defense. "Actually, this guitar could be more valuable than you think. I'd have to have it checked out, of course. Do you suppose I could see it?" He paused and straightened in his chair. "And by the way, my name is George Rawson. You ladies may call me George."

I shook my new friend's hand. It was nice to be on a first-name basis with the mark. "Deborah Gleason. And you may call me Deborah." I smiled, then gestured at Bea. "This is my mother, Bonnie Gleason."

Rawson pulled his chair over to our table and continued his pitch. "I'll have you know that I'm very knowledgeable about guitars. As a matter of fact. . ." He puffed out his chest and smiled proudly. "I'm the manager of the 'Lord of Rock and Roll.'" Keeping in character, we stared at him with blank faces, forcing him to explain who that was. After a few seconds, he clarified his boss's name, speaking quietly as if saying it out loud was somehow sacrilegious. "Alejandro." He reached into his wallet and handed us a card.

I took the card and shrugged, pretending to be unfamiliar with the Lord of Rock and Roll. When I handed the card to Bea, she studied it and tucked it in her purse. George beamed at my pretend mother. "Mrs. Gleason, could I convince you to let me see that guitar? I'd like to take a closer look."

"Wait a minute." I gave him the stink eye of a protective daughter. "What would this guitar be worth, if it really *was* Stevie Ray Vaughan's?"

"Oh, I don't know." He fidgeted, obviously trying to avoid showing too much interest. "A few thousand, perhaps. You certainly don't want to throw it out."

A few thousand! Classic. He was low-balling us with that figure, which he assumed would be enough to interest us, but not enough to force him to pay what it was worth. Now was the time to get serious.

"Well, if anyone's going to bring that guitar to you, it'll be me. I don't want Mom dealing with these sorts of things."

George smiled, apparently happy to be dealing with me. But he wanted to confirm this with Bea. "You don't mind?"

She flipped her hand. "Debby takes care of business for me. If you want to buy it, talk to her." Then she pointed her finger at me. "See? I told you it was worth a lot. Just don't let him cheat you."

George slapped a hand to his chest. "I promise I wouldn't do such a thing. Call me up, Deborah." He smiled and leaned closer. "Bring the guitar. I bet Alejandro will be interested in it, too. And I'm sure you'd like to meet him." He winked.

I gave him a quizzical look, still feigning ignorance of Alejandro. But on the inside, my heart was beating just a little faster at the thought of meeting the man. This con was going to be ridiculously hard to pull off.

Eight

Alejandro's mansion sat high in the Hollywood hills, up a winding road only occasionally interrupted by the gated entrance to some other rich person's estate. I pulled up to his imposing stone pillars, and a woman's voice interrogated me at length before letting me in. After that, I approached the house slowly, taking in every detail so I'd be prepared for a quick escape. Just in case. You never know.

I rounded a curve and the house appeared before me. Low and wide, I barely noticed it at first. It blended in with its surroundings as it spread across the hillside. Modest, in a way. But as I got closer, more of it came into view, and by the time I'd pulled up to the front, I knew that there was no way this house could ever be called modest. The only difference between it and the houses I grew up in was, well, everything.

I'd been in fancy homes when I was young but always for one reason: to swindle people. When I was eight, Bea and I visited a home like this, pretending to be new neighbors. She settled me in a small room so I could watch television while she chatted with the grown-ups. But I didn't watch for long. My job was to sneak into the master bedroom so that I could swap an oversized diamond ring with an imitation that Bea had made. They never found out. In fact, a few years later, Bea showed me a picture of the woman at a gala ball, still proudly flashing her fake diamond.

Now here I was again, preparing to swindle another rich person. Only this time, it was Alejandro, someone I admired for his music and his incredible good looks. Everything about this was wrong.

Wearing a blue floral-patterned maxi dress, a khaki cloth hat and tan heeled sandals, I felt demure yet edgy, just enough for rock and roll. I quickly rang the bell while I still felt confident. The door was opened by a short, attractive woman with long dark hair. She wore a blue tailored business suit with black edging that matched her blouse. At least my choice of clothing was more-or-less correct, but my dress went almost to the floor, whereas this woman's skirt barely covered her thighs. Undoubtedly short enough to satisfy a rocker like Alejandro.

As her eyes scanned me, a small smile crept onto her face. "Ms. Gleason. Right this way. I'm Karen Summersby, Alejandro's personal assistant." I noticed that she emphasized the word "personal," and she walked with a sway to her hips, daring me to be as appealing. Either her famous boss demanded that his employees dress revealingly, or this woman routinely competed with every female who came to the house.

She led me through an expansive home that boasted open rooms, high ceilings, and picture windows that framed Los Angeles like a postcard. Along the way, I noticed a big man in black—serious black, including his suit, shirt, and tie, with some really dark sunglasses. Alejandro's bodyguard, no doubt. Arms folded tightly, he watched me from down the hallway. I forced myself not to think about what would happen if he found out who I was.

Karen opened a door and waved me into an empty room. "Alejandro is just finishing an interview and photo

shoot with *No Moss*. You can wait here. He won't be long."
She quickly left the room.

No Moss magazine was the premier destination for
everything music-related. They had been one of the first
media outlets to recognize Alejandro ten years ago, before
anyone else had heard of him. So it amused me that he
continued to be involved with them. Yes, even someone as
well-known as Alejandro still needed to feed the fame
machine.

As soon as Karen stepped into the hall, George Rawson
walked by. She propped her hands on her hips and gave him
a distinctly unpleasant look. "Your *dealer* is here." She said
it like I was selling drugs. Then she walked away, heels
tapping loudly on the tile floor. Good riddance to her—I
didn't like her any more than she liked me.

But George was much more friendly and came right
over to chat. "Deborah, hello again." We shook hands. "I'm
sorry, but the *No Moss* shoot is running late. Ivory Doe is
interviewing him for a ten-year retrospective, and she does
love our boy. They've been at it for hours. Anyway, why don't
you come to the pool and you can wait while they wrap up. I
know he'll want to see this guitar." He led the way, and I
nervously followed him onto the back deck.

This was getting to be very intense. First, I was meeting
Alejandro, who made me all fluttery inside, and now I was
also going to meet Ivory Doe. Ivory was a famous journalist
who wrote in-depth stories about the world of rock and roll.
Musicians knew they'd made it when she came to interview
them. In Ivory's original coverage of Alejandro, she dubbed
him "The Crown Prince of Rock and Roll." But by the time
his fourth album came out, his popularity had grown so
much that she upgraded him to be "The Lord of Rock and

Roll," which became his unofficial title. When Ivory Doe laid down an epithet, it stuck.

The pool looked like the set of a movie. Camera tripods, photographer's umbrellas, and lighting reflectors were everywhere. People ran around the deck with clipboards, makeup kits, and cameras. In the middle of it all, sprawled out on a recliner wearing only a tight bathing suit, was Alejandro. Sex personified, seeing him like this made my jaw hit the floor.

I took a moment to reflect. Arguably the most famous performer in the entire world was in front of me, wearing a striped bathing suit so brief and body-hugging that it was easy to imagine the rest. But I didn't do that, because I was a professional, here to con this man. I barely noticed that his wavy black hair had a wild and wet look that caught the sunlight just right. And I didn't pay any attention to his incredibly handsome face, chiseled and sharp, with full lips that screamed to be kissed. I also didn't spend any time staring at his spectacular build, and I paid no attention to his muscular arms and legs, his breathtaking torso, or the trail of hair diving suggestively below the waistband of his swim trunks. Yes, I was as calm as a fan girl could be, sitting in the front row of an Alejandro concert. At least I wasn't screaming his name.

And just to add even more hotness to this scene, the iconic Ivory Doe was sitting in a nearby chair, chatting away. Her little black dress gave new meaning to the notion of "little," showing off every inch of her long legs and challenging her ample bust to remain covered. I felt like I was on the set of a porn movie.

Ivory owned the action here by the pool. She directed everyone, from Alejandro to the lighting people, posing

Alejandro while consulting her notes. From her perch near the Lord of Rock and Roll, she was a blur of motion.

Alejandro, by contrast, was barely moving. He sprawled on his back with his eyes closed, seeming to be asleep. But he occasionally spoke to Ivory in response to something she said, which proved he was less inert than he appeared. I even saw him reach for his phone at one point, and after that, he took a sip from a drink on the table. But he always laid back down when he was done. The man seemed tired.

George and I watched this scene for a few minutes, then George broke in. "Ivory, are you done yet? Alejandro has an appointment now."

She ignored George and turned to Alejandro for an answer. "Are we done, baby? I've got enough for a smashing article."

Alejandro chuckled. "We're *well* done." He took another sip from his drink and sank back down into the lounge.

"Strike it!" she barked, causing everyone around her to change direction. Then she ran a hand up Alejandro's arm. "Got to run now, doll—meeting my editor for tea. But don't worry. . ." She smiled and gave him an exaggerated wink. "I'll be back at midnight." She stood up, straightened her skirt, and walked away. Behind her, wires got coiled up, umbrellas came down, and everything got hauled off.

In the wake of Ivory's departure, Alejandro remained on the lounge chair with his eyes closed. A photographer was snapping his last few shots on the way out, his camera clicking continuously as he took a final pass by the lounge. Suddenly, he swung around and took a picture of me, catching me with an embarrassed look of surprise.

This was bad. I was trying to be anonymous here, but now he had my picture. I quickly turned away, but the photographer was curious. "Who are you, honey?" He looked at me hard, trying to figure out if I was worth another shot.

I needed to become uninteresting, so I stooped over and snorted, then I worked my jaw for a few seconds and sniffled. "I'm with the guitar shop," I snorted again. "Just delivering this to Alejandro." I nodded to the guitar, then turned away to chew on a fingernail in as unappealing a way as possible. With any luck, he'd deem both me and my picture mundane enough to ignore. The photographer frowned for a few seconds, then shrugged and walked away.

When the last of them had gone, George walked up to Alejandro and kicked his lounge. "Get up, idiot. Interview's over and your next appointment is here."

Alejandro raised a hand in the universal fuck-you signal. "Go away, dammit. I've done enough performing today." He let his hand collapse against his side, and he rolled away from us.

George kicked the lounge again, stirring Alejandro. "What the hell, George?" He rolled back to us and squinted, one hand shading his eyes.

"That guitar I told you about—the Stratocaster—it's here. Check it out. And try to act your age for once." With a shake of his head, he muttered, "Jerk."

Alejandro slowly sat up and turned to look at me. When he initially spotted me, his half-closed eyes and lethargic movements made him seem exhausted. But as soon as his eyes found me, they widened, and he sat up straighter. He stared at me for a second, his mouth open as if he was about to say something. Suddenly, he dropped his gaze over to his phone. "Hang on a sec."

He snatched the phone from the table and spoke into it. "What, Karen?" As he listened to his personal assistant, he stood up and started to pace, his eyes darting back to me occasionally. I even caught him doing a full-body sweep, after which his gaze intensified and he stared even more. I watched him too, trying but failing to ignore his hungry leer.

Talk about hot! Alejandro's eyes were all over me, stripping me bare. I felt prickly heat run all over my body from his infrared intensity. No wonder people called him seductive. I'd worried that he'd be hard to resist, but I never imagined he'd be this provocative. Did he do this to all women? Not that I minded—I was enjoying the view myself. Who could resist that dark, sculpted face, those luscious lips, that spectacular physique?

As his hard gray eyes bored into me, I felt something strange—a disturbance, a jolt, a shift. It was like when you step off a treadmill and your whole body wants to keep moving, but the floor doesn't do that anymore, so you're forced to slow down. Whatever this sensation was, it threw me, and I stood helplessly enthralled in Alejandro's captivating eyes.

As I'd suspected, conning this stunning man would be impossible.

Nine

Alejandro continued to talk on the phone while his eyes stayed glued to me, leaving me completely confused. It couldn't be that he lusted over every pretty woman. First of all, I wasn't that pretty. And second, he'd been laying down five minutes ago, practically comatose, while the sexy and scantily clad Ivory Doe fluttered about. Why would he ignore a woman who had promised herself, come midnight, then suddenly pay so much attention to me?

Alejandro's eyes dropped away as he continued the conversation. "Yes, I saw the samples. Wait. . ." He pulled the phone away and worked it for a while, his eyes still sneaking a look at me occasionally. "I like the blue one. Go for it." A busy man.

His pacing had taken him back to the lounge chair. He reached down to exchange his phone for his drink and upended the glass to finish it off. Finally, he stepped up to me with his arms folded and smile gone, silently staring.

Perhaps this was a test, a way to separate the drooling fans from the serious visitors. I needed to impress Alejandro, so I gave him a light smile. "You seem busy. Should I come back later?"

He shook his head with barely a smile. "No, it's fine. I remember now. You're here about Stevie Ray Vaughan's guitar. Ms. . ." He paused with his hand held out, waiting for me to fill in the rest.

"Deborah Gleason." I reached out to shake his hand, and the simple touch of his skin took my breath away. His eyes continued to undress me while his smile now promised to do it for real. What was going on? I normally didn't tolerate men leering so obviously, but this wasn't some drunk I was talking to at a bar. This was Alejandro, a man who could have any woman he wanted, and he undoubtedly got them, too. Nothing made sense.

He let go of my hand to reach up and gently pull off my hat. My wild bleached hair must have flown out like a bunch of pickup sticks, because his eyes widened, and he smiled broadly. "Nice hair." Under his watchful gaze, I ran my fingers through it. Of course, any grooming attempts were pointless.

He chuckled at my failure to neaten up, then he reached out to try it himself. Sweeping one errant strand from my forehead, his strong yet gentle touch left my scalp tingling. I clamped my mouth shut to keep from sighing, although I think I failed. I even laced my fingers together to keep from throwing myself at this powerfully seductive man. His looks were hard to resist, but his unexpected tenderness disarmed me completely.

One thing was certain: now was a terrible time to try and swindle him. Regrettably, I had to do it. In an attempt to pretend that I was mostly ignorant of his fame, I made a lame attempt at conversation. "You must be George's employer."

Alejandro's eyes flashed, and he arched a mesmerizing eyebrow. "You don't know who I am?"

I squinted at him. "You must be Mr. Alejandro. I've heard of you."

He laughed, loud and hearty. "*Mister* Alejandro? Seriously?" He laughed a bit more, then propped his hands on his hips. "For your information, 'Alejandro' is a mononym, my first and only name. To everyone in the world, I am simply, *Alejandro*." He gave it his usual Spanish accent, overemphasizing the third syllable. Truthfully, I knew all about him, including his full name: Alejandro Muñoz-Perez.

But at the moment, I had to pretend that I knew very little, so I continued to make small talk. "You could simplify the name even more and call yourself Al." Now I was being coy. It helped quash my nerves.

Alejandro gave me a throaty chuckle. "*You* can call me Al." He hummed the Paul Simon song and danced around the pool deck for a few seconds. Then he closed the distance between us. "Tell me you don't know my music." Standing this close to me, I could feel heat rising from his scantily clad body.

The prim-and-proper Deborah I was pretending to be took a step back. She needed to get some distance from the burning cauldron of lust simmering in the body of this sultry rock god. Too bad I wasn't Dee today, because she wouldn't have to retreat from such a seductive and eye-popping man, especially one who was being this friendly. Not that I understood the reason for his friendliness.

I continued my banter. "I've heard of *you*, but I don't know if I've heard your music." I shrugged. "If you're that popular, then perhaps I'd recognize some of your songs. But I prefer jazz." I offered a shy smile. "Sorry."

He narrowed his eyes at me. "I'm not sure yet, but you may be one of the most interesting women I've ever met." He waved his arm toward the chairs by the pool. "Sit."

Excuse me? Was I hearing this right? Why was Alejandro offering me superlative praise? His undisguised desire was making me lightheaded. This must be some sort of trick he liked to pull.

George had been watching the two of us without saying a word, evidently used to this level of fervency from the renowned musician. It explained everything—Alejandro probably did this all the time. Stranger stories had been told about him. For most women, the standard response would be to dive right in. But I wasn't playing that game today, which was really a shame. It would certainly be more fun than conning him.

I sat down opposite Alejandro and George, a small table between us. George fidgeted like a kid awaiting Christmas and reached out to take the guitar from my side. He set it on the table and opened the case, staring with reverence. Then, slowly, he lifted the guitar out and blew off some dust. "Stunning." He held it out to Alejandro. "What do you think?"

Alejandro glanced at the guitar and nodded, then he grinned at me. "Yes, stunning."

Oh, please! Why wasn't he treating me like a normal person? Could it be that he did this to every woman he met? No wonder everybody loved him.

Then, I was even more surprised when he reached across the table and took my hands in his. "What would you like to drink?"

Wow, he was so intense—way too intense for me. His eyes were burning me up. It made me wonder who, exactly, was being conned here.

As much as I might have needed a glass of wine to steady my nerves, I did not need anything that would reduce me to a puddle on the deck of the pool. So I pulled my hands away from his and sat up straight. "Nothing for me, thanks."

George set the guitar back in its case. "You don't mind if we have this guitar authenticated, do you?"

I shook my head and tore my eyes away from Alejandro, relieved to be looking at George instead. Released from the gorgeous rocker's overpowering energy, I was able to focus again. I gave George a steely stare. "I'm not leaving it with you, but I'll bring it to your authenticator and wait while it's being examined." I put on my business face. "And by the way, I've done some research on this since we last spoke. Seems to me that it's worth much more than a few thousand dollars if it's real."

Alejandro curled up one corner of his mouth. "And just what do you think this guitar is worth?" He considered the guitar briefly, then returned his gaze to me.

"Well, let's see," I forced myself not to stammer. "George offered me a few thousand dollars, but I know it's worth much more. So I'll counter by asking for six hundred thousand." I let a partial smile sneak onto my face. "Your turn."

George's head snapped to attention, and he glared at me. In the ensuing silence, Alejandro just sat there, his grin even wider. After a few seconds, George grunted. "You *have* been doing your homework, haven't you? Okay, let's split the difference and say three hundred thousand. But I doubt we can go much higher."

Good. At least they were talking about real money. I got up and paced around the pool, letting the tension build. Then I fixed my gaze on Alejandro, purposely ignoring the man I was negotiating with. Another of my mother's rules for conning was to seem disinterested in the deal, never too eager. But today I didn't have to pretend. I had my eyes on something much more interesting than a fake guitar. And he seemed to agree.

I continued the bidding. "I'll drop to an even half million."

Alejandro approached me slowly, his gaze on me the whole time. His face hovered inches away from mine, and I could feel hot vodka breath teasing me. I steeled myself and stood my ground, pretending to be unintimidated. We faced off for a few seconds before he stepped back and took over the negotiation. "All right, Ms. Gleason. How about four hundred thousand?"

George quickly added, "That's the best you're going to get. We can't go a penny higher. And it will take me a week to get that much money together."

Four hundred thousand was a great price for a fake guitar, especially since I knew that the real one would go for six. Bea liked to tell us that in a con, you offer them something for nothing while actually giving them nothing for something. So giving it to him for much less than its book value meant he would think he was getting a steal. It would also make me seem less professional and less threatening. I pretended to consider his offer.

After a few more seconds, I conceded. "Well, I suppose that's acceptable. I could shop it around, but I have a lot of work to do with all the stuff in mother's house. So, fine— you have a deal. But I want cash or an online funds transfer. I'm not handing this over to you until I have the money."

Alejandro wrapped his arm around my shoulders and pulled me close. Wow, did he ever feel good! Hard and muscular, I wanted to take a bite out of his ripped biceps. Instead, I struggled to maintain steady breathing while trying not to lose myself in his embrace.

Through the rush of emotions flying in my head, I heard him ask, "Don't you trust us?" Not surprisingly, when he acted so attentive toward me, a complete stranger, I trusted him less. But I couldn't deny that I *lusted* for him more.

I let a light laugh come out as I forced myself to push away from this most perfect man. "I don't trust the media circus that hovers around you. The last thing I need is an article about me in *No Moss*."

He let out an unamused laugh, then dropped his head. "You're right. My life is a circus—I'm never alone. Wherever I go, a crowd follows and pictures show up on the Internet." He shook his head, then pulled me back to his side. "Sorry, Deborah. Welcome to my life." He flashed beautiful gray eyes at me, shattering my defenses.

I couldn't understand what was happening. This super-famous man was practically making a pass at me, and we'd just met. The fierceness of his stare made my head spin, causing me to inhale sharply. Something was wrong here. I couldn't imagine any world in which Alejandro wanted to be with me, and now I felt certain I was being conned. That seemed to be happening an awful lot lately.

But since con games were my specialty, I gave my face a mental slap and resolved to handle this man. Let him play me all he wanted; I'd simply play him back. "Oh, no you don't," I chuckled. "I'm not joining your circus. I want nothing to do with your ridiculous celebrity—you can keep it for yourself."

He wrapped his other arm around me and pulled me into a hug. "Oh ho! A challenge." He nodded his head. "Accepted. I want to get to know you." He let go of me and stepped away, pointing his chin toward the guitar. "But for now, I want to know more about that guitar. Bring it back tomorrow, and we'll authenticate it. Then, tomorrow night, come out with me."

Wait, did I hear that right? Did Alejandro just ask me to go out on a date? He seemed to be attracted to me, which was the fantasy dream of millions of women. I couldn't deny that I liked where this was going, but I knew it meant trouble. It violated a cardinal rule of conning people.

Bea always told me when I was younger, "Never fall for the mark." She insisted this was a significant rule, even though when I first heard it, I couldn't imagine why. Boys were yucky back then, so there were no situations I could imagine where that rule would be relevant. As I got older, I understood better, and these days, I understood perfectly.

Never fall for the mark.

Unfortunately, I'd fallen for Alejandro years before we'd even met. So it was far too late for that particular lesson.

Preparing For the Deal

Ten

I was about to drive over to Alejandro's estate the next day to get the Stratocaster authenticated. But before I did that, I needed to talk to Vance, so I wandered over to his car and knocked on the window. He rolled it down with a sneer. "What?"

"Hey, Vance. I'm heading over to the mark's place now. Could you do me a favor? Since you can't come into the estate, would you please park a little farther than normal from the gate? They have cameras all over, and I don't want them to know I'm being followed."

Vance nodded with a big smile. "You're good, Dee. I like working with you."

What was his problem? "You're not working with me, Vance. You're working *against* me."

"Aw, don't be angry. We make a good team. Maybe some night we can get a drink together. Beats sitting in your room watching television, I figure."

Poor Vance. He still had a thing for me, even though the only intimacy we ever shared happened once, over fifteen years ago. After that first kiss, he started acting even more mean, which baffled me at the time. Unwilling to suffer his attitude, I got over him quickly. And Vance seemed to get over me, too, never giving me any indication to the contrary.

Suddenly, though, he liked me again. I could see how spending all day watching someone could affect a person's feelings, so I tried to let him down lightly. "Don't go falling for me just because you're stalking me. You have to keep your emotions separate from the job." I figured he could use a little advice, even if it was the sort of advice I needed myself.

Vance laughed. "Following you around isn't making me like you, Dee. I've liked you for years. And by the way, love what you've done with your hair."

Of course. I understood men much better now than I had back then, and I realized that his mean act had merely been a way of covering his feelings. I'd thought we had a mutual dislike going on. Now it turned out he had a crush on me the entire time. How annoyingly typical. For some reason, I kept running into these damaged men, from Vance all the way to Roman.

"Sorry. Not happening, Vance. Besides, you're married now, and you've got a kid, right?"

He nodded.

"How is little Roger?"

"Smart as a whip." Vance laughed. "Sharper than his old man." Yeah, I believed that.

I drove to Alejandro's estate with Vance in tow. When I was a few blocks from the mansion, I got a call from Elle. I knew she was concerned about me, but this wasn't the best time to talk. Nevertheless, I always made time for my sister, so I pulled to the side of the road and took the call.

I started by bringing up something I'd forgotten to mention the other day. "Hey, happy birthday, sis. Big one coming up." Elle was turning twenty-one in just five days.

"Yeah, yeah." She was plainly disinterested in her new adult status. "Listen, I have big news for you on the parent front."

"Oh, no!" A nervous jolt shook me. Elle had promised to find my birth parents, and in a moment of weakness, I'd let her. Now I was about to be confronted with their identity. A tiny part of me was curious, but the bulk of my being still didn't want to know. "You found them?"

"Yep. I could have gone through regular channels, but that would have taken months. So instead, I let the hacker on my crew handle it. She got into the adoption system and found your info. I'll send you the details. But get this! When she probed the agency, she noticed that someone else had pulled the same information a few hours earlier. Was that you?"

A tight knot welled up in my throat, and I had to swallow it down. I felt certain that Bea had done this. She already had Vance following me. Now she was gathering more dirt so that she could guarantee my obedience. More than ever, I needed to find those fingerprinted drugs.

"No," I whispered. "It wasn't me. Can you tell who made the inquiry? Could it be our dear, sweet F.M.?" A nervous laugh broke through my defenses. "She's been really controlling ever since I got here—even has Victory Vance following me. Maybe she's planning something."

"*Maybe she's planning something?* Are you nuts? She's *always* planning something. And by the way, I spoke to her yesterday. She told me that you two are in the middle of a big con."

I groaned in defeat and took a long hard breath. "Yeah, she talked me into one more con. We're close now, ready to set up a deal."

"And you think you can satisfy her by doing this?" That made me pause. I knew that doing this con would make Bea happy—cons were the only things that ever made her happy. But would this *satisfy* her? That was a different question. I'd come here to help Uncle Carl, but instead, I'd gotten myself completely back in the game. Here I was, doing things I'd promised myself I would never do again.

I silently cursed Elle for seeing more than I did, for being wiser. She might be three years younger, but she'd spent more time with that woman, and I knew she was right. I was in trouble.

I pretended to know what I was doing and repeated the story I'd been telling myself for days. "Don't worry. This should go down fine, and then I'll return to New York."

"Well, I hate to be the bearer of bad news, but Bea thinks you're back on her crew for good. She told me that the two of you are starting up again, and that after this con, she's got lots more planned."

I felt a weight descend on me, and I sank down in my seat. I had assumed that Bea would only blackmail me once, but now I realized that was foolish. Unless I got that cocaine back, I would never be free of her.

"Damn. Thanks for the warning."

Elle growled. "Dee, do I have to come down there and help you?"

"I can manage. Besides, aren't you busy with your Robin Hood gang?"

Elle laughed at my reference. She had a crew of con artists who considered themselves to be ethical. They only attacked people who had too much money and abused their power. Dubbing themselves "The Adjusters," Elle's gang swindled rich crooks, teaching them lessons and redistributing wealth to their innocent victims. Elle was the mastermind of the crew but also their cat burglar. Always a good runner and gymnast, she could sneak in or out of any place without being seen.

The Adjusters got their start a few years back, when Elle went looking for her birth parents. She found them in

Oregon, barely holding on to their home because of a predatory lender who had tricked them into an expensive refinance. Elle assembled a crew and pulled a long con that took the finance company for millions of dollars. Then, she gave most of it to the people they had cheated.

After that, the crew was hooked. They soon built a reputation among disadvantaged people as a gang that could right the wrongs of the world. I was simultaneously proud of her and worried. One day, Elle was going to take a big fall. But right now, she was having a blast, still running strong. She often sent me encrypted messages detailing their scams.

"Robin Hood, huh? I like that. And from the sounds of it, someone needs to swoop down and save your poor ass. I'm coming there—don't try to stop me. Besides, I owe you big time for all the things you did for me when we were kids."

She was right about that: I had been watching over her all those years ago. When I was fifteen and she was twelve, she messed up a job we were pulling. It was a real-estate scam, where Uncle Carl pretended to be a crooked government employee who could manipulate deeds. He promised each mark that for a mere hundred thousand dollars, property worth millions could be theirs. We even had a convincer to make the mark happy: Bea. Using a classic "In-and-In" scheme, where you convince the mark to go in by having someone else also go in, Bea pretended to be another investor who would also contribute a hundred grand.

But Uncle Carl, known to the mark as the crooked government employee who was selling cheap property, didn't want to deal with a bunch of investors. He insisted that only one person bring the money for all of them. Bea then gave a big speech about how honest the mark was and how much she trusted him. To prove her trust, she offered to hand over her hundred thousand dollars and let him be the one to buy the deeds. She had brought her money in a special case that locked to her wrist, so she insisted that the mark use it, for added security. The trick was that the case also had a trap door on the side that would let us remove the money without him knowing.

They met in a secluded nook of a hotel bar where Bea handed over her hundred grand. Right after they combined their money and sent the mark off to see Carl, the rest of us were supposed to take it back. Hale and I would create a distraction, a loud and disruptive argument, during which Elle would sneak up to open the trap door and remove the cash. Hale and I did our part, getting into a huge fight in the hotel lobby. We crashed into everything and everyone, surrounding the mark with a noisy ruckus. He stood there and watched us, exactly as planned.

But sadly, Elle wasn't there at the moment. She'd gotten distracted, texting with her friends, and she missed her opportunity. By the time she was ready, the mark had left the building, tired of our squabbling. And Uncle Carl wasn't actually going to meet with the man—we were supposed to have the money by that point. In the end, we had to let the mark walk away with his money and ours. We were screwed.

This was a serious offense. Bea had expected to get her money back along with the mark's contribution. But now it was all gone. Elle would be in for a beating like we'd never seen. We got walloped when little things went wrong, so the loss of this much money was sure to elicit harsh punishment. Bea once locked Jay in the basement for a week because he lost a thousand dollars, which was nothing compared to the hundred grand Elle had just blown. I needed to help her.

Jay had died two years before, and I was already planning my escape. I'd been skimming from jobs by that point, which was easy because I was often the "inside man" for our cons. That meant I was the one who negotiated prices with the mark. When we agreed on an amount, I would tell Bea it was for less and keep the difference. The trick was to stash the extra money somewhere before I got home, so Bea wouldn't find it. My secret nook in the library was perfect for that.

After two years, I'd squirreled away a hundred and fifty thousand dollars. I didn't want to have to start all over again, but my money could well save Elle's life. I had to give it to her.

I stuffed my hundred and fifty grand into a paper bag, then padded some of the bundles with blank paper so it would appear that there was a full two hundred in there. When we brought it to Bea, she found the padding but convinced herself that the mark had done it behind her back. Then, since she still made fifty grand from the deal, she was content, and we all got our candy bars. Without a doubt, the most expensive chocolate I'd ever eaten.

After that incident, Elle shaped up and started to pay more attention to each con. She knew how much that money meant to me, and she promised it would never happen again. In fact, from that point on, she became an active participant in every con and even started to help Bea with the planning. She had blossomed into a full-fledged grifter.

So I suppose I'm the one responsible for turning her into the mastermind of The Adjusters. Her work as the head of that team demanded exacting focus, from planning their elaborate stings to keeping her entire crew in motion. Elle had become quite the professional.

And now I had the mastermind of The Adjusters coming down to Los Angeles to help me out. This could be very helpful. I'd be happy to run my plans by her to see if I'd missed anything. In the meantime, I had something important that she could help me with: find those fingerprinted drugs. I intended to get them back, one way or another. Bea did not get to use those drugs against me for the rest of my life.

"Say, would you happen to know where Bea's storage locker is? I'd like to make a withdrawal." Hale had hacked into a number of Bea's accounts, but he hadn't found any payments to a storage locker yet. It wouldn't hurt to try other options.

Elle was no help. "Beats me. She never trusted anyone with that information. But if you do find it, let me know and I'll help you clean it out." My sister may have stayed in touch with the nefarious F.M., but I was glad to see she had no loyalty to her.

"You've got a deal. And thanks for coming down. I may just need your help."

"You *definitely* need my help."

Eleven

I quickly got to Alejandro's place. Carl had assured us that the fake guitar would pass their authentication tests, but I still worried. At least if it failed, I could plead ignorance. After all, my mother had found the instrument in her attic and had no idea where it came from. Still, this was one of those moments that I hated about conning.

I buzzed at the gate, and Karen let me in. Thankfully, Vance had driven past the gate and parked out of range of the cameras. At the mansion, I gripped the fake Stratocaster a little too tightly as I stepped up to the front door. Today I wore a dark gray V-neck sweater over a knee-length pleated black skirt. I didn't need to cover my hair anymore: Alejandro had seen it yesterday, so he knew exactly what he was getting.

Karen answered the door in a little black dress with long sleeves, a high neck, and a very short skirt. Her heels looked uncomfortably high, too. With a brusque, "Come on in," she led the way.

My curiosity got the best of me, and I stopped her. "Does Alejandro make you dress like that?" The way he'd leered at me yesterday made it seem that the horny musician chased every woman he could find.

Karen turned to face me with a look of shock. "Don't be ridiculous. There are no dress codes here. But I know he enjoys looking at me—we hooked-up once, you know. And since I'm his personal assistant, I like to look the part."

This introduced a whole new possibility into her story. She wasn't being forced to dress this way by her employer, and she wasn't competing with everyone who came to visit. Instead, she was doing it all for Alejandro, vying for his attention and hoping to win him back. "Did you hook-up before or after you became his personal assistant?"

She sniffed, obviously annoyed by my question. "I've been his assistant for the past three years, but we got together nine years ago, when he first became famous. Didn't last long, but none of the others do, either." She eyed me carefully. "You wouldn't last two days."

I couldn't stop a laugh from bursting out. "You're right. I have no intention of lasting for even one day." I cocked my head. "Do you think that every woman who comes here wants to seduce him?"

She propped her hands on her hips. "I don't *think* it. I *know* it. In all the time I've been his assistant, I have never met a woman who didn't want to have sex with him." She squinted at me. "You do, too, so stop lying about it."

"Hey, I won't deny that he's gorgeous. But I'm just here to sell this guitar, then I'm gone." She stared at me for a second, then gave me a derisive snort and walked on.

When we gathered in Alejandro's living room, I was slightly disappointed to see that he was more fully dressed in jeans and a white Fiery Boys T-shirt. Truthfully, I'm a sucker for hot rockers, so the Fiery Boys were also on my short list of favorite bands. Their lead singer, Chuck, was nearly as absurdly good-looking as Alejandro. I heard that their recent tours had intersected in Seattle, and the bands dropped in on each other's shows. I would have liked to have seen that!

But today, I had to pretend that I didn't care about the Fiery Boys *or* Alejandro. I might not get distracted by his scantily clad body, but his handsome face and piercing gray eyes were trouble enough. He didn't make it any easier on me when he gave me a huge smile and a big hug. That smile alone could melt steel, and when he hugged me, I felt all the air rush from my lungs. What was going on between the two of us? At least he pulled away after the hug, which gave me a moment to regroup and pretend I wasn't left buzzing from the contact.

George was there, as was the guitar authenticator, a man named Oscar Peters. Peters gave me his card, then he went to work on the fake Stratocaster. All business, he barely said a word before starting. Instead, he saved his breath for the exam, which he narrated in great detail. He measured and photographed every part of the guitar, examined the lacquer carefully, applied chemical tests, and shined black light everywhere. He spent nearly an hour, testing the guitar and explaining each test. An oppressive hour that felt like ten.

Karen left after a few minutes, but George watched the entire process with fascination. Alejandro seemed less interested. He checked his phone, gazed out the window, and even worked on a song, humming and writing down notes on a pad of paper.

I tried to act cool during the examination, but inside, I was as nervous as I'd ever been. This was another one of those con moments when things could go bad. I'd even parked my car close by so I could make a run for it, if necessary. In fact, moments like this were the reason I got out of the con game—the tension was so severe that I could barely hold myself together.

Finally, Peters smiled and pronounced the guitar authentic. Before I could censor myself, I cried out, "Really?" which elicited a laugh from everyone else. I covered my gaffe by enthusing about how amazing it was to have found something this valuable among my mother's old junk. But in truth, I was surprised that Carl could make such a high-quality fake. I had new respect for my uncle.

George continued to focus on the guitar. He reminded me that they still needed six more days to arrange the funds. Payment would be in cash, because he preferred to make these deals with as little oversight as possible.

George asked that we do the exchange at his home in Bel Air. He gave me another card and wrote his home address on the back. The man was clearly relishing the moment, happy to be doing this deal.

I was also happy. The con was on and would be over in less than a week. I wouldn't have to deal with Alejandro anymore, which would make this so much easier. And Bea would be delighted with cash—she hated electronic funds transfers. An attaché case full of cash always caused a celebration when I was young. If I could find that blackmail evidence, I could even leave town safely.

I packed up the guitar and headed to the door. The sooner I got out of there, the better. Alejandro was also happy but for a different reason. "You're coming out with me tonight, Deborah."

Oh, right. I'd forgotten that he'd said that yesterday. Well, maybe I hadn't forgotten, but I'd tried to put it out of my mind because it didn't make any sense. I assumed that he'd forget all about it. But he hadn't.

It seemed like a thoroughly bad idea, so I tried to beg off. "Oh, come on. I know you were just teasing me yesterday. I've done some checking on you, and you're always with beautiful models and sexy movie stars, not someone like me. Wouldn't you prefer to be with your real fans?"

"My real fans bore me. You can help me forget them." He stepped closer to me and held my face with both hands, caressing my cheeks and sweeping strands of hair away from my forehead. "I'd rather spend time with you."

Whoa, he needed to stop this now! Even his gentle touch was exciting me. And the intensity of his eyes as they roamed over my face made it impossible for me to think straight. "No, I can't." I pulled away, just in time, avoiding his gaze. Any longer, and I would have thrown him to the floor and kissed him madly.

Alejandro shook his head with a smile. "Sure you can. Give me your phone." Unable to resist his request, I handed over my phone and watched as he programmed his number into it. "There. Now you have something valuable: my personal phone number. You *have* to go out with me." He grinned. "Give me your address, and I'll pick you up at seven. Perhaps you can give me a tour of your mother's attic. I bet your uncle left other valuable items there, too."

Bea and I had been worried about this. We wondered if they would want to see the secret attic where the guitar had been found. She had even prepared for this—a friend of hers lived in an old house that would be perfect. But it would be difficult to arrange an attic full of old musical instruments on such short notice, so I tried to deflect him.

"I'm not staying with my mother. Her place is a mess with all the packing up, so I got a motel room. Tell me where we're going, and I'll meet you there."

"No. It's a surprise. Tell me where you're staying."

Damn. Nothing stopped this man. I could have him meet me at the strip mall, but then I'd have to sneak out of the bathroom window all dressed up for a date. I decided that since I was already spending time with Alejandro, perhaps it would be okay to walk out my front door and let

Vance see us. I could always excuse the dalliance as a necessary coddling of the mark. Before I could find another reason not to do it, I gave him the address of my motel.

Alejandro wrinkled his nose. "I know that area. I used to live around there when I was little. Not the nicest neighborhood."

"Hey, it's cheap." I shrugged. "What should I wear?"

"This is a formal event tonight. I'll be wearing a tuxedo."

Alejandro in a tuxedo? My head grew light from the thought. I'd seen pictures of him at award ceremonies in tailored formal wear that hugged his body so well it made gossip columnists pant. If he showed up looking that glamorous, I'd probably self-destruct.

But the real problem with going out on a date with Alejandro was the paparazzi. I worried about too much exposure. Some people might recognize me as New York artist Dee Frank. I was building a reputation for my pottery, and although I tried to keep my picture out of the media, there were occasional photos of me on the web. But even worse, others might remember the young girl who had swindled them years ago. In either case, any recognition would spoil it all.

I swallowed and asked meekly, "Formal? Will there be many other people around?"

He grinned with a light laugh. "Wherever I go, there are always other people around. But tonight I want to keep you to myself, so I promise not to let you out of my sight." He pulled me into a hug.

Oh my God, he felt so good. And he smelled spicy, like hot, buttered sex. I wanted to lick it off his chest, inch by inch, then nibble on his kissable lips. No woman could ever get enough of this incredible man. How could I survive a date with him?

I started to say something, but he cut me off. "Please say yes. I'd love to spend more time with you."

"Oh, God, you're making this so hard."

"No, I'm not. It's not hard at all. Just say, 'Yes, I'll go out with you.' Easy!"

I laughed. "What was that first word, again?"

He wrapped me in his arms and brought his lips up to mine. "Yes," he reminded me, his lips hovering so close.

I looked up at this beautiful man and knew I was helpless to resist him. "Yes," I conceded.

Alejandro smiled broadly, then pulled away. "Good. I'll see you tonight."

Numb, I turned to leave. Now that I had accepted a date with Alejandro, things were officially messed up. I needed to get out of there before I did something even more stupid.

As I approached the front hall, Karen came up to me, all smiles. "Your guitar is real! I didn't think it would be. So many of them are fake, you know." She gave me a playful elbow in the ribs.

To my surprise, Karen was suddenly much more friendly. Maybe now she believed that I wasn't trying to bed her boss. Too bad I no longer believed that.

Twelve

I groaned inwardly when I saw a limousine pull up to the motel office. The driver, a burly man dressed in black, was familiar. I'd noticed him at Alejandro's place, lurking in corners. He spotted me as soon as he came inside. "Zere you are, Ms. Gleason. I am Udo." He spoke with a German accent. "Follow me, please." He led me out and opened the limousine's back door.

Alejandro was sitting on the far side of the big bench seat in a tuxedo that fit him so well, I wondered if it had been painted on. He was tan and fit and mind-numbingly beautiful in his sharp clothes. I glanced at my strapless gray and white floral print dress with a flowing, layered skirt. I had bought it this afternoon, after agonizing for hours. It looked formal, but next to this hottie in a tuxedo, I felt inadequate.

Alejandro leaned away from me, against the opposite door. From across the car, he regarded me with an appraising smile. I sat on the other side of the bench, mimicking his posture and leaning against my door. Safe on the far side of the limousine, I returned his smile.

"Deborah, you look great." Yeah, right. Such a line. And the way he said it seemed to lack conviction. But then again, he lived in a world of artificial praise, so perhaps this was just his way of talking. Besides, I looked okay, but that was all.

I gave him a bashful smile. "You're the one who's dressed to kill." If anyone looked great, it was Alejandro. He always did, especially now.

"Good, because you're the one I was hoping to impress tonight." In a snap, he closed the distance between us. Before I knew it, he had scooted over next to me and wrapped his arm around my shoulder, pulling me close. His solid body and powerful embrace made me shiver and left me momentarily disoriented. He even had that spicy outdoor scent I'd noticed before—too damn good. Why was this incredible man coming on to me so strongly?

"Alejandro, I. . ." Before I could say another word, he cut me off with a kiss, hard and greedy. No! Yes! My mind fought a losing battle against this onslaught. It was as if he had leapt from a video and landed next to me, dreamy and unreal.

How could this be? Alejandro was kissing me! I'd only imagined doing this for a decade. Now, the world-famous heartthrob was coming on to me in the back of his private limousine. There were no words for this. There were no thoughts, either. My brain fogged over as I lost all rational control. So I did the only thing left to do. I wrapped my arms around him, pulled him closer, and deepened the kiss.

And wow, did he ever feel good. His body was superbly hard and muscular, enveloping me in heated need. His mouth was soft, yet firm as his warm lips crushed onto mine. My tongue met his halfway in a gentle dance of exploration, playing like lost lovers starved for affection. I felt myself start to fall apart.

This couldn't possibly be happening. It certainly wasn't supposed to, anyway. I was trying to swindle this man, not seduce him. Besides, he notoriously threw himself at hundreds of women, so perhaps this kiss was nothing special to him. But for me, it was pure fantasy gold. A dream I'd be able to replay for the rest of my life.

In the meantime, though, we had to stop. As soon as I could gather my wits, I'd end this. Any time now—perhaps after this kiss. Not that either of us was showing any sign of stopping.

After a dazzlingly long time in his arms, I opened my eyes and looked around, mentally applying the brakes. Then I pushed him away.

He resisted at first, then loosened his grip and let me go. "Too much?" He squinted one eye.

"No, it was good." I paused to take a breath. "But I can't do this. Sorry."

"It was *good*?" He grinned. "You can do better than that —I thought it was great. What are you hiding? Do you have a boyfriend?"

A boyfriend! That was a laugh. If Roman saw me kissing Alejandro, he probably wouldn't care at all. That's how much of a boyfriend he was. Pathetic hipster.

"I do have a boyfriend, but I don't think either of us feels very strongly about it. That's not why I stopped. And you're right—that kiss was much more than good." I held a hand to my chest and took a long breath to show him just how good it was. "But I'm trying to sell you a guitar, so I don't think this is the right thing to do."

He stared deeply for a few seconds, then relaxed into the limousine seat. "Okay, I understand. Perhaps when this business of ours is finished?"

"Maybe. I can't think about that right now." I fanned my face with my hand but failed to get any relief from the searing heat that still enveloped my body. "This is all so strange for me. Please don't be mad."

Alejandro shook his head and offered me a light smile. "I'm not even the slightest bit mad. I apologize for being too forward, but I just couldn't resist." He slid away from me on the seat while both of us straightened our clothes and hair, pretending that we hadn't just kissed madly. It was easy. All I had to do was convince myself was that I wasn't alone with one of the most famous, talented, and sexy men alive. How hard could that be?

After neatening himself up, Alejandro turned to face me. "So, Deborah, tell me about yourself. What do you do?"

And just like that, he was back to being civilized, and I was back in the con. I allowed the truth to make its way into my answer, even though I should have lied. "I'm a painter, living in New York City right now. I manage to sell enough of my art to pay the bills."

Alejandro nodded at me and let a tiny grin creep onto his face. "You won't have to worry about bills after I buy that guitar."

"You'd think that, wouldn't you? But Mom will keep the money—it's her guitar."

His eyes flared, and his mouth twisted into a frown. "You won't get any of it? Why not tell her that it sold for three hundred? Then you can pocket the extra hundred thousand."

"Do you think I'm a thief?" This conversation was verging into dangerous territory.

Alejandro burst into laughter, slapping his knee. After a few seconds, he got himself under control. "Sorry about that. It's just that everyone's a thief. Look at me—millions of poor kids love me so much that they pay money they can't afford for my music. It makes me feel like a swindler, a con artist." I struggled to control my breathing at his choice of words. Good thing he didn't stop to dwell on it. "And your mother is getting way too much money for a simple guitar. Hell, even George takes my money."

Now it was my turn to laugh but not nearly as hard. "Maybe you pay him too much."

He quickly sobered up, no longer amused. Then he checked to make sure the glass separating us from the driver's compartment was all the way up. Secure from eavesdropping, he took a deep breath and lowered his voice. "When I say that he takes my money, I'm not talking about what I pay him. George embezzles from me. I've known about it for a few months now, but apparently he's been doing it for years." He grumbled his displeasure.

I was shocked. "That's terrible. What are you going to do?"

"Not sure, but I'll figure something out."

"Why don't you fire him?"

"Can't. He has too much power, and he's ruthless. With access to all of my finances, he could ruin me before I could get control back."

"Well that sucks. How did he get so much power?"

"George has been my manager since before I got famous. He promised me greatness back then, which he delivered. But he also insisted on complete control. It seemed like a good deal at the time, but in retrospect, he cheated me."

I felt bad for Alejandro, and I wished I was conning George instead. Elle's team would love to take that guy down. But I had a job to do, so I tried to focus.

"Should I worry about George when I sell my mother's guitar to him? Will he cheat me?"

"No, he won't cheat you if you do an honest deal. But if you ever tell anyone you sold a guitar to me, he'll come after you, and I promise it won't be pleasant. He hates it when people use my name to their advantage."

"How can that be? You're famous—people must use your name all the time."

"They do, but not without permission. Let me give you an example of George's handiwork." He shook his head with a downturned mouth. "Last year, George noticed a beauty salon that had my picture in their window. The photo was a popular one that showed me with Talia Dare." He looked at me to see if I'd respond to his name-dropping. I kept a straight face, so he explained. "She's a famous rocker."

"I know who Talia Dare is."

He widened his eyes. "You've heard of Talia Dare, but not me?"

That made me laugh. "I never said I hadn't heard of you. Just that I didn't know your music. I'm not sure I could recognize a Talia Dare song, either." Another lie—I had nearly all of her music.

"Right." He grinned. "Anyway, that photo made the rounds back when the two of us were on tour together. So it had been published everywhere. But the beauty salon had edited the photo. They'd removed Talia's face and replaced it with some other woman. That bothered George.

"He went in there and asked about the picture. They told him it was part of a 'digital makeover' system where customers could see how they'd look with various hairstyles, in this case, Talia's. And the picture was perfect because women love to imagine themselves with me." He winked and grinned, then his face fell. "Well, some do, anyway."

I flushed lightly, embarrassed to be one of the few women alive who didn't claim to want his body. "So I'm guessing he sent them a cease-and-desist letter to force them to stop using your picture."

"Yeah, *right*." Alejandro shook his head. "That would have been the proper thing to do. But not George. He came at them with both guns blazing."

I frowned. "What did he do?"

"He hired thugs to go in and intimidate the owner. They started by ripping up all of the posters, including the pictures of me, Talia, the Fiery Boys, and a few others. Then they trashed the shop and actually roughed up the owner."

"George beats people up for something so minor?" Perhaps I shouldn't be worried about Alejandro's bodyguard. It was George I needed to avoid. Would he send thugs to attack me after this deal? Now I really wanted to get out of town.

Alejandro's face fell as he sighed. "George does whatever it takes. He's brutal. And after everyone heard that thugs busted up a beauty salon and beat up the owner, nobody wanted to go there anymore. It basically drove them out of business."

"What an ass! I can see why you don't want to mess with that guy." *I* didn't want to mess with George, either. This con might be much more difficult than I expected.

Suddenly, the intercom beeped next to Alejandro, and he picked up the handset. "What, Udo? . . .Really?" He squinted at me. "Udo says that someone's been following the limousine since we picked you up."

Stupid me! This date was a huge mistake. First I was fraternizing with the mark, and now I had to explain to him why Vance was following us.

I looked out the back window to be sure, then I grabbed the handset so I could talk to Udo. "Is it that skinny guy in the dark gray sedan?" Udo confirmed my suspicions, so I spoke to both him and Alejandro. "It's my cousin, Vance. He gets a little overprotective of me sometimes. Sorry about him, but he's harmless."

Alejandro chuckled and hung up the intercom. "I hope he doesn't make a scene. I'd hate to have to sic Udo on him."

The limousine slowed down as it approached a huge building. I saw a large crowd of formally dressed people milling around. Too many, in my opinion. "Where are we?"

"It's a party being thrown by *No Moss*, the magazine that interviewed me yesterday. Lots of rich and famous people here tonight. You'll love it. Plus, you get to be my date." He grinned. "Make your friends jealous."

A streak of panic shot through me. He'd promised that he would keep me to himself tonight, but I should have known that could never happen. It was one thing to be with the incredible Alejandro but another thing entirely to be at a venue so full of famous people and no doubt plenty of paparazzi, too. They'd say, "Oh, are you dating Alejandro?" And I'd struggle to avoid saying, "No, I'm just stealing his money."

Sooner or later, someone was going to recognize me, for my pottery or for my youthful exploits. I had to get out.

"I'm sorry, Alejandro. I can't do this."

"Of course you can. It'll be fun. The *No Moss* people will love you. Wouldn't you like to be seen with me in their gossip pages?"

That was the last thing I wanted, and he needed to understand that. "Absolutely not. And keep me away from their skanky reporter."

Alejandro threw his head back and howled his laughter. "You think Ivory's a skank? Yeah, she does like to flaunt it, but believe me, underneath the skank skin is a hard-edged woman." He leaned closer and whispered. "You want to know what I think? I think you're better looking than she is."

"Okay, now I *know* you're lying. Besides, I heard her say that she'd be back last night. Don't tell me you two played Scrabble."

Alejandro hitched one side of his mouth into a smile. "Good! You're jealous. That means you want me." He leaned over and stole a kiss. "Ivory means nothing to me. Come to the party, and I'll prove it to you."

The door opened, and he stepped out to camera flashes and cheering fans. He held out his hand to escort me, but I shrank back in the limousine. No way was I stepping out at this party holding hands with Alejandro. In addition to being seen by everyone here, pictures of the two of us would flood the media. I'd be yet another woman spotted on the arm of the rocking hottie. Now I understood why there were so many. But right now, in the middle of a con, I couldn't do this.

I looked around in a panic. After a few seconds, Alejandro's hand disappeared, and Udo ducked his head inside to escort me out. "Zey are vaiting for you, Ms. Gleason." I stared at the big man.

"Sorry, Udo. I'll get this back to you." I grabbed his hat, shoved it far down on my head, then escaped through the door on the other side. Some people tried to talk to me and take my picture, but I covered myself and quickly disappeared into the crowd. A few blocks over, on a quiet street, I found a cab and made my escape.

Five Days
Until the Deal

Thirteen

I woke up the next morning feeling slightly numb. It couldn't be a hangover because I hadn't been drinking, so it must have been the fact that Alejandro had kissed me. Had that really happened? My memories of the limousine ride felt like a dream, something that couldn't have been real. But it *was* real, and my lips still burned from the heat of that kiss. Too bad I also remembered that Bea was forcing me to swindle this man. No wonder I felt numb.

I stumbled to the bathroom while I contemplated my bizarre life. The most desirable man I could think of wanted me, for no reason I could figure, and I had to push him away because I was being forced to cheat him. Reality had taken a vacation, leaving me neck-deep in surreal stew, and no amount of water splashed on my face was going to make things normal again.

So I called the most real person I knew: Wanda. She represented everything normal about my life. Only she could give me what I needed.

The blast of her voice warmed me like a hot shower. "Dee, love! Good to hear you're still with us. You're not going to believe this, babe, but you've become the hottest thing in New York City! Your pottery is *flying* off the shelves. Everyone, I mean *everyone* wants a piece of you. And that includes me, honey. You've got to come home."

"Oh, Wanda. It's good to hear your voice."

She paused. "What's wrong?"

"What's right? I'm spiraling out of control here." I stopped to take a breath. "Bea's got me doing things I shouldn't be doing. I just need you to tell me that it's all gonna be okay."

"I can do that." She cleared her throat and spoke with authority. "It'll. Be. Okay." Then, back to being Wanda, she added, "Do you need me to say it three times?"

I smiled. "No, that did the trick. So what else is happening?"

Her answer surprised me. "We've had two unusual visitors at the shop. One good and one bad. The good is a *New York Times* reporter who came by looking for you. I told her all about the shop, but now she wants to meet you even more. Could be big."

This was a good visit? Wanda understood that I liked my anonymity, even though I'd never told her I was in hiding. But she still courted fame for me, somehow managing to ignore the disconnect between these two things. I might not be hiding from Bea anymore, but I still couldn't handle notoriety, especially in the middle of this con. I couldn't allow a piece about me in the *New York Times* any more than I could appear with Alejandro at a *No Moss* party.

But on the positive side, if everything turned out well with this con and I found that blackmail evidence, I might be willing to reveal myself, for the first time in my life. If I could stop hiding from Bea and didn't alienate Alejandro too severely, I might be able to return to New York and live openly. Imagine a world where I didn't have to run from *New York Times* reporters and *No Moss* parties. It seemed like a dream.

In the meantime, such a world didn't exist. So given that Wanda's good visitor wasn't very good in my book, I asked her with trepidation, "Who was the *bad* visitor?"

"This strange guy came into the shop and asked all about you. Something about him set off my cop-alarm, so I clammed up. Told him I hardly know anything about you." She giggled. "He got the message and left."

A cop or just an investigator? Dee Frank hadn't done anything illegal, so it probably wasn't a policeman. Could the investigation of my birth parents have triggered some trouble? Or was this another of Bea's tricks, checking up on me so she could gather more dirt? Whatever was going on, it was annoying.

Wanda shifted to serious. "If you're doing something that you shouldn't, Dee, then maybe this is a good time to stop." She paused, trying to use the silence to draw me out. But I couldn't share my illegal exploits or my romantic ones, so I had nothing to say.

"Don't worry. I'll tell you all about it when I get back."

"Come home soon. I miss you! We'll go dancing and drinking. Ooh! I know! Let's throw a huge party at the shop and invite everyone, even that *Times* reporter. Put you even more on the map. Just pick a date, and I'll set it up."

I loved this woman's energy, her enthusiasm, and her insistence on grabbing life with both hands and giving it a shake. Perhaps she was right. If things worked out well, a party would be exactly what I needed when I got back home. I knew Wanda would be able to cheer me up—I felt better already. "Yeah, that sounds like fun. And I'm coming home soon—hopefully less than a week. We'll do all those things and more, I promise. Thanks for being there for me."

"I got you covered, Dee. And I'm glad you're nearly done out there. See you soon." I hung up, feeling much better.

Then it all got ruined. Bea called and started screaming at me from the moment the call went through. I had to hold the phone down at my waist to prevent damage to my eardrums. Thanks to Vance, she knew about my date with Alejandro and had many choice words to describe the foolishness of it. I tried to get her to admit that she'd hired him to follow me, but she refused to concede anything.

I endured a few minutes of her angry con lessons, with extra emphasis on the perils of falling for the mark. I wanted to point out that I was just keeping the mark happy until the deal was complete, but all the voices in my head reminded me that she was right. "Never fall for the mark," they screamed in chorus with Bea. I really needed to take that advice more seriously, if possible. By the time I got off the phone, I was back to feeling like crap.

And then, just to keep my emotions yo-yoing some more, Alejandro called. I stared at his name on my phone and my mouth fell open. Why was he doing this? I didn't merit so much attention, especially after running away from him last night. If he were any other man, he'd stay clear of me after a stunt like that.

But not Alejandro. "What happened last night? Why did you run away?" The concern in his voice was sincere—I felt it in my gut. Suddenly, my head was spinning in a blurred daze, lost in his kiss, unable to hear the bells of alarm warning me against getting romantically involved.

"I'm sorry. I just couldn't handle a media event that big."

"You're the first woman I've met since I became famous who didn't want to be seen with me. Are you secretly married? In witness protection?"

I laughed. "No and no."

"Can I meet you in private? I have to see you some more."

There it was again. A strange sensation that I'd somehow been dropped into a dream where the world's most handsome and popular musician wanted me. My whole body buzzed at the thought of meeting him in private. "Okay, sure." Oops! Why did I say that? I meant to tell him to leave me alone. What was wrong with me?

"Good. How about right now?" There was a knock on the door of my motel room, and I jumped so high that I nearly hit my head on the ceiling.

"Is that you at my door?" I ground out the words.

His answer came at me from both sides. "Open up, Deborah. Let me in."

I went to the door and looked through the peephole. Alejandro! Wearing a gray hoodie, jeans, and sunglasses. I quickly opened up and ushered him in. "What are you *doing* here?"

"Obviously, I'm here to see you. I didn't get enough last night."

He didn't get enough? Oh, please! Regrettably, he was right—neither of us got enough last night. I definitely didn't. But nobody ever promised me enough from life, so I was used to it by now.

Also, I was not here to give enough of anything to this man, except perhaps confidence. My job was to take, not give. But instead, he was the one who was taking. Already, he had taken much more than I'd ever expected. And all I wanted to do was give him more.

But one thing I didn't want to give him was my room number. I thought motels didn't release that information. "How did you know my room? Did the office tell you?"

"Your cousin told me after I gave him a signed photo."

How annoying! I was about to tell him that my cousin was doing a lousy job of protecting me, but before I could say anything, Alejandro pulled me into his arms and planted a kiss. All of my defenses were instantly obliterated by his steel-gray eyes, his rugged beard shadow, and wisps of his jet black hair. Those irresistible lips drew me in, and I fell gladly. Oh yes, I remembered that kiss, one of the best I'd ever had.

After a nice long one, he pulled back, hovering inches away from me. His fingers ran through my hair a few times. Then suddenly, he stopped, staring at my head. "So you're a natural blonde. The hair under the bleached part looked dark to me, but now I can see that it's not."

I turned to stare at him. The world-famous musician, who women everywhere fawned over, was looking closely at me. I didn't expect to be treated with such consideration, such loving attention. I thought that he simply wanted to seduce me, but instead, Alejandro was acting like he cared. He was noticing things about me, learning what he could. And my confusion grew deeper with every encounter.

Interestingly, although I'd been with Roman for the past five years, he'd never noticed anything about my hair. One time, two years ago, I asked if he knew what color my hair was. He started by telling me it was white, but I pointed out that I bleached it and wanted to know if he could name my natural hair color. By this point in our relationship, he'd seen me naked plenty of times, so he must have seen my blonde pubic hair. And my roots were easily as grown out then as they were now, so Roman could simply have looked at me to find the answer. But he never really put much thought into my appearance, and he didn't bother to look that day, either. Instead, he told me that my natural hair color was black. I never bothered to correct him.

Alejandro, by comparison, instantly knew better. "Yeah," I laughed. "I'm a dirty blonde. Next to the bleached hair, it seems darker than it is."

He chuckled then stepped away. "I don't have a lot of time right now. Certainly not enough to make love to you properly." He sat on the sofa, patting the cushion next to him. "Sit. Talk to me."

Did Alejandro just profess a desire to make love to me? The way he spoke with such conviction was overpowering. I had to curl my hands tightly to keep from grabbing his chiseled face and lunging for him. That still didn't help, so I counted to five, slowly. Then I let a shuddering breath rumble from deep down. "Okay." A little calmer, I sat down carefully, pasting a shy smile on my face. "How was the party?"

He leaned back to look at me. "Boring. The same old crap. You really should have been there—you'd have made it much more interesting."

He had no idea how interesting it might have gotten if I'd gone to that party last night. And if I hadn't been conning him, it would also have been fun. How I wanted to scream out my guilt and stop all this. Take me to jail—I don't care. As long as I could have one night with this incredible man.

"I'm sorry, Alejandro. Part of me wants everything you're offering, and more. But another part of me is scared senseless. Maybe we should finish this guitar business first."

"I disagree. If you're willing to explore this after I buy your mother's guitar, why not do it now?"

Ugh! Did he have to be desirable *and* reasonable? Why couldn't he just be a sexist egomaniac? Then I'd be happy to take his money, and I wouldn't want to get naked with him. Both of which are important factors of any successful con.

"Look, I don't like the spotlight, and you're way too famous."

He grinned. "So you *do* know who I am."

"I've been doing some reading. Enough to realize how incredibly well known you are. I don't want any of that."

"Trust me, I understand. I'm not totally comfortable with my fame, either. Nobody treats me like a human being anymore. And it's depressing to have to hide all the time or need a bodyguard just to go out for a walk. My old friends rarely come by, and when they do, it's not the same as it used to be. Even my bandmates treat me with too much deference. Instead of seeing me as a friendly musician, I'm now their rich and famous boss." He let out a dark laugh. "The worst is my parents, who treat me like a hero—their famous son. Back in high school, they wanted me to be a lawyer. They thought music wasn't a respectable career. Now they tell everyone they meet that the 'great' Alejandro is their son."

"Did they dislike your music, or just careers in music?"

He nodded his head with a smirk. "You're right: it was a money thing with them. They were poor immigrants from Chile. My dad worked hard on a construction crew, and he wanted me to do better. But my mom loved music—she even gave lessons to make some money. There was a beat-up piano in the basement where we lived, so she occasionally took me down there to teach me."

I'd never seen him play a keyboard in the ten years I'd been following him, so I was curious to know more. "I thought you played guitar. Who taught you that?"

Alejandro's eyes glimmered as a smile grew on his face. "Mom. She had one that she'd brought from Chile. One day, I picked it up and started to strum it like she did. I'd been watching her play, and I'd learned a few chords. Before I knew it, I could play the guitar, too. The piano didn't get much use after that."

He took a long breath. "Look, Deborah, I get that you don't want to go out in public, but I want to see you again, get to know you better. I've got to go now—I'm meeting some people about a tour later this year. But I want you to come to my place tonight for dinner. I promise I won't make you into the next tabloid sensation." He grinned. "It'll just be us. No fans, no reporters, no manager."

I arched an eyebrow. "No personal assistant?"

He laughed at my question. "Karen means well. But no, she won't be there tonight, either. I want you all to myself. I'll send Udo for you at six."

That sounded like a terrible idea. Going there for dinner would only heat things up between us. I could never resist his advances, and I knew he'd make them. Then it would be even harder to con him. This date was completely and utterly wrong.

"Alejandro," I took a deep breath. "We can't. . . I'm not ready."

"Don't worry. This doesn't have to be anything more than dinner. I like that you're not a desperate fan girl, and I enjoy spending time with you. That's enough for tonight. No sex. Although both of us want it, so I'm not sure why you're holding back." He grinned and pulled me into his arms. "Just come over for dinner, then Udo will take you home. I reserve the right to kiss you madly, though." He did that a few times, just to make sure I understood.

It really seemed like Alejandro wanted to see me. And refusing his advances could potentially be worse than accepting them. He was the mark, after all, and needed some attention. Attention that I wanted to give, as well. Also, I couldn't have him showing up randomly at my motel room—he might see something he shouldn't. I wanted to conclude this deal as soon as possible, so I simply *had* to go there for dinner. There wasn't any choice.

Proud of my ability to take a really bad idea and convince myself it was brilliant, I gave him a hesitant smile. "Okay but tell him to meet me at the coffee shop in the strip mall around the corner. That way, I can sneak out without Vance seeing me."

He laughed. "Fine. And by the way, I'm sorry you and Karen started off badly. I actually think you two would like each other. She means well, and she's damn good at her job." He paused with a thoughtful smile. "She's got me totally organized."

I shrugged. "Sure, but she still thinks she has a chance with you."

"Yeah." He took a long, noisy breath. "We had a one-night stand when I first got famous, but it was just one night—we both knew that. Then she got the job as my assistant, and on her first day, she reminded me about our hook-up. I didn't even *remember* her, that's how bad I am. So I warned her that it wasn't going to happen again, and she understood."

"I don't think she still feels that way."

He grunted. "You're right. Things have changed recently. Last month, she asked me if I could ever imagine the two of us getting married. I reminded her that this was not going to happen, and she nearly burst into tears."

"If she's as good an assistant as you say, then she must devote her life to you. Does she deal with your fan mail and social networks, too?"

"Yeah, and my calendar, my shopping, my homes. . ." His head spun around in a little circle, showing how overwhelmed he was by her efforts. He concluded the list with, "My life."

"See? That's a lot of work. No wonder she expects something in return."

"She gets my admiration and my money, but she doesn't get my love. Sorry."

"Hey! Don't apologize to me—this is between you and her. I understand that you can't give her more love, but you do owe her, if she's as good as you say. So maybe you should give her more money. It might help her let go of the need for love."

Alejandro hummed for a second, apparently considering my suggestion. "Good idea. I'll work on it." He stood up. "Anyway, I have to go." He grabbed me and stole one last kiss. Then he put on his sunglasses, flipped up his hoodie, and left.

I watched him walk out to his car. When he got there, a woman who had been standing next to Vance's car shrieked and ran up to him. Leave it to Vance to blow the rocker's cover. The woman jumped a little and pulled out some paper and a pen.

Alejandro signed his name and briefly chatted with her. Ever the generous performer, he managed to make time for all of his fans. Udo waved his hands and said something, probably trying to keep Alejandro on schedule. He nodded to the bodyguard and turned to the woman again. That's when she made her move.

She threw her arms around him and tried to kiss him. He was so surprised that he nearly fell over. I watched as he regained his balance, pulled her arms from him, and held her at a distance. Udo quickly came over and took her away while Alejandro got in the car. Then they drove off.

I was right about him being too famous. Even when disguised, people found him and attacked him on the street. The poor guy had no private life.

Fourteen

The limousine picked me up at the strip mall's coffee shop promptly at six. Alejandro wasn't in back, so I chatted with Udo. "You're more than just a driver, aren't you?"

"You are right, I am his bodyguard. But I also drive him around, since he got famous."

So this was the guy who watched the parade of women. I was sure he'd seen it all. "Is it true he's with a different woman every night?"

Udo frowned. "It is true zat most vomen only spend one night. But zere are far fewer than you zink."

"Oh come on! I see him with a different woman every day."

Udo laughed. "Zat is how zee media sees him, but it is not so."

"Yeah, I guess the media could make up stories about me, too. That's why I ran from the event yesterday." I pulled his hat from my purse and handed it back to him. "Thanks for the loan."

"If you do not vant zee media to make up stories about you, zen you should not be vith him. Zey are going to find you eventually, you know. Zey even follow me. My vife calls me each time she sees me in a picture vith him."

"Your wife *calls* you? Where is she?"

Udo slumped his shoulders. "She does not live vith me right now. It is a long story."

I understood that he didn't want to discuss his marital problems, so I let it drop. "Well, the media may be lying about some things, but I know he and Karen got it on."

Udo flipped a hand out to the side. "Yes, yes. She tells anyone who asks. But it is over between zem." He regarded me in the rearview mirror. "If you do not mind my saying, Ms. Gleason, I zink he is quite taken vith you. I have not been sent to fetch many vomen, and never one who had run away from him zee day before."

Oh God! I did not need to hear this. Not only was I swindling this beautiful and talented man, but I was stealing his heart, too. Not that I understood how such a thing was possible. Still, I hated myself even more for conning him.

I slumped back in my seat. "I guess I should be honored." But honor was the furthest emotion from my mind and certainly the last thing I deserved. I rode quietly the rest of the way to Alejandro's mansion.

When we arrived, he greeted me at the door with a modest hug. His spicy outdoor scent reminded me of his kiss. And his kiss reminded me that I shouldn't be there. But then he wrapped an arm around me, solid and cozy and impossible to resist. So I gave up trying.

Alejandro stepped back and smiled. "How about a tour? You've been here twice, but you haven't really seen the place. Let me show you around." He escorted me down the hall.

It turned out that Alejandro collected much more than rare guitars. His house was full of interesting artifacts, including paintings, sculptures, weavings, and rare books. Some people place their collections on pedestals, behind glass, or in locked rooms. Not Alejandro. He believed that his possessions should be touched, even used. He encouraged me to feel the texture of an oil painting, we walked over fine silk rugs, and he handed me a rare first-edition book of Pablo Neruda's poems, pointing out his favorites.

We entered his study, a beautiful dark-wood room with shelving all around. I saw books, vinyls, and CDs. A few awards decorated another shelf—he had gold and platinum records, some Grammys, an MTV award, and more. One corner of the room was piled with band equipment: guitars, microphones, and speakers. Over by the side of the room was a small collection of drinks and snacks. And on the left, a solid wood desk faced the window. I'd been taking in all the fascinating things on his shelves, so I hadn't noticed the desk. But as soon as I did, I nearly fainted.

Oh. My. God! How could this be? Right in the middle of his desk, close to where he sat, was. . . trouble. I hoped I was wrong, but the more I stared at it, the more I knew I was right. He had one of my pieces of pottery—a small vase that was being used to hold pens. I started to back up to the door.

Did he know who I was? Had he found the one or two obscure pictures of me that my friends had posted to the Internet? Suddenly, I worried that he was about to expose me.

Alejandro waved toward the desk and I sucked in my breath. I knew what was coming next: some comment about the vase, revealing my true identity. I could feel a cold sweat crawl across my body. Damn these con games—I was so done with them.

Alejandro smiled and sat down at the desk. "This is where I write my music." He looked at me, then straightened with a frown on his face. "Are you all right?

You seem pale." He stood up and came over to take my hand.

I fanned myself. "I'm fine, thanks. Just a bit nervous." I didn't even have to fake a nervous laugh. Much to my relief, he didn't seem to know who I was. But my tension over being exposed nearly gave everything away. I exhaled slowly, letting my nerves relax.

I needed to change the subject, so I walked across the room to the wall of awards. "Are these Grammys?" I liked how they were shaped like old-fashioned gramophones.

He smiled, then came over to take down the one in the middle and offer it to me. "This is the first Grammy I ever won." I hefted it in my hand, surprised by how solid it felt.

"You have an awful lot of stuff here."

He laughed. "That's a good way of putting it: stuff. Sometimes I feel trapped by it all. Good thing Karen keeps it all organized. I've got an entire room full of things that I don't know what to do with. The original lyrics for many of my songs, less-important awards, the first guitar I ever bought. . ." He smiled, his dark features lighting up my deepest recesses. "Stuff."

With a nod, he turned and started to leave the room. "Speaking of guitars, let me show you my collection. Your mother's will soon be there." He led me to a large room that was full of guitars. Like everything else he collected, these weren't secured in any way. Instead, each one hung on hooks that made it easy to remove. He even took down an acoustic guitar and strummed it a few times. "This belonged to Eric Clapton." He hung it back up.

Each electric guitar had a cord attached to it, connecting it to the wall. He picked one of them up, slung it around his neck, then flipped a switch on the wall. When he strummed it, the chord reverberated through the room from hidden speakers. Then he started to play an old song from his first album.

My mind reeled, struggling to accept what was happening. A personal performance by Alejandro—nobody would ever believe it. I had to force myself to stand still and not move to the beat. After a few bars, he stopped. "Do you know this song?"

I pretended ignorance. "Is it one of yours? I think I've heard it. It's nice."

He burst out laughing. "'Nice,' eh? Of all of the songs I have written, this one is my personal favorite. And I just played it on a guitar that Jimi Hendrix once owned."

I hung my head, glad for any excuse to look away from the great rocker. "I must be a disappointment to you."

He put the guitar back on the wall, then he lifted my chin to look at me. Warmth radiated through my body, and I allowed myself to return a smaller smile. This was so messed up! All I wanted to do was throw myself at him and kiss him again. Instead, I had to kick myself on the inside to keep myself focused.

Alejandro shook his head slowly. "No, Deborah. You've yet to disappoint me." He let go of my chin and walked over to a big metal door by the side of the room. "Are you ready for the special guitar collection?"

"You have even more?" I looked around the room, which had over fifty guitars in it. "How many guitars can one man own?"

"The ones out here are mine. But George has his own collection that he keeps at my place. Let me show you."

So the rumors were true. I was about to see George's fabled collection of stolen guitars. Alejandro turned to a keypad next to the door. Although he covered it with his other hand while he entered the code, I could see the movement of his button-pushing hand, which was enough. Aunt Franny, a keen observer of the human body, had taught me when I was little to read the muscles and bones in a hand pressing a numeric keypad. What can I say? Old habits are hard to lose.

The room with George's collection was more like a vault: austere, windowless, and protected by a door that belonged on a bank safe. A dozen guitars hung on the walls of this room, and a thirteenth was displayed on a pedestal in the center. In stark contrast to Alejandro's guitars, these were much more securely protected in glass cases. I noticed alarm wires on each case and quickly spotted cameras, laser beam emitters, and a few other high-tech security features. George clearly had a different approach to the care of his valuables.

I gave Alejandro a grin. "Nobody gets near George's collection."

"No. He doesn't even like it when I show it to people. Don't tell him I let you in here."

"If he's so sensitive about it, why does he keep it here?"

"Because I've got space for it and better security. And because he can come here whenever he wants."

Alejandro pointed to one guitar on the wall. "This one was stolen from Paul McCartney."

"George stole it?"

Alejandro blurted out a laugh. "No, he wouldn't do that. But he bought it on the black market." He waved his arm across the room. "Every guitar here was stolen. I like rare guitars, but George has a thing for 'missing' ones."

"Isn't he worried about buying them and getting busted?"

Alejandro rolled his eyes. "George has balls the size of Jupiter. He once boasted to me that he could buy a stolen guitar while cops watched him do it. Claims that as my manager, he can get away with anything. And he thinks the police are stupid." He nodded toward the guitars all around us. "So far, he may be right."

I walked to the display case in the middle of the room. The guitar sitting there looked very simple, just a plain old acoustic guitar. "This doesn't seem so special."

Alejandro nodded. "You're right. It's not that special. It's just a basic Martin guitar—a Dreadnought, or 'dread,' as they're called. But George had one of them when he was a kid, so he's got a soft spot for them. This one here is a rare prototype of an original D-1 model—stolen, of course."

"So George plays guitar?"

Alejandro groaned. "Not very well, but he likes to pretend. Still has his original dread at home. And he's so sentimentally attached to it that he paid seven hundred thousand dollars for this prototype. They only made eight of them, and four were destroyed in a fire. The others mysteriously disappeared thirty years ago." He pointed into the guitar's sound chamber. "See how it's stamped 'D-1' in there? They've been making dreads for a long time, and each model gets a new number. The D-27, the D-45, and so forth. But a D-1 is a rarity, and the prototypes are even more valuable. Notice how underneath the D-1, instead of a serial number, it says 'Prototype 6.' That's a true collector's item."

"And stolen, too. Aren't you worried about getting in trouble?"

Alejandro just shrugged. "Not really. Besides, there's nothing I can do about it. If George wants them here, it's his business. Also, these are incredible instruments, so I don't mind too much. I guess my morals are somewhat imperfect. Besides, I appreciate beauty." He turned to face me with a lusty grin.

I'd seen that look before, on countless Alejandro videos, a come-hither smile that nobody could resist. Damn, he was hot—it burned deep into me. The long black hair, the irresistibly alluring grin, those intense gray eyes. I stood there transfixed.

I began to wonder how much he knew. Was it possible that when he talked about imperfect morals, he knew how it applied to me? Or was he referring to only himself and George? Perhaps he simply had the hots for me and wanted my body. Not that I had any problem with that, but I still didn't understand how it could be possible.

Four Days Until the Deal

Fifteen

Alejandro called me the next day, first thing in the morning. We'd had a lovely dinner at his place, after which Udo had brought me back, early in the evening. But dinner with this man was difficult enough, and the intensity of his parting kiss had left me shaken. So I hadn't slept much last night.

I managed to grab my phone and squinted at his name. Was I the only person in the world who was unhappy to be awakened by the Lord of Rock and Roll? I scooted farther under the covers to take the call.

"Deborah!" He enthused a little too much, which made me wonder what was going on. A man so famous and desirable couldn't possibly want me this badly. Sure, in my fantasies, we fell instantly in love. But in real life, it didn't happen. So I couldn't figure it out.

I mumbled my response through a pre-caffeinated fog. "You seem happy." Some people are more chipper in the morning than others, and Mr. Sunshine seemed like one of those early risers. His gentle laugh warmed me and brought me fully awake. Okay, perhaps it really wasn't so bad to get a personal wakeup call from a world-famous rocker. So what if his desire was mysterious? Just thinking about his hot mouth made me start to liquefy. I had to take a moment to make sure I wasn't still dreaming.

But what he said next assured me that this was no dream. "I got the money early, and I'm ready to buy the guitar today. When can you bring it over?"

Whoa, what? He was rearranging the deal? Not good. Now I understood why he seemed so excited—he was playing games, being the important person and commanding others. I needed to be careful here.

He seemed to be cutting out his business manager, doing the deal himself and at his place. I wasn't sure how I felt about that, so I probed politely. "I thought we were doing the deal at George's."

"I'm relieving him of his duties for this deal. I don't trust him anymore, so I got the money myself. When can you bring over the guitar? To my place, by the way."

So George was out. For the most part, I was relieved by this change. First of all, I'd get to finish the deal four days early, which would get me home sooner. And secondly, I wouldn't have to deal with George. The stories of his thugs and their aggressive tactics fed directly into my fear of bad con repercussions and disturbed me more than I wanted to admit. All in all, I was glad to be done with Alejandro's ruthless business manager.

But now I was swindling the rock god directly, and that raised other concerns. Like my ability to pull it off at all. Also, I suspected he was cheating George with this deal, so I needed to watch my step or else I might get caught between the two of them.

Predictably, even the barest hint that the deal was going to go down today caused my con fears to start up. "You'll get caught," they warned. And even if I didn't get caught, I'd have to face my guilt about robbing this wonderful man. How could I take his money when flashes of lust sparkled in the air all around us? This deal was so incredibly wrong.

I was also unsettled by his change of plans. Things were supposed to happen in order, not get rearranged at the last minute. But con artists have to keep their balance while floating on the currents. I would simply have to adapt—we'd do the deal sooner. This also meant I wouldn't see Alejandro after today. One last visit, one last kiss, and then I'd run back to New York where I'd be safe. Certainly safer than here in Los Angeles.

I looked at my watch and calculated how quickly I could make it to Alejandro's place. Then my training kicked in and told me to stretch it—make him wait. Alejandro's mother may have taught him to appreciate music, but mine taught me how to work a mark. Don't appear bored, but don't appear too eager, either. Let them be the ones who are desperate to do the deal.

Deborah Gleason was a busy woman. She wouldn't drop everything and run at the chance to sell this guitar. She'd take care of her personal business during her lunch hour. So if I wanted to be professional about it, I'd delay my visit until then.

I nearly started to laugh out loud at myself. Yeah, I was being *such* a professional in the way I handled Alejandro. I kept my focus all the time. I didn't grope him, throw him to the floor, or lose myself in his intoxicating kisses. Much. At least I hadn't ripped his clothes off and had wild sex with him. Although it *did* happen in my daydreams.

Without a doubt, I was losing it. I was doing so many ill-advised things that even Bea had to keep her eye on me. But interestingly, thinking about the nefarious F.M. had a positive effect. It woke me up, as thoughts of her usually did. And it helped me get back to the deal.

"I'm busy right now. But I can be there at noon. Is that okay?" It was.

I debated telling Bea about this change. She'd be upset about it, which could start all sorts of trouble. She'd insist things go back to the way they were, with the deal concluding in four days. But I liked the idea of finishing this now, so I convinced myself to leave Bea out of it. I had the guitar—why not just go to Alejandro's and get the cash?

Also, I knew Bea would be thrilled to see the money sooner. Maybe even thrilled enough to offer me a deal that would stop her blackmail. Then I could go back to my simple life in New York, free of grifters and con games, free of people following me, and free of overexcited musicians who called me too early in the morning.

Four hours later, I arrived at Alejandro's estate, dressed nicely, as befits a woman about to make a huge sale. No longer hiding my hair, I dressed to complement it by wearing a black knit pantsuit over a crisp white blouse. Light gold trim on the collar framed my neck.

I didn't want Vance to know about this change of plans, so I'd sneaked out the bathroom window with the guitar, and driven to Alejandro's in my black SUV. He was waiting for me at the front door, all smiles. "Good to see you, Deborah. Come in." We exchanged a hug and a brief kiss, then I followed him in. My feet bounced a little as I carried the guitar, watching his muscles flex under his thin T-shirt as he moved through the house. I tried to remind myself that I was a con artist, not a groupie, but whenever I was around him, the two seemed to get confused.

On the way to the study, I saw Udo, watching from a corner. That helped sober me up. With a jolt, I remembered where I was, what I was doing, and why I shouldn't feel so damned happy. Did Udo carry a gun? Could he run as fast as I could? Did he know how much money his employer was about to spend?

Alejandro led me to his study where an attaché case sat on his desk, next to my pen-holding vase. I set the guitar down next to his case, and we turned to face each other. Despite my fears, this was going very well so far.

Alejandro's look completely captivated me and put me at ease. He warmed me with a spectacularly intense smile, twinkling gray eyes, and a pounding heart. No wait, that was *my* heart doing all the pounding. I was definitely having trouble staying focused.

Since this would be the last time I saw Alejandro, I let myself get lost in his eyes once more. The deal could wait— he obviously didn't seem too anxious. We gazed for a few minutes.

Suddenly, my guilt overcame me, and I felt awful about the whole deal. I wanted to scream out the truth, admit my lies, refuse his money, and tell him about my childhood as a con artist. I didn't care about the money. I wanted him. I wanted to sweep that fake guitar off the desk and kiss him right there.

But those thoughts made my con fears get worse, and the threat of being busted by my mother held me in place. I had to finish this deal. It would be the easiest path forward —the money was sitting right there. Besides, whatever emotional entanglements Alejandro and I had built were destined to go nowhere, so I might as well take that pile of cash.

I sighed, and he broke away from our stare. Then he slid the attaché case across his desk toward me. "Four hundred thousand dollars." I pulled the case closer and opened it up.

The sight took my breath away. It was filled to the top with neat piles of fifty-dollar bills. That meant I was looking at 8,000 bills. From my experience with cash, it looked about right. I nodded my head and smiled, our gazes once again locked.

His smile managed to kick my con fears away, even if only for a moment. It made me happy, and all I could think about was his mouth on mine, his arms holding me tight, his hot body pressed close. Those incredible gray eyes seemed to be looking deep into me, to the core of my being. It was as if he saw things that nobody else had ever seen.

Stop! What was wrong with me? I should be checking his money, not standing there, thinking about his kiss. Why couldn't I concentrate on this deal?

I knew the answer, and it was only partly about this man. My con-game fears were scaring me, pushing me to avoid the deal. Anything could happen at this point, and my brain kept churning through the possibilities. I tried to stop the images bubbling up from the past, but they fought with each other to play in my head. I saw a mark get scared and run away when he looked at his own money and realized how much of it he was about to spend. I saw a deal that ended with police lights flashing behind me as I ran down the street and into an alley. I saw my brother, dead on the ground with blood running from his forehead. Please—my mind screamed—don't make me con anymore.

There was no way out—the deal was nearly done. I had to calm down, this was crucial. So I took a few seconds to breathe, then I pasted an easy smile on my face. Casually—like I did this every day—I reached for one of the piles of cash and thumbed through it. Just a spot check.

The blur of the bills going by looked good, so I stopped at one of them to examine it more closely. And that's when all the air rushed from my lungs, snapping me to full attention. Something was seriously wrong. At first I couldn't believe what I was seeing, but realization pierced through my denial and forced me to accept the truth.

I was staring at a three-dollar bill.

I felt my blood chill hard, like flash-frozen vegetables. The deal was definitely dead, and I might be, too. I needed to run now—I had to take action. But I couldn't seem to move my body. I was physically immobilized with fear. Caught! Again! Damn if I wasn't the world's worst con artist.

How had this happened? Did he know the guitar was a fake? What else did he know about this con? About me?

My best guess was that the authenticator had changed his mind. Carl said that the guitar wouldn't pass all tests, but that it would pass the initial examination. Perhaps Peters took a sample and had it more thoroughly tested later. Whatever the reason, Alejandro had learned the truth. I'd been swindling him.

Standing there unsteadily, I felt all my walls start to collapse. The lies and the con began to fade, and I could barely remember what name I had used. All I could see was the end of my life, dying in a prison cell.

Then, with a mental slap to the face, I confronted my reality. The first order of business was escape, so I dropped the pile of cash and turned to the door. Good thing I'd parked my car close.

But Alejandro had beaten me to the door and stood there with his arms folded. "Is there a problem?" His smile was gone, replaced with an emotionless mask, hard and opaque.

Bea always told me, "Never let them see you sweat." But it was far too late for that. I gathered as much of myself as I could and folded my arms, too. "I don't know what you're talking about."

He blew out a harsh laugh. "You're right, there's nothing wrong here. Fake money in exchange for a fake guitar." He leaned closer and squinted. "You tried to cheat me, didn't you, *Ms. Dee Frank*."

His words were like a kick to the gut. He knew my New York name, so he must have known that I'd painted the vase. This explained why it sat in such a prominent position on his desk—he was sending me a signal.

How did he discover who I was? I never did any social networking, so he couldn't have looked me up online. Granted, there were one or two photos of me on other people's social media accounts. One of my friends posted my photo from a party last year, with the caption, "Dee Frank, New York Artist," but it wasn't that easy to find. I doubted someone as famous as Alejandro would spend the time to locate it.

The other explanation was that *he* hired the New York investigator. Perhaps all those people checking on me were his, not Bea's. The famous man had a bodyguard, so he probably had a security team handy, too. Either way, Alejandro knew much more than he let on. He might even know my childhood name and how much of a con artist I once was.

What would happen next? Was Udo standing on the other side of the door with his gun drawn? Were the police on their way? I hadn't done anything illegal yet. Nothing had been sold. So perhaps there was hope. One thing was certain: I really hated this con game!

Alejandro and I stared at each other for a few seconds, this time without the longing. Instead, there was amusement in his eyes, an almost gleeful pride, like a hunter who had just bagged some big game.

I broke the stare and dropped my head. "How long have you known?" I did my best to appear only mildly curious.

"I knew who you were the moment I met you." He picked up my vase from his desk and held it out. "I was in your gallery in New York a few weeks ago, and I bought this.

I'm sure you noticed it yesterday. You weren't in your shop that day, but I looked you up afterward and found a picture of you." He shook his head with a grin. "Not an easy picture to find—you keep yourself pretty well hidden." He set down the vase. "So when a beautiful and reclusive New York artist showed up at my home with a different name and a supposedly rare guitar, I had to wonder." He shrugged. "I told Peters to declare the guitar real and tell me the truth later. And the truth is, the guitar is fake."

"If you knew I was cheating you all along, why the loving attention? Why the kisses? You should despise me for trying to swindle you. Or were you just trying to throw me off?"

"I was curious to watch you con me, and honestly, it was fun unsettling you. I knew you'd hate going to that *No Moss* party, though you really surprised me when you ran from it. And I thought you'd pass out when you saw your vase on my desk. But make no mistake, I'm very much attracted to you —it wasn't all a ruse."

So his interest in me had been real. I wondered if it would be helpful. "Well, I'm *very* much attracted to you, that's for sure." I raised my chin proudly. "What happens now?"

"I'd say the possibilities are vast. I could call the police, I could have Udo kick your ass, or I could take you to bed." He let a sly grin creep across his face. "Why don't we sit and talk about it, Ms. Frank." He motioned to the sofa, and we sat down, not too close.

I was in a precarious position. I could weave a new web of lies, or I could just kick the whole mess to the side and tell the truth. Under Alejandro's guarded but still-somewhat-warm gaze, I opted for the truth. I doubted I could manage much else.

"My name isn't really Dee Frank—that's just what people call me in New York. My real name is Dee Kirkland. I grew up here in Los Angeles and spent my youth as a thief, con artist, and forger. I'm really sorry I tried to swindle you. Believe me, I didn't want to do it. But I. . ."

He held up a hand to stop me. "Thank you for telling me the truth. It's a rare thing when people do that." He picked up a folder of papers from the coffee table by the sofa and handed it to me. "My private investigator already told me this. He also told me that the woman calling herself Bonnie Gleason really *is* your mother, Beatrix Kirkland. And your so-called cousin, Vance Geiger, is a small-time grifter you've known for years. So I imagine you hired him to protect you."

As he laid out the facts of my life, my mouth fell farther and farther open. Alejandro must certainly have hired the man who'd visited my New York shop, and he may have hired the people who pulled the record of my birth parents just before Elle did. But he clearly hadn't hired Vance, because he thought I had done it. That meant that Vance wasn't part of the investigation.

"Not exactly," I whispered, barely able to speak. "I didn't ask Vance to watch me. My best guess is that Bea hired him to keep me in line. She probably thought I'd run away or screw it up." I let out a short, sad laugh. "Turns out, she was right."

He nodded. "That makes sense. The woman's got a long record, with many entertaining tales, including some scams where you figure prominently. I was most impressed with your forgeries—my favorite was the Monet."

Shocked, my mouth fell open even more. He actually knew about the theft of that Monet, which was pretty impressive, given that it had taken the museum a year to figure it out, and then they'd made a concerted effort to keep it quiet. Good thing I'd opted for the truth.

I looked up at him with a grin. "Thank you."

"You're welcome." He was giving me that look again that I'd seen so often since we met. Those bedroom eyes, that incredible smile.

He knew so much about me, I figured he ought to get the full story. So I took a deep breath and let it out. "And by the way, Beatrix Kirkland isn't my mother—I've never met my real parents. Bea is my *foster* mother, so she's the closest I've ever had to a mother, even though she's never acted like much of one."

"Yes, I know about Bea. I'm surprised you've never met your birth parents." He pointed to the folder in my hands, which I still hadn't opened up. "I investigated that, too. Your birth mother's name and address is in there somewhere. I think she lives in Ohio."

As I suspected, Alejandro *was* the other person who had pulled the record of my birth parents. It seemed as if everyone but me knew about them, but I still wasn't ready. Right now, I had more pressing things to think about. Like getting free of here. Like not going to prison. Like having sex with Alejandro, if I could believe that was an option. These things were more important than the parents who left me behind twenty-four years ago.

Suddenly, there was a clatter on the other side of the room. We turned to look as Karen burst out of a closet, unsteady as a drunk getting up from a barstool. She wore her usual skimpy outfit: an ultra-mini aqua skirt with black tights and a black blazer.

Alejandro reached her quickly and helped her steady herself. "What are you doing here, Karen?" He evidently did not expect to see his personal assistant.

She waved her phone in the air. "Don't worry, I've called the police. They're on their way." She straightened her skirt and glared at me.

Great. Now I desperately needed to leave. I jumped to my feet and faced Alejandro with a silent plea for mercy. He shook his head and returned to the study door, making a big show of locking it, pocketing the key, then tapping his pocket to be sure it was safe. He faced me and pointed to a chair by his desk. "Sit down."

With Karen ready to lunge, Udo on the other side of the door, police on the way, and Alejandro blocking the locked exit, I decided to do what he said.

Sixteen

I sat in Alejandro's study, ruing the day I decided to come to Los Angeles. Furtively scanning the room, I searched for air ducts, passageways, or secret panels. Unfortunately, I had a sick feeling that this wasn't the first time a guitar forger had been caught here. And Alejandro didn't seem too worried that I would escape. Tougher people had probably tried and failed.

I started to speak, but Alejandro shot a stern look and shook his head. So I closed my mouth again and sank down in my seat. Just as well—I had no idea what to say.

Alejandro walked over to Karen and took her by the shoulders. "You sit, too." He indicated the chair next to mine.

Looking like she wanted to rip me apart, she sat down with her arms folded. Alejandro stood in front of her chair. "Karen, I need to tell you something before the police arrive, both good news and bad news. I haven't got much time, so let me get right to the point." He leaned over the chair with his face close to hers. "First the bad news. I do *not* love you. I never have, and I never will." He spoke slowly and evenly.

As this information sank in, Karen's face fell. She seemed washed out, drained. "Oh, Alejandro." She sniffled and slumped down in her seat.

He put his hands on her shoulders, drawing her gaze back up to his. "But there's good news, too." He smiled at her. "You are one of my best friends, and you're a great colleague. Without a doubt, you're the best P.A. I've ever had. In fact, you're so good that I've decided to double your salary. You work incredibly hard, and you deserve more. But. . ." He gave her shoulders a little shake. "You have to accept the fact that all we will ever be is friends and coworkers. Got it?"

Her eyes widened as she digested this information. "You're doubling my salary?" She paused for a few seconds while her mouth churned and her eyebrows bobbed. Finally, she nodded. "I guess you're right—I got too close." She took a long breath, exhaled, then smiled. "I can do this."

Alejandro nodded and stepped back from her chair. "Good, let's test that. You know how the two of us sometimes discuss other women I'm attracted to? God, we must have spent hours talking about Zenith last year, and you never got jealous."

Karen shot him a half grin. "I was right about her."

Alejandro smiled back. "Yes, you were right about her. I've had a rough year, partly because of what she did. But I'm getting over it. In fact, I've got my sights on someone new I want to tell you about." He cleared his throat and glanced my way.

"Her name is Dee." He winked at me with a friendly twinkle in his eye.

I swallowed and sat up straight. This was really happening. Alejandro was on my side, and despite my inexcusable behavior, he wanted me. Even if he was just doing this so he could have his way with me in bed, I didn't mind.

And perhaps I was even safe. This new development seemed to indicate that he wouldn't turn me over to the police. But the police were still on their way, so I couldn't be sure. I held my breath and waited.

Karen looked at me with hard eyes for a few seconds. Then she shrugged, admitting a little smile. "Okay, I get it." She turned back to Alejandro, now fully engaged. "What are we going to tell the cops?"

He patted her shoulder. "Thank you, Karen. I'll take care of the cops. Just back me up." I resolved to do the same.

The police arrived, and Alejandro unlocked the study door. He made us wait there while he went out to greet them. I stayed silent and remained in my seat, but Karen got up and waited by the door. Soon, Alejandro led two young-looking policemen into the room, both of them clearly in a good mood from having met the famous rocker. They were tall and lanky, one blond and the other with dark hair.

"Boys." Alejandro nodded to the officers. "This is Karen, my personal assistant, and Dee, my security specialist." Karen and I exchanged smiles about my new job title.

Alejandro then turned to the officers and introduced them. "This is Lucky." He pointed to the blond man. "And this is Myles." He pointed to the dark-haired man.

Myles took off his hat and bowed with a flourish. "Ladies, a pleasure." He ribbed his partner in the side. "Show some respect, Lucky."

Lucky arched an eyebrow, then doffed his hat, too. He turned to Alejandro. "So there's no emergency here?"

Alejandro shook his head. "No. Sorry about that. My security specialist was testing the systems and made the alarm go off." He scolded me with a wagging finger and an impish grin. "You should have told me you were working on the system." He turned back to the officers. "So you see, it was all just a mistake."

Myles shrugged and smiled at me. "Hey, hey! No harm done, little lady. You'll remember to tell people next time."

"Say, Myles. . ." Karen smiled at him then stepped back to include his partner. ". . .Lucky. Could I show you around? Perhaps we can find some Alejandro T-shirts or CDs?" She hooked her arms through theirs and led them from the room, chatting happily as their voices faded down the hall.

Alejandro and I stared at each other for a few seconds. He still had that twinkle in his eye, but his expression was stoic and impenetrable. I couldn't tell what he was thinking. He knew I was a crook, but he liked me. As I'd been doing for days now, I continued to wait for any of this to make sense.

I finally found my voice, although it was barely a whisper. "Why are you protecting me? I get that you're infatuated, not that I understand why, but shouldn't I be prosecuted for what I've done?"

Alejandro chuckled. "I have plans for you. Quite a few, in fact. One thing I need is a con artist who can take George down." He grinned. "I think you'd be perfect for the task. Wait until Karen's finished buttering up the cops. Then we'll talk."

So I *was* safe, and now I understood why. We were some kind of a team now. I doubted he trusted me very much, but then again, I barely trusted him. And there really was an attraction between us. Who knew where that might lead?

I decided to probe a little deeper. "Is that why you want me, because I can help you take down your manager?" Not that I minded any attention from this man, but I was curious.

"No, the attraction is real—you're very pretty. Of course, I can't lie—your con skills are a strong factor in your appeal. Help me take George down, then I'll let you know if there's more to it than that." He shrugged, then pointed at my vase.

"Also, I like your art, both the pottery and the forgeries. You've got talent, Dee, and I appreciate that."

I exhaled, letting this huge change sink in. Alejandro was on my side here, which opened up significant opportunities. Including the promise of some forbidden delights. If I could just take care of Bea, life would be perfect.

In the meantime, we waited for Karen to get rid of the policemen. Then, we'd get serious. Until then, I indulged in some idle conversation. "So, Karen gives out free CDs?"

"And T-shirts and candy bars and all sorts of crap. She knows how to keep the fans happy."

"Since when do cops take gifts? Isn't that against regulations?"

He shrugged. "She offers gifts to every visitor. It's up to each person to accept them or not. When it comes to the police, about half of them stand on principle, but the rest are happy to take our gifts. Besides, they're not worth that much, so it's hardly a bribe."

"No one ever gave me gifts. I didn't get a candy bar or anything." I pretended to pout.

He allowed a sliver of a smile. "You weren't interested. What was it you said?" He mimicked me in a light falsetto. "'I prefer jazz,'" That made us both laugh. "And if you want a candy bar, we've got plenty here. I have a secret fondness for Low-Hanging Fruit bars, myself."

I curled my lips in disgust. "You've got to be kidding."

Alejandro shrugged. "Hey, they're not so bad. I used to eat them when I was a kid, now I use them for hangovers. The sugar rush helps clear my head the next morning." He held the sides of his head to mimic morning-after discomfort.

I blurted out a laugh. "Well I used to eat them when I was a kid, but now I can't stand them. Back then, Bea gave them out as prizes for pulling successful cons."

"Chocolate is a great motivator for kids. I used to get them after music lessons. Good thing I like music."

"Hey, I *liked* conning people when I was a kid. I didn't know any better. Bea would tell us how bad someone was, then praise us for punishing them. The better we got, the more she praised us and the more candy we got. My favorite used to be the Nuts To You bars. These days, just give me a churro."

"Well, since you didn't pull a successful con today, no candy bar for you. And no churro, either." He wagged a playful finger at me.

I smirked. "That's quite all right. So do you keep my vase on your desk all the time, or did you set it there just to stick it to me?"

Alejandro laughed. "No, it isn't a prop—I like it. I've had it here since I bought it. And now that I've met the artist, I don't think I'll ever put it away."

My heart jumped from the thrill of his praise. I couldn't wait to tell Wanda about this—she'd be so excited. Then, as if he could read my mind, Alejandro picked up my vase again and held it next to his face. "I should pose with this—help your business." He smiled artificially and gestured to it like an actor in a low-budget ad.

I chuckled, then continued his joke. "I could start a new line of pen holders—the Alejandro series."

"Now you're talking. And another thing. . ." He pointed to his attaché case. "I'm a little disappointed that you didn't get to admire all the fake cash I put together." He couldn't stop talking about my failed con, reliving it as if it was a famous sporting event. Boys love their toys, and Alejandro wanted to show off the effort he'd put into tricking me.

"The three dollar bills were a nice touch."

He groaned. "I was just getting started with that. Check it out." He slid the case closer.

I picked up another pile of money and examined it. This one also had three-dollar bills below the real fifty. The next pile was padded with Monopoly money, a thick pile of green twenties, complete with little houses and trains. The pile after that had trillion-dollar bills with zeros running halfway across the top. I even found a pile of very convincing fifties that had only one flaw: the president featured on the bill was George W. Bush. I laughed at each new way he'd found to fill the case with phony money.

"Very funny. But I have to tell you, nobody uses toy money in a con. All you need to do is cut up blank paper, or scrap. Anything, really. But no con artist would actually spend money on fake bills." I laughed sadly, remembering more of my ridiculous childhood. "When we were kids, Bea occasionally made us cut up paper to use in cons like this."

"And that's exactly why I bought phony money. I haven't got the time to cut up that much paper. Besides, I couldn't wait to see your face when you realized you'd been had. I wanted the full effect."

"Well, you got it. I hope you're happy. That three-dollar bill nearly gave me a heart attack."

Alejandro laughed. "You see, I'm a con artist, too. We're similar, you and I."

I doubted that. "We couldn't be more different if we tried."

"No, it's true. We're both artists, and we've both played con games. In fact. . ." He chuckled. "I've tricked you a few times, now. Remember when you first came to visit me and

I had a phone conversation with Karen? That was a fake. I just pretended she'd called so I could search my phone for that picture of you I'd found on the Internet."

I'd wondered about that at the time. As soon as he saw me, he'd reached for his phone. He'd recognized me and needed to see the picture again to be sure, but he covered it by pretending to talk to Karen. Not bad.

Alejandro went on with his résumé of deception. "I played cons when I was a kid, too. Don't forget that I grew up in the same neighborhood that you did, so I had to do some unsavory things to survive."

"I've read that you grew up poor. But I didn't know about anything illegal."

"There are a few shady things in my past. My parents came to the United States illegally back in 1984 after some really rough years in Chile. I was born two years later, an anchor baby, if you will. We lived in a filthy tenement building, which—coincidentally—George now owns." He shook his head darkly. "Anyway, I learned to play tricks there. When I was a teenager, I played Three Card Monte for a year, tossing three cards around on a table and challenging people to follow the queen. Thanks to that game, I was able to buy my first guitar."

"Okay, I'm impressed. Did you have a crew, or did you play alone?"

"Initially, it was just me. I was a pretty good tosser. But after a month, a friend of mine started playing the shill and lookout. I would signal him so he knew which of the three cards were the one, and if anyone bet on that, he'd bet a higher amount on a different card. Then I'd take his money, and I wouldn't have to pay the person who guessed right. Eventually, we'd hit someone for big bucks, then it would be time to wrap up. My buddy would yell out that the police were nearby, and we'd run away. That's the way the game goes, you know."

I laughed. "Oh, don't worry, I know. Bea taught us to play when we were kids. Back then, Jay was the tosser. Hale, a friend of ours, was the shill and lookout. But our team had a roper, too. Me. I'd find a guy and bring him to the table, pretending that I loved the game and could always follow the cards. Jay would signal me and let me win a few hands to show the mark how good I was. Then, when the guy started to bet on my advice, I'd be right next to him and could check out his wallet, see what he was holding. If he was just making tiny bets, we'd let him win once or twice. But as soon as he bet anything serious, it was time to take him down. I'd feed him the wrong card, then run away. Jay would take his money, and before the guy could complain, Hale would pretend to spot the cops. Then they ran, too."

Alejandro grinned. "Wow, you had a full crew. What happened to them?"

"Hale's still around—you might like him. He and his two friends were also part of our crew. But the people I did the most cons with were my sister, Elle, and my brother, Jay. Bea raised us and taught us everything she knows. If you ask me, she was just conning the foster system when she took us in. Never cared much for us, unless we were helping her cheat someone. The rest of the time, we were on our own. She didn't even do much to feed us—she'd just buy extra groceries occasionally and assume it would be enough. She was always out somewhere, eating on her own. So if the food ran out, she didn't even notice."

"She sounds pretty nasty. You seem to have survived her, though. How did your sister fare?"

"Elle left home a few years after I did. Lives in Oregon and is still playing con games. Jay. . ." I dropped my head. "He wasn't so lucky—he died when I was thirteen."

"Yes, I saw that in my investigator's report. Murdered. What happened?"

I shook my head. "Please, not now. I'm having enough trouble keeping my sanity around you. I mean. . ." My hands fluttered for a second, then I deflated. "You're Alejandro! I've been a fan for years."

His lips curled into a smile. "So you *do* like my music. And what about those kisses? Were they just to fleece me? Did you feel anything?"

I wrapped my arms around his neck again and gazed into his eyes. "Those were real kisses, and I liked them a lot. In fact, I'd like some more."

And just like that, we fell back into kissing. I didn't care anymore; the deal was over and a new deal was being formed. If, after exposing myself so completely, he still wanted another kiss, who was I to refuse?

He wrapped me in his arms and pulled me tight against his solid chest. Submerged in his incredible body, I dove deeper. He smelled great, as always, and I savored his spicy scent. We wrapped each other tight, tangled arms and legs grappling for more.

The clacking of Karen's heels roused us from our kiss. Her voice rang out as she led the officers closer. "Thanks, boys," she concluded. "Call me when he next plays Los Angeles, and I'll get you tickets." The front door closed and the house dropped into silence.

Karen came back to the room, all smiles. "Everything's taken care of." She waved two business cards. "Got their contact information, too, in case we need any more assistance." She had really dealt with this change well and seemed quite comfortable with my presence. Perhaps her new salary helped.

Alejandro nodded with a tight smile. "Good work. Go ahead and take the rest of the day off."

"Thanks!" She nodded at me, gathered her things, and left the study. I heard her heels clicking away in the distance. Then the door closed, leaving me alone with a dangerously sexy man.

Seventeen

After Karen left, Alejandro sat on the sofa and motioned me over. "Now let's talk." I made sure to sit far from him, as I'd done before. His allure was as strong as ever, but I wasn't sure about my own feelings anymore.

Alejandro chuckled. "You can get closer—I won't bite."

"You already have."

He curled one side of his mouth into a smile. "Point taken." He took a long breath. "Look, Dee, you've been living a clean life since you moved to New York. What made you come back here and start up again with Bea?"

Wow. He really did know all about me. "She forced me to do it—she's very persuasive. And she's going to be pretty annoyed that this deal fell through." I gave him a sly smile. "I don't suppose you'd let me finish up with George? If I don't do this deal in four days, as we planned, Bea will get suspicious."

Alejandro pursed his lips. "You probably could—George still thinks your guitar is real. But since it was supposed to be for me, he's paying you with my money. I can't allow that, so I'm afraid you'll have to think of something else." He quirked his lips. "Nice try."

I shrugged. "You can't blame a girl for trying. Old habits, I suppose. Bea and her friends taught me everything I know."

"Oh? And just what do you know?"

I understood what was going on. This was a job interview. He needed someone to take his manager down, so he wanted to know if I was qualified. What, indeed, did I know, and how good was I at it? This might be fun.

I gave him a grin. "Let me show you." I got up and walked to his shelf with the Grammy awards, moving them away. Behind it was a loose panel I'd noticed earlier. When I slid it to the side, it revealed what I knew would be there: a wall safe. "You think your home is secure? This is one of the most obvious hiding places for a safe that I've ever seen. Any thief would notice these awards, and a good one would spot this hidden panel."

He got up and approached the safe. "But it's state of the art. I was told that nobody can open it."

I examined it for a few seconds, rapping my knuckles on the door to check its construction. "You've been handed a line. This is just a home model. I could open it in a half hour if I had a stethoscope. And my brother, who was great with safes, could have done it in ten minutes. Also if I drilled right here. . ." I pointed to a spot above the dial. "I could stick a mirror in and see the works. Then it would open in seconds."

Analyzing his security was fun, so I kept going. "Also, George's private room of stolen guitars isn't too safe, either." I pulled out my phone and consulted the note I'd made when I was here last. "The combination is 527903."

Alejandro's eyes bugged out. "How did you get the combination? I covered the keypad when I entered it."

I gave him an embarrassed smile. "But you didn't cover your whole hand, and I know how to read the musculature." His smile grew broad, which made me grin. "My Aunt Franny taught me that. Is she in your report?"

"Franny? I believe so. Mother of the guy who's following you, right?"

"That's her. She and her husband were good friends with Bea, so I grew up with them in my extended family. They taught me all sorts of things."

I was starting to have fun now, so I decided to give him a demonstration of what I could do, up front and personal. I stood up straighter and gave him a smile. "See if you like this."

Stepping close to him, I ran my hands up and down his arms, hugging him and roaming all over his remarkable body. He responded and pulled me into a hug. When I fell upon his fabulous mouth with my lips, his eyes blazed. While we kissed, my arms continued to roam.

I could have remained happily in that kiss for much longer, but I had an ulterior motive, so I pulled away. Alejandro squinted at me and shrugged. "I've had better kisses."

"Sure, but how many of them included a fleecing?" I held out his wristwatch.

He looked down at his wrist and started to laugh. "Nicely done."

"I also got your wallet and the key to the study door." I handed them back to him with a proud smile.

Alejandro shook his head and laughed. "Very impressive. I love the way you do those things."

How could he love skills like that? Skills that once earned me Bea's praise, but now only caused me trouble. "Come on, Alejandro. These are dangerous skills. I don't know if I'd call them lovable. I don't know if I'd even call *myself* lovable."

"Oh? Why not?"

I gave him a derisive snort. "Well, let's see. I'm a thief, a forger, and a cheat. My real parents abandoned me when I was a baby, so no love there. And Bea's idea of love is a candy bar when I steal money for her. The only long-term boyfriend I've ever had doesn't love me at all. And I've hardly known *any* relationships that worked. Not mine, not Elle's, and certainly none of Bea's. The only couple I know that are still together are my Uncle Carl and Aunt Franny." I sighed. "I suppose I wouldn't know what to do with real love."

His gray eyes focused on mine. "My parents loved me, but no woman has, since I got famous. Now they just want a piece of my fame. So, in a way, I wouldn't know what to do with real love, either."

"Don't be ridiculous! You're world famous for your love songs. You must have experienced love more recently than that. I mean, hey—I don't know much about love, but I can feel it in your lyrics."

"I thought I was in love last year with a woman named Zenith. But I was wrong—something I'm not proud of. The only other time was long ago. . ."

"Your first?"

"No. But early. In high school. Went out with her for nearly a year, then she dumped me. It hurt badly, and that's part of the reason I left Los Angeles. Two months after the breakup, my parents had to move back to Chile, so I went with them."

He shook his head slowly. "I really loved her. And I still did, five years later, when she showed up in my dressing room one night after a show. I almost didn't recognize her. She looked different, weathered and hard. Still, meeting her again was wonderful, therapeutic. We even had sex again. But the love was gone—I could tell. She was strangely possessive, as if she had some sort of claim on me because we'd gone out once. She'd become clingy and artificially cheerful. It was sad. She couldn't treat me the same way anymore—my fame had killed it." He shook his head. "Still, she taught me my first lessons about love, which I still draw on for my songs."

"Wow. So you've been faking it with all the love songs? Good thing I can't tell the difference between real and artificial love."

Alejandro stepped closer to me, close enough that I could feel his warmth and hear him breathe. "We may not know much about love, you and I, but I bet we know a few things about lust. And right now, I've got that for you. . . in a big way." I felt my heart skip when he said that, and I leaned back to take in his brilliant gray eyes. He combed his fingers through my spiky hair and dropped a quick kiss to my lips. "I've wanted you since I saw that picture on the web. And when you showed up in my home, I wanted you even more. Now I intend to have your body before this night is out, Dee. You may not *do* love, but do you *make* love?"

His words ignited my body, fanning hot flames of excitement. "Yeah, I do that." I grinned. "I've wanted to for about ten years now." With an arched eyebrow, I leaned farther away to give him the once-over. "I must say, you've still got it and then some." I giggled as I wrapped my arms around his incredible chest.

He dropped his lips down on mine, hard and quick, and we fell to the sofa, rolling around like teenagers in the back of a car. His phenomenal body surrounded me, and his incredible kisses went on for a blissful eternity, leaving me breathless and raw. Wrapped tightly against his body, I could feel him hard and ready. I ground myself against him as we continued to writhe.

In the middle of a hard and hungry kiss, his hand slipped into my pants and found me ready for more. Sensation swam around me as I thrust my tongue deeper into his mouth, desperate to quench my desire. Firm fingers drove my arousal steadily higher until it couldn't go any further. When I finally unraveled, I moaned my climax into his mouth and trembled in his arms.

Alejandro pulled away and stood up, one hand extended toward me. "My bed is much more comfortable." He gave me his world-famous bedroom eyes.

Oh, yes! His bed was quite luxurious. It came with an outrageously beautiful man who, besides being an expert at playing guitar, was also an expert at playing my body. We continued to kiss while we finished undressing, his level of excitement now plainly on display. I was so ready for him that I let my legs drift apart. But he surprised me by thrusting his face down there, insisting on tasting me first. How could I refuse a second blazing orgasm?

Afterwards, Alejandro hovered over me with a lascivious grin, waving a condom package. By this point, there was only one thing left for me to do, so I threw him on his back and straddled him. With a growl, he grabbed me hard. We rode higher and higher, bursting forth when we crested the peak together, then coming down the other side, snuggled in each other's arms.

Our lust didn't end there. We spent the next few hours entangled in each other's bodies. I'd never encountered a man with so much sexual energy. But then again, Alejandro was famous for that, so I shouldn't have been surprised. Still, he was an amazing lover, strong and hard as well as tender and sweet. Much more than I bargained for.

At one point in the evening, we found ourselves in the shower, making love under the water. After a spectacular climax, we collapsed against the wall, staring at each other. I sniffed his soap. "What is this? I smell it on you all the time."

"Clove soap. Like it?"

I licked his cheek. "Mmm. Yes, very much."

"You should try the shampoo." He squirted some in his hand and started to massage it into my scalp. His hands felt heavenly as they roamed over my head. This tender gesture made me feel so happy that I sighed with pleasure. I didn't expect him to continue to treat me with such devotion once he'd achieved his goal of seducing me, but Alejandro still acted like he cared.

I shouldn't have been so surprised by this. After all, letting a man wash my hair was no big deal. But I'd taken a few showers with Roman over the past five years, and he'd never attempted to do this. Instead, he always stood on the other side of the stall, bathing himself. I don't think we ever had sex in the shower—he only joined me to save water. Sex while the water ran would be an offensive waste of resources to him.

Alejandro, by comparison, took every opportunity to touch me, to observe me, to care for me. As he rinsed off the shampoo, he inquired about my hair. "Did you ever let the blonde grow out?"

"Never. Bea always said that blonde attracted too much attention. It's one of the cardinal rules of conning—'Don't stand out.' She made me dye it brown when I was a kid. I bleached it when I moved to New York, intentionally spiting her by making it noticeable." I laughed as I held out my hair. "She really hates this. Insisted I keep it covered when I was around you."

He smirked. "Didn't work. I recognized you immediately. You see, my place in New York is only two blocks away from your shop, and I've been there for years, so I remember when you opened. I've checked your place out a few times and liked what I saw. I kept waiting for you to be there, but now I understand why you rarely do that.

"When I finally broke down and bought your vase, I became curious to check you out. I found that picture of you at a party. The white hair is distinctive and so is your face. So you can imagine my delight when you walked right into my home." He held my shoulders and stared at me with such intensity that it knocked the air out of my lungs.

I forced myself to resume breathing, little half-breaths that went silently through my parted lips. He looked so damned wonderful, dark and strong, with those intense eyes.

And how nice that he found me to be a delightful surprise. "Lucky you." I gave him a shy grin while my heart fluttered.

"I think my luck's about to get even better." He lunged into another kiss, making me hot and wet, inside and out.

We spent the rest of the night together in bed.

Three Days
Until the Deal

Eighteen

A beam of sunlight woke me up early, forcing me to shade my eyes and turn away. When I looked around, I found myself in a strange bed with a sinfully beautiful man. A man straight out of my most cherished music videos, whose powerfully rugged face now slumbered next to me. And to make the fantasy even more intense, both of us were naked. I must have jolted at the realization, because he stirred and awoke with a smile. "Good morning, my hot little con artist." Now there's something I'd never heard before.

"So it wasn't a dream." I'd made love, all night long, with the most famous and sexy musician alive. I could die happy now.

Alejandro laughed. "Maybe you're still asleep." He got up and wandered to the bathroom, every muscle in his stunning body flexing as he moved.

"In that case, don't wake me." I sat up in bed to see more.

We'd hardly slept last night. Besides the awesome sex, we talked and played and snuggled for hours. Definitely the best con I'd ever botched.

Except for one little detail: Bea. I wanted to call it quits, forget this entire mess and go home. But she was far from done. When I was a kid, Bea would never let a little hitch like this stop a deal. She always had a plan B, as well as a plan C, and sometimes even a D. She undoubtedly had a backup plan for this little problem as well, but I'd be damned if I was going to use it. I needed my own plans, especially now that Alejandro wanted me to swindle his manager. So I was back to being a scheming con artist. We even discussed my new plans last night, in the few moments when we weren't completely consumed by passionate pursuits.

Eventually, the plan coalesced. It even seemed to be good—a way to solve multiple problems at once. We would cheat George to recover Alejandro's embezzled money. In my plan, I would find a second guitar in my mother's fictitious attic. This would have to be a stolen guitar, so George would want to buy it. He was already roped-in and believed that I could produce rare guitars. All I had to do was find something that he wanted for himself.

Then, on the day I sold the guitar to George, the police would arrive and take everything away. Cooperating police, that is. Lucky and Myles seemed like perfect choices, especially since they weren't above an occasional gift.

A cool-out was essential for this new con. Alejandro might not go after me if he got cheated, because it would be bad publicity. But George would attack with everything he had. And he had some serious resources, including thugs who did his dirty work for him. If I stole that much money from him, he'd probably have me killed. But if George and I both got busted during the deal, he wouldn't blame me for it, so he wouldn't retaliate.

Once they arrested us, the fake guitar and the money would get confiscated. Then, depending on how far Lucky and Myles were willing to go, I'd either get them to give me some of the money, or I'd pull a maneuver from Bea's playbook and invade the police evidence locker. Either way, I'd recover the money and destroy the fake guitar. George would never see either again.

In the meantime, I would hopefully have the tainted cocaine from Bea, thanks to Hale's hacking. I would be free of her, and Alejandro would get George's money. Perfect.

Interestingly, Alejandro did not want to know my plan. This wasn't because he didn't care; in fact, his care ran deep. But he needed deniability, so he insisted that I not tell him everything. I could ask him for background information and for things that I needed. I could even get him to do small tasks. But he would not allow me to tell him the whole plan. The con was entirely up to me.

I told Alejandro a few things about the con, but made no mention of the police action at the final deal. I did tell him about the second guitar, because I had to involve him in its authentication. He'd been able to influence the analysis of the fake Stratocaster, so I asked him to speak to Oscar Peters again. The man was obviously for sale, and I wanted to purchase more of his good graces.

The only other aspect of the plan—which I'd already told to Alejandro—was that I intended to stick to the original schedule and sell the guitar to George in just three days. If that slipped, Bea would get even more suspicious, and she was already suspicious enough—look how she had Vance following me. Add to that her understandable concern over my tryst with the mark, and I knew I was too close to the line. If I alarmed her any further, she'd make even more trouble for me and Alejandro, and she'd have me pulling cons for the rest of my life. Oh wait, she was already planning to do that. Well, I didn't need any more of her displeasure.

Given that I couldn't tell Alejandro everything, I worried that his ignorance would get in the way. He was a part of this, and if he didn't know what was going on, he might not react properly. So he suggested that Karen be the one who knew my full plan. Apparently, she disliked George and wanted to help take him down. And since she knew Alejandro's schedule, she'd be able to keep him out of trouble.

I wasn't terribly excited about bringing Karen into this, but he wanted her to do it, so I decided to give her a chance. She seemed much more friendly after Alejandro had talked to her, but I still wasn't convinced of her loyalty. I decided to bring her in slowly so I could watch her. If she worked out, I'd have a definite advantage. I even had some ideas about things that would be perfect for her to do. This con might succeed, after all.

Alejandro returned from the bathroom and climbed onto the bed, hovering over me. His lips toured my mouth, my face, and my throat, quickly heating me up with their promise. I responded by exploring his muscular chest, his steely arms, his smoking physique. With one last kiss, he got up and put on shorts, a ragged T-shirt, and running shoes. "I'm going for a run. You can get breakfast if you like."

I sat up quickly. "You're a runner? Me too. I did it all the time when I was a kid, although I haven't done much lately. Where do you run?"

"I've got my own private track that runs through the woods around the edge of my property. Keeps the fans away, usually."

"Usually? They attack you when you're running here?"

"They attack me everywhere. Did you see that woman at your motel the other day? Typical."

"You handled her quite gently."

"I have to. I can't have pictures of me fighting with women. That doesn't look good in the media, so I tend to retreat from any physical interaction with fans. Sooner or later, they give up."

He held out his hand to me. "Want to come along? We've got some track shoes here that might fit you."

"Sounds like fun. I don't know if I can keep up with someone as fit as you, but I bet I can beat you in a sprint."

"A sprinter? Sure, we can do some of those. Did you do that in high school?"

I laughed. "I've been a sprinter for as long as I can remember. Bea insisted that all of us learn to run. Comes in handy when you're being chased down the street."

"Aha, so it's not about fitness. That explains why you favor sprinting. Sure, come along." He flashed a wicked grin. "We can pretend you just stole my money, and I'm trying to get it back." It wasn't funny, but I laughed anyway.

We jogged around Alejandro's private track a few times, a pleasant run through the trees lining his property. As I knew would be the case, he had far greater endurance on the long haul, but I could beat him in a sprint every time.

We came back and shared a shower that consisted of brief bathing and luxurious lovemaking. Then, suddenly hungry, we settled down to a big breakfast.

When we were finished eating, I leaned back in my chair. "God, Alejandro. I wish I could spend all day with you, but I have too many things to do."

"So do I. And by the way, you seemed interested in my Grammys earlier. Can I offer you one?"

I raised an eyebrow. "You're kidding! You'd let me take one of your Grammys as a gift?"

"Well, sure. I've got plenty. Check this out." He led me to a room that looked like a hoarder's paradise. The walls were filled to bursting, and most of the floor space was heaped with piles of junk. Papers and trinkets and statues and even a few guitars. Colorful and disorganized, most of it seemed like garbage. I did spot a few things that looked valuable, including an entire shelf of Grammys and other awards. Alejandro waved his arm across the piles of rock-and-roll leavings. "Take your pick."

I squinted at him. "What is all this?"

"Stuff from the bottom of my pile. Even Karen doesn't know what to do with these things, so we just throw them in here."

"I can't believe you throw all your Grammy awards in with the rest of this." I walked over to where the awards were stockpiled and picked up a sporting trophy that was wedged between two music awards. When I read the plaque, I laughed. "Your Grammys have no more meaning to you than this tenth grade swimming award?"

"Well, first of all, I was a really good swimmer. But secondly, these Grammys were for crap songs. I'm not really proud of them." He nodded toward the awards. "I've got eighteen Grammys, you know. The only three that mean anything to me are in my study. The rest are here." He picked one of them up and handed it to me. "Go ahead, have a Grammy." He chuckled.

I hefted the golden award as I read the plaque. "Oh my God! This is the Grammy you got for 'Body of a Woman!' I love that song. I can't believe you're willing to give it to me."

"Well, it depends on what you plan to do with it. If it means something to you, and you want it, then it's yours. If you're just going to sell it or melt it down, then maybe you should leave it here."

I had to think about that. I'd had a spectacular night with this incredible man, so perhaps I wouldn't mind a little keepsake of our time together. Also, I needed something nice to defuse Bea's anger with me, now that I'd had sex with the mark. I could give this to her and make her happy. Of course, *she* might melt it down or sell it, but that could make the difference between the success and failure of the con, so regardless of what happened, this little Grammy award would surely be nice to have.

"Thank you, Alejandro." I blew dust off the award and cradled it to my chest. "It's beautiful."

He leaned down and kissed me. "*You're* beautiful. Like a starburst of delight from the miracle of love." I was amused to hear him quoting lyrics from one of his old songs. Men rarely used song lyrics on me, certainly Roman never did. My so-called boyfriend was too cool for—as he put it— sappy love talk. The last thing he would do was compliment me on my looks. But it made sense that the world famous composer of love songs knew how to do sappy. Even though I knew he was handing me a line, I had to admit that I liked it.

I put the Grammy award into my backpack and prepared to leave. "I have to go, now. But I *will* call later. Don't worry, though. If you're busy, I'll understand. I know how it is with you."

He shook his head. "You clearly *don't* know how it is with me. I'll just have to show you." He gave me a parting kiss, leaving me weak and happy.

Nineteen

I left Alejandro's place to begin managing the crazy pile of details and backup plans I needed to get done in the next three days. Too bad sleep wasn't on the list, but I'd sleep when this was over.

As I returned to the motel in my black SUV, I wondered if Vance would be suspicious. I'd left the television running in my room all night. But even Vance needed to sleep sometime, and the man didn't overthink much, so I trusted that he'd be waiting for me without question.

I peeked through the curtain and looked down at his car. The newspaper shield was down, so I could see him sitting there, watching. He fidgeted, then reached over and brought a bottle up to his mouth. Poor Vance—he needed a drink to keep himself going through the long days. As much as his presence irritated me, I felt bad for the guy.

I sneaked out the bathroom window once again. Unfortunately, the con was very different now. And with the police involved, I needed to stay out of sight, more than ever. Cameras were ubiquitous these days, and I didn't want my movements around town to be discovered after Lucky and Myles arrested me. Good thing I'd used a fake ID when I rented the SUV.

Bea may have taught me to hide in plain sight, but my new rule was to simply stay hidden. I went to a costume shop where I got an assortment of wigs: a short red pixie cut, a stark black bob, a long blonde wig that danced across my shoulders, and a brown one with tight curls that ballooned about my head. I decided on the red pixie for today and hid my bleached hair from sight.

Next, I did some errands. I went to an art-supply store to get a set of fine woodworking tools. Then I bought rubber gloves and an assortment of bags, so I wouldn't leave any fingerprints behind. Another lesson inspired by my foster mother. With the gloves and the wigs, I could more effectively hide my activities and leave as tiny a trail as possible. Now I was ready for anything. Hopefully.

The final thing I needed—the most important item— was a second fake guitar. This guitar had to be the shiniest of bait, something that George Rawson couldn't live without. More than a rare musical instrument and more than a simple investment, this guitar had to *mean* something to him. It had to evoke his strongest feelings, grabbing him so hard that he'd be unable to live without it. I needed such a guitar, and I needed it fast.

Only one guitar could do all that. I would offer George another Martin Dreadnought, the same guitar that was in the center of his shrine. He had one of the four remaining prototypes in the world, so I would offer him another one. Since all of them were currently reported stolen, George would jump at the chance to get a hot pair. Also, having two of the series would make each one more valuable. He'd be on his way to getting all four—a great opportunity.

Another reason to choose the Dreadnought was that it was a simple-looking guitar. I needed a copy quickly, so it had to be easy to make. With any luck, Carl could knock off a copy in time.

When I arrived at the music shop, I took a moment to talk to Franny. The last time I was there to pick up the Stratocaster, I came and went through the back entrance. And before that, when Bea and I came to talk Carl about which guitar to use, I'd been whisked in and out the door so quickly that I didn't get any time with Franny. Today, I stopped to visit.

Franny looked the same as always, her gray hair swept back over her thin face. Today, she was done up in orange. An orange patterned blouse, a solid orange skirt, and big orange glasses. Her lipstick was still quite red. I loved everything about this woman—when I grew up, I wanted to be like her.

Before I could say anything, she launched in. "So my eyes weren't deceiving me. White hair or red hair, I still know it's you, Dee. Been a long time."

"Too long." I gave her a hug. "It's good to see you, Aunt Franny. How are you?"

She inhaled with a snort. "The usual." With her hands on my shoulders, she studied me for a few seconds. "You're working a job, aren't you?"

I was back to being a kid, pulling cons as if the last seven years had never happened. I took off the wig and held it in front of me. "How did you guess?"

"Wasn't the wig. I spotted it when you were here last week, and I can see it in your eyes now."

Nobody could hide anything from Franny. "I've got that con energy—you can always tell." I stared right at her so she could observe me more closely.

Franny smiled. "You and Carl. I can tell he's been up to something. When he's just repairing guitars, there's no edge. But lately, he's got an extra level of energy." She leaned back. "Who's the mark?"

I laughed. Franny didn't let any secrets into her shop. But then I hesitated. "Um, can you keep a secret from Bea?"

"Gladly," Franny grinned. "So who are you after?"

"Guy named George Rawson. Manager for Alejandro, as a matter of fact."

She slammed a fist on the counter. "Nail that bastard!"

Whoa! Where had that come from? I narrowed my eyes. "You know Rawson?"

"Never met him, but I've heard stories. Guy's got his hand in all sorts of trouble. Even owns a few slum dwellings a mile from here where some of my friends live. They say he's the meanest landlord they ever had. One guy I know got into serious shit from him when he fell behind on his rent. Instead of evicting him, Rawson planted drugs in the guy's place and called the cops. Can you believe that?" She shook her fists in the air.

"Drugs? Rawson doesn't seem like the type."

"Aww, that's adorable. 'Doesn't seem like the type.'" She stared at me, letting her gaze roam up and down. "You don't seem like the type to be a con artist. But you *are*."

Franny never minced words—I'd learned some important lessons from her. I paused for a few seconds while I thought it over. "Let me rephrase that. George seems so proper and upstanding. I can't imagine him consuming anything stronger than a martini."

"Well, you're right about that: he never touches the stuff. But he knows it's good money, so drugs are part of his plan. He's got a crew that works his buildings. Lets him offer the complete slum experience."

"Huh. So he deals drugs. Seems like it should be easy to bust him."

"Can't. He never gets close to the merchandise. Just lets his people do all the dirty work. That's why no one's been able to take him down. He's got dealers, procurers, enforcers, the whole shebang."

"Wow. So that explains his thugs. I heard he put a beauty salon out of business by beating up the owner."

"Yep. I've been following him for a few years now. If you're conning him, I've got some dirt you'll want to see. Not enough to put him away, but I've got the names of all of Rawson's people on the street. Might help you to take that shithead down."

I nodded. "It might just. From the sounds of it, I'm going to need all the ammunition I can get."

While I had her in a talkative mood, I tried to figure out her son. "By the way, how's Vance?"

Franny gave the barest of shrugs. "We hardly see him anymore. He lives over in Highland Park. Married now, with a six-year-old kid who's cute as the devil. Other than that, Vance keeps to himself."

Good. Franny wasn't part of the whole Vance-and-Bea act. I gave her a hug and then headed back to see Carl.

My uncle was no less embroiled than the last time I'd seen him. He tapped on something with a small hammer, then straightened up from his table. "Hello, Dee. How's the guitar?"

"It's fine. But I need another."

He took in a long breath. "Now what?"

"I need a simple acoustic guitar: a Martin Dreadnought. George Rawson has one of the missing D-1 prototypes. I want to sell him another."

His mouth dropped open in a look of shock. "Tell me you're kidding."

"Uh, no. Why?"

"Because it's very hard to fake that. Sure, it's a basic looking guitar, but the prototypes weren't lacquered as well as the production models. To make a guitar with perfectly aged lacquer will take over a month. I'll have to bake it just right."

Damn! There went my plans for a simple guitar that would be easy to fake. But my plan had backup plans built in, so I wasn't overly worried. I could get a cheap guitar authenticated, one way or another. Alejandro was going to try and influence the authenticator. And if that didn't work, I could arrange to get Oscar Peters out of the picture in some other way. He might suddenly fall ill or have to leave town. Then George would need to hire someone else. My mind raced through the possibilities while I decided how to handle this. Not a problem—I told myself with crossed fingers—this little snag meant nothing.

I shrugged at Carl. "I haven't got a month. I need it tomorrow." Carl arched an eyebrow and let his silence say "no."

After a few seconds, he squinted at me. "And by the way, how do you know what's in his collection? Did you see it?"

"Yep. He has thirteen guitars, including the prototype Dreadnought. He even has a guitar that was stolen from Paul McCartney."

"So that's where the McCartney guitar went." Carl smiled. "Look, I can knock off something for you by tomorrow, but it'll be crap. The D-18 guitars are almost the same as the D-1s, especially the vintage 18s. I know a guy with one and can get it for you. Then it's a simple matter to file-down the serial number and stamp a new one. But like I said, it won't pass even the most cursory authentication."

"That's all right, it doesn't have to pass any tests. Just make it look right, so nobody notices anything at first glance."

He blew out a long breath. "Okay."

"One more thing." I caught Carl rolling his eyes, so I finished my request before he could say anything. "Don't tell Bea about this."

Carl laughed. "Not a problem. She and I don't get along as well as we used to." I wasn't surprised to hear this after what Franny had said about Bea.

"Oh, and don't stamp the number inside the body—just stamp the word 'Prototype,' and leave the number off. I haven't done enough research to know which of the D-1 prototypes is the most likely one to sell him, so I'll stamp the number myself." That's why I'd bought the woodworking tools.

He nodded with a smile. "You got it. This is gonna cost you four grand. And for all that money, you'll have a fake guitar that will be obvious to any expert."

I smiled and handed him the cash. "That's my little problem." Inside my head, the more sensible part of me was rolling on the floor with laughter. Calling my problem "little" was the understatement of the year. Tomorrow I would pick up an embarrassingly fake guitar and have just two days to get it authenticated and sold. Yes, I had more than a little problem.

Twenty

With my red pixie wig and my anonymous black SUV, I drove to the pizza place and found Hale at his usual table. He was the only one in the restaurant today, hunched over a table covered with tiny electronic toys. "Hey there," I called as I walked toward him.

"Hang on." He played with a tiny circuit board for a few seconds before turning to me. "What's up, Dee?" He arched an eyebrow, clearly waiting for an explanation of my wig.

I ignored his look and swept my hand over the table. "There's no place to put a pizza."

He leaned back, smiling. "I overdosed a few years ago and stopped eating pizza. But I still love this place. I even helped out the owner at one point when he had some financial difficulties. So now he lets me work from here, and he's even happy to let my new crew use the place as a hangout, just like we used to." He slid over and motioned to the seat next to him. "What's up?"

I noticed that harried look in his eyes, his con energy. Hale was busy, so I sat down and quickly got to the point. "Any luck with Bea's finances?"

Hale made a grumbling sound that was not encouraging. "Sorry, I've been over everything, but I can't find any payments to a storage facility. She probably pays them in cash. I know I'd do that if it were me. Afraid you're out of luck."

"Okay, thanks for trying, Hale." Great. Now I didn't have a way to recover the tainted cocaine. On top of everything else, I needed a backup plan for that, perhaps a way to get Bea out of the house so I could search the place. Things were getting complicated.

In the meantime, I had other problems. "Can I ask you for another favor? I'm working a man named George Rawson, and I need him followed."

He gave me an exasperated look. "Sorry, Dee, not happening. I'm in the middle of something now." He returned his attention to the electronics.

As I'd suspected, he was busy with a con. But I didn't need much from him, and he hadn't heard my offer yet. I scooted close, resting my hand on his shoulder. "This is a great job, Hale. It pays well, and it will be over in three days. Also, you only need to watch him for a few hours."

"I don't know." He shook his head. "Surveillance is such a bore."

"Then let me make it interesting for you. This guy is big in the music industry." I reached into my backpack and pulled out Alejandro's Grammy award, setting it down on the table.

Hale squinted at the golden phonograph, then his eyes shot open as he read the inscription. "Whoa! Are you serious? You're conning Alejandro?"

"Right now, it's his manager I'm after. I need you to follow him because I've got too many other things going on. Also, as you know, Victory Vance is still following me, and he reports everything to Bea."

With a look of alarm, Hale quickly got to his feet and ran to the window. I laughed. "No, don't worry. I always ditch him before I come here. You're safe. But that's why I don't want to do any surveillance—it's already tricky enough avoiding Vance."

I nodded at the table full of electronics. "While I'm at it, I need some toys from you. Hmm. . ." Such a dazzling array of devices, I hardly knew where to begin. "Got any wireless spy cameras?" I might need to bug George's place. The guy was dangerous, so I needed to keep my eyes on him.

Hale glanced down at the table and picked up something that looked like a fat button. "One free spy camera, on me. This one does audio, too." He explained how it worked.

Hale was happy to offer me his electronics gear, but that was the extent of his interest in my con. "Please don't make me follow this guy."

"Look, Hale, if easy money isn't enough for you, I have something else you might like. You'll probably get to meet Alejandro."

"Whoa, really? Now you're talking!" He grinned. "I'm in." I knew that would sway him.

Suddenly, a woman's voice inserted itself into the conversation. "Don't trust this man to follow anyone! He's a terrible tailer." We turned to look, and both of us recognized her at the same time. "Elle!"

Like a true cat burglar, Elle had slipped into the pizza place without anyone noticing. She now stood a few feet away from us. Hale and I ran up to give her hugs, then he pulled back and stared at her with wide eyes. "First Dee, and now you. What's going on?"

She shrugged. "I came to help out my big sister. Seems she's in too deep." She grinned as she tugged on my wig.

Elle looked the same as I remembered. Short, with long straight brunette hair, she wore jeans and a green T-shirt. The two of us didn't get together very much anymore. The last time I'd seen her was two years ago when she was doing a job in New York.

Elle stepped away and ran her gaze all over me, shaking her head and clucking like a disappointed parent. I folded my arms and frowned. "I am *not* in too deep! I've got this whole thing under control."

"Like hell, you do. What do you need, Dummy?"

I laughed. "You know, I think you finally have the right to call me that. I've been such a dummy with Bea."

"Hey, the F.M. is a wily old broad. She still fools me sometimes. What can I do to help?"

"Can you keep an eye on my mark? Hale doesn't seem to like surveillance."

"Sure. Are you really conning Alejandro's manager? I thought you were doing the big man himself."

"Yeah. Bea thinks I'm conning Alejandro, but it's his manager I'm after. Guy's a scumbag, so you'll enjoy helping me take him down."

"I don't need an excuse to help you out, Dee. I'll keep an eye on him. And I'll get my crew's hacker to dig into his financials, just in case you need more ammunition."

"Thanks, Elle. Also, can you find Bea's storage locker? Hale hacked her financials, but he couldn't find anything."

Elle smiled. "Sure, I'd love to see that place. I'll get my hacker on it, too."

"Great." I exhaled my relief. With Elle on this, I had renewed faith that my problems with Bea would get solved. "And one more thing. . . Can you manage the F.M. for me? Pay her a visit and tell her that you and I are spending some time together while I'm in L.A. That way, I can avoid seeing her without raising too much suspicion."

"You got it. See? I knew you needed me."

"I guess I do. And thanks for the electronics, Hale. You guys are the best." I gave them both hugs.

Hale grinned. "Just like old times. Except no Jay."

"I think Jay would have been proud of us, still working cons after all these years. He really thought the world of you, Hale."

Hale squinted at my compliment. "We were rivals. Two kids the same age, competing with each other to run the cons."

"Yeah, but he loved to watch you work."

Hale shook his head. "You're just trying to butter me up so I'll help you with this con."

"No need for that, you already agreed to help."

Elle jumped in. "Dee's right. Jay was happy when you and your friends joined our crew. And he'd be happy to see you now, still running things from the pizza place. Let's help Dee with this deal. Jay'll be smiling down on us."

Twenty-One

I returned the SUV to the strip-mall parking lot and climbed back into my room. No sooner did I get settled than I got a call from Bea. "Get your ass over here, now!"

"What's wrong?"

"I'm not doing this on the phone. Get. Over. Here." She hung up.

I knew this would be about my inappropriate visits to see the mark. Of course, I would have preferred to keep my nocturnal delight a secret from Bea. But Vance had followed us on the first date, and he'd seen Alejandro come to my motel room. So Bea knew what was going on. It looked like I was in for another lecture.

I got cleaned up and dressed for my foster mother: casual jeans with a plain white T-shirt, a navy jacket, and a baseball cap to cover my white hair. Then I walked out the front door and got in my brown sedan. Vance spotted me instantly and raised the newspaper too late to hide himself. The poor man was so incompetent.

Bea sat at the kitchen table, snacking on a Low-Hanging Fruit bar. She eyed me carefully as I walked in with the backpack holding Alejandro's Grammy award. This was a peace offering that I planned to use to keep her from getting angry. Or at least any angrier. She seemed quite upset already, so it looked like I wouldn't get to keep this particular memento. Alejandro would simply have to deal with the fact that his gift wasn't going to end up on my bookcase as a remembrance of our night together.

"You fucked him!" She scowled at me. "How many times do I have to tell you. . ." and the lecture went on from there. She covered basic facts like the proper way to deal with a mark, the reasons why it's wrong to fall in love with one, and the importance of focusing on the goal at all times.

As an added bonus, I got to hear about another of Elle's screw-ups, from years ago. This happened soon after I left town, but I already knew the story—Elle had told me all about it. Now Bea laid it out for me, and I acted appropriately shocked by a story she thought I didn't know.

Back then, Elle had ruined a huge deal by dating the mark's son. She didn't know she was doing that at the time: she just liked the kid. But when Bea started conning his father, Elle felt bad and told the boy. A total mess. The con went sour, and the boy broke up with her. The moral of the story was not lost on me: never fall for the mark.

And I got it. Because honestly, I wasn't falling for him. First of all, he wasn't the mark anymore, although Bea didn't know that. Also, this wasn't about love and relationships and so on. All I wanted was a fling with the hottest rocker on the planet. Was that too much to ask? Regrettably, it was too much to ask of Bea, so I kept the question to myself.

When she started to rerun the lecture for the third time, I'd had enough. I cut her off with a wave of my hand. "Stop worrying so much. Everything's fine. We're still on for the exchange in three days. And I brought you a present, hot off Alejandro's walls." I reached into my backpack to pull out the Grammy award.

This did not make her any happier. She pulled it close to examine it, then pounded her fist on the table and screamed at me. "You stole this from him? Fucking idiot! What on earth would possess you to do something so stupid? This could alert him and curdle the whole deal!"

She swore a non-stop blue streak at me until I was able to cut her off.

"Can it! I didn't steal this from him. He gave it to me as a present. Take it, and stop yelling at me about this deal."

Bea's anger seemed to lessen as she reached out for the Grammy again. She lifted it up and hefted it in the air, feeling its weight. Then a smile slowly formed on her face. "This could come in useful someday. You might need it."

"*I* might need it?" I already knew what she meant by that—I was her permanent partner now. Thanks to Elle, I already knew that Bea would never let go of her blackmail evidence. But I wanted to hear this directly, to drive home the reality of my situation. I needed her to think she was in control, even if I had no intention of letting things stay that way. "What are you talking about?"

"We're a team now. Just like the old days. After this con, we've got plenty more to do. And you can be sure that this little award will be useful at some point."

Her grin cut deeply, reminding me that I had work to do. If I didn't find that cocaine, I'd never leave Los Angeles. Suddenly feeling a little sick and desirous of some air, I made my excuses and left.

Free of my foster mother, I went back to the motel. I was about to call George when someone knocked at my door. Vance stood there, wavering unsteadily on his feet. "Hi, Dee," he slurred. "Want some dinner?" He held up a bag of food.

"Vance, you're drunk."

"And you're beautiful. Don't make me sit in my car all night. Let's have dinner together, maybe go out to a bar. I bet Alejandro never takes you out for drinks."

"Oh, Vance. I can't go out with you."

"Why not?" He stepped into my room and started pulling food from the bag.

I ran over to him, grabbed it all away, put the food back in the bag, and handed it to him. "We're not doing this, Vance. Besides, Bea will be angry if you get too close. Stay in your car—it's best for both of us. Sorry." I guided him to the door and pushed him out, trying not to laugh as he flashed his classic scowl.

I found myself torn between being creeped-out and feeling sorry for Vance. I didn't want to be rude, but it seemed like the only way to keep him from barging into my room. Too bad he didn't understand that any relationship we might have had ended a long time ago.

After a few minutes, I was calm again, so I called George. He picked up quickly. "Hello, Deborah. Is there a problem?"

"Not at all. In fact, there's an opportunity. I found another guitar in Mom's attic and wondered if you'd like to see that, too."

"What kind of guitar?"

"Just a plain old acoustic guitar. Not very exciting, but if I've learned anything from you, it's that you never can tell with these old guitars. And on the inside it says. . . Let me see. . ." I crinkled some paper so he'd think I was fumbling through my notes. "Ah, here it is. 'Martin D-1 prototype.'" I heard a gasp across the phone line and went on with my pitch. "Don't know if that means anything, but the word 'prototype' seemed unusual, so I thought you'd want to know."

I thought I detected hyperventilating on the other end of the line. "Can you send me a picture of the guitar? And. . ." He paused to take a breath. "Is there a number after the word 'prototype'?"

"Sorry, I don't have the guitar with me now. I just noticed it when I was at mother's place today. If you're interested, I can get it and bring it over to Alejandro's."

George had gathered himself into full deal mode. "Tell you what, Deborah. Why don't we keep this between you and me? I don't want to bother Alejandro. And besides, I'll be the one who buys this guitar, not him. Let's meet at *my* place tomorrow evening, six o'clock. Okay?"

I paused, pretending to think. "Yes, that would work. See you tomorrow." We hung up.

I was happy to see that some of my plans were proceeding as expected. On the downside, I'd lost the trail of the cocaine, and the second fake guitar was going to be a challenge to get authenticated. But I'd faced Bea and roped in George. Elle was in town, and Hale was helping out, too. As much as I didn't want to give myself false hope, I had to admit that things were going acceptably well.

Twenty-Two

With my day done, I called Alejandro as he'd asked me to do. We'd had mind-blowing sex last night, which, if this were any other man, would make me think that another night might be possible. But this wasn't any other man. This was the world-famous Alejandro, the love-em-and-leave-em rocker who—according to Karen and Udo—didn't do relationships. So even though he had expressed his devotion, I knew the Lord of Rock and Roll was a busy man. He might not have time for anything more than an update on the con.

The call picked up quickly. "What's up, Dee?"

"Not much. Done for the day."

"Good. I can't wait to see you."

I didn't expect that. This sounded like a second date to me. I gave a silent cheer for the chance to have more fun with this incredible lover.

In the background, I heard a familiar woman's voice. "Who did you just invite over, baby?" The formidable and highly desirable Ivory Doe cooed. "Is it her? The mystery mousy woman?" Ivory must have gotten very close to Alejandro, because her voice was now at full volume. "Whoever you are, darling, you'll have to get in line for this man. Behind me!" Her lusty cackling faded into the distance along with the echo of her heels. With a final, "Ta, ta," I heard a door slam.

Alejandro laughed. "She's something."

"The mystery mousy woman?" I wasn't that bad looking. Sure, I had a small mouth and nose—but I always thought it made me look younger. When I was feeling generous, I even considered it to be cute, although I never got much agreement on that from the men I dated. But mousy? That was new. Perhaps I *was* mousy, especially compared with Ivory and all of the other beauties who flitted about Alejandro. Leave it to her to hang that epithet on me.

"I'm afraid she means you. Her photographer took a shot of you when they were here for the interview. Then, believe it or not, someone got a grainy photo of you from the night you ran from my limo. Now you're a minor sensation, made even more intriguing by the fact that nobody knows who you are. Ivory dropped in just to harangue me about you, but I wouldn't say a word. I know you don't want the publicity, and besides, you're my little secret."

"Good God, Alejandro. You're impossible to be with."

He let out a little laugh. "That may be true, but I'm sure it won't stop you from coming over."

"Oh, please!" I teased him. "We're just working on a little project here."

That made him laugh harder. "Bullshit, sweetheart. You want me as much as I want you—I know how this works. But you don't have to admit your feelings with words. Just get over here and show me with your body."

I took a long, loud breath. "Now that you mention it, I believe you're right. I *do* want your body." Good thing he couldn't see the giant smile on my face. "I'm on my way."

I made a big show of stepping out of the room and driving off in my brown sedan. Visits to Alejandro's place were expected by this point, so I figured I'd give Vance something to do.

When I got to the mansion, Karen let me in with a nod. "He's in the study." She started to walk the other way.

Karen really had changed since the first time we'd met. She saw me as a threat then and hated me. Now I was even more of a threat, but she was professional and supportive. I wouldn't have imagined a change like that. Perhaps she *would* be a good member of my team.

I stopped her before she could run off. "Karen, I need your help. Can we meet somewhere tomorrow?" I explained one of the details of the con that she could help me do. I didn't explain the whole thing yet—perhaps I'd get to that tomorrow. Karen was delighted to help and promised to meet me at a coffee shop. Then she left, walking down the hall with a definite spring to her step. Who would have thought that she'd be so happy to pull a con?

I opened the study door to find Alejandro playing his guitar, a pencil between his teeth. His black jeans and tattered T-shirt showcased his powerful body, thrilling me more than anyone else possibly could. He nodded to me and played a few more chords. Then he stopped, made some notes, and played it again, staring at me the entire time.

When he was finished, he set down the guitar and leaned back in his chair, giving me a sultry look that lit me up from the inside. "I can tell you've been working hard."

Oh, yes! This was what I needed after a day of juggling the con: a safe place to unwind with some of that raw passion I could see in his eyes. I started off coy, swinging my hips and giving him my best hard-day-at-work swagger as I walked across the room. "You know how it is," I grinned.

"Dog eat dog." I stopped in front of him and propped my hands on my hips.

He stood up and pulled me into his arms, wrapping me snugly. "Bow wow. Need something to help you relax? A drink?" One hand ran up and down my body while the other held me tight.

I let my head rest against his solid chest while my hands busily explored the sculpted landscape. "It's okay," I smiled as I gave him a squeeze. "I've got one right here. A tall, cool drink that smells like cloves and tastes like sin." I brought my mouth up to his and took a long, refreshing drink. As I suspected, this tall, cool drink was sizzling hot.

His kisses still managed to surprise me, a beautiful dance of lips and tongues submerged in overwhelming sensation. We groped each other for several minutes, desperately trying to find ways to get closer.

Finally, we pulled back, heated stares still linking us together. "Bedroom," he growled. I nodded and stole another kiss. I couldn't resist. After all, his mouth was world famous for its incredible sexiness. And it turns out those millions of women were right.

He led me to his bedroom where we threw ourselves onto the bed without letting go, landing as one, kissing and hugging tight. His hands roamed my body, caressing me and slowly stripping me down. When he'd taken it all away, he ravaged my body. His hands and lips were everywhere, touching, massaging, tasting, and exciting; driving me to an exquisite high.

Breathless and dizzy, I lay naked on his bed in a crumpled heap. "God, you're good. And look!" I pointed at him. "You're still dressed." I got up and quickly remedied that situation. Then things really went wild.

We managed to eat dinner at some point, takeout from one of his favorite Middle Eastern restaurants. Then we fell back into the bedroom again, snuggling, discussing the con, and making love.

Later that night, we took a break and stumbled into the kitchen, half naked and grabbing at each other like children. He opened the refrigerator and smiled. "Excellent! Karen got them." He pulled out a foil-covered package and set it in the oven.

"What's that?" I walked over to the oven, but Alejandro stopped me.

"Something special for you. Don't look. Besides, you'll know what it is when it warms up. In the meantime. . ." He opened the freezer and pulled out two tubs of ice cream. "We've got vanilla and mint chocolate chip."

"What? No Nuts to You bars?" We laughed, then we sat and snacked. After a few minutes, a sweet smell filled the kitchen, and I knew what he had in the oven. "Oh my God! Churros! You remembered."

"Are you surprised?"

"Frankly, yes. I'm not used to people paying so much attention to me."

"Well, perhaps you should start getting used to it, because I can't stop thinking about you." He leaned over to kiss me, then got up to pull the churros from the oven. I devoured mine quickly and gave him a sugary kiss.

Full, and unreasonably happy, I looked around the kitchen. What an incredibly lovely home. Even the kitchen was inviting, all Spanish tile and wood. This little nook was a cozy place for a midnight snack. Yes, Alejandro's home was a spectacular setting for the high life. The sort of luxury most people saw only in movies. Or in my case, the sort of luxury I was taught to steal.

Alejandro ran his hand up my thigh and I remembered how I was dressed. I'd come here from the bedroom in panties and a blouse, barely covered. I suddenly felt exposed.

"Are there other people in the house? Is Udo protecting you?"

"No, he's gone for the night. Karen was just leaving when you got here."

I laughed. "Guess that makes me the night shift." I loved every minute of this, spending another night with Alejandro.

"It's true. Hey, I have an idea." He gave me a devilish grin, his face lit up as if he'd just invented the wheel. "How about a game of Truth or Dare?"

That sounded like fun. "Sure, you're on."

He leaned back with a nod. "You're up first, truth or dare?"

"I'll tell a truth." He knew most of them anyway. But I should have known better from this man. He wasn't going to ask me to tell him some boring truth—he went directly to the core.

"My investigators told me that your brother, Jay, was killed at age fourteen. What happened?"

I sucked in a breath. "That's a big one. And it's not pretty. Are you sure you want to know?"

He stood from the table and pulled me to my feet. Then he silently escorted me to the living room where we sat on a sofa amid piles of pillows and blankets. When we were firmly snuggled in, he gave my hand a squeeze. "Yes, I'm sure. Tell me about your brother."

I took a long breath as it all came swarming back. "He was the oldest of us, a year older than I was. We were doing a Three Card Monte scam one evening. As usual, Jay was the tosser, Hale was the shill, and I, the precocious thirteen-year-old girl, was the roper."

"Didn't Elle ever work with you?"

"She was only ten—too young to play. Besides, as the only one of us who still looked like a child, she often worked with Bea to do parent/child games. That's where they were that evening."

I let a long breath slowly cycle through me, then I jumped right to the heart of the matter. "It was my fault. As the roper, I was supposed to spot the perfect mark. Rich and greedy, slightly helpless, and not too dangerous. But I totally blew it. A man approached us and asked some questions about the game. He was well dressed and seemed eager to learn, so I chose him. Worst decision I ever made."

Tears started to build up in my eyes, but I forced myself to go on. "Using Jay's signals, I whispered the correct card a few times while we watched other men play. Soon, the guy started betting, using my advice. We let him win some low bets, but when he pulled a fat chunk of cash from his wallet, we knew it was time to take him. I signaled Jay, and he spun the cards around the table, finally stopping and presenting the three choices.

"I told the guy that it was the left card, then I turned to run. But he grabbed my wrist, holding me there. With his other hand, he reached out to point to a different card. I was already nervous about not being able to get away, but things got much worse when he raised his arm to point to the card. He had a gun in his jacket." I shook my head. "Huge trouble."

"A cop?"

"Worse. A vigilante." I shuddered just thinking about him, a face I'd never forget. "Some crazy guy from our neighborhood who decided to single-handedly get rid of card games." I sat up to shake off the sensation of watching Jay die again. It crept along my skin, chilling me in its path. Alejandro noticed this and scooted closer on the sofa, wrapping me in a hug.

After a few seconds, I continued my story. "Back then, I had a signal that I used when it was time to abort a con. I kept a little toy tiger in my pocket. In case of any problem, I'd let it fall to the ground. Jay and Hale would notice, then we'd all run away.

"But the guy was somehow on to this, and as soon as I pulled out the tiger, he snatched it from my hand. So I switched to a more direct approach and yelled out that the cops were coming. Hale took off, but the guy grabbed Jay's wrist and held both of us tight. He said, 'There's no cops, and we're going to finish this game.'"

I swallowed and rocked in my seat, hating what came next. This was an event I didn't want to discuss. Without a doubt, the most terrifying day of my life—I was starting to sweat just thinking about it. Perhaps I shouldn't have agreed to play Truth or Dare.

Alejandro hugged me tighter. "You don't have to finish this if you don't want to."

I took a deep breath. "I'll finish." I hadn't told this story to anyone in New York, so I'd been able to put it out of my mind for years. And I never expected or wanted to tell it to Alejandro. He didn't need to know how badly these confidence games had screwed up my life. I wanted him to trust me, not think of me as an unreliable partner. But for some reason that I couldn't put into words at the moment, I also needed to tell this story. Perhaps it was the fact that he gave me permission to stop, which let some of the pressure off. It let me go on with a measure of safety and freedom.

I stared at the floor for a few seconds, then continued. "He was bigger and stronger than either of us. He pulled us away from the table and kicked it over, spilling the three cards. They landed face-up on the sidewalk, so now he could tell that none of them were the queen. Jay had palmed it off and replaced it earlier, before he started to mix them up. This is Three Card Monte, you know—the mark never wins."

Alejandro rolled his eyes. "I know how it works. So now he knew you were cheating him."

"Yeah, that was bad. He dragged me and Jay into an alley, pushed us to the ground, and pulled out his gun. Jay tried to be brave. He called the guy a big talker who wouldn't commit murder over a stupid card game. I'll never forget his answer. He. . ." I shuddered and bit my lip. "He gave us a cold smile and said, 'You're wrong.' Then he shot Jay in the head. He must have used a silencer, because I barely heard the puff of the pistol. But blood started to run from a small hole in Jay's forehead, and he collapsed on the ground."

"Jesus, Dee. That's awful."

I nodded and felt tears welling up, but I forced them back down. With a swallow, I went on. "I must have freaked out when I saw Jay lying there. I screamed and cried, but the guy pointed his gun at me and warned me to keep quiet. He dragged me to the end of the alley and threw me in the trunk of his car. Then he drove off. It completely freaked me out. I hit bottom that day, bouncing around in that dark trunk, crying for Jay, and waiting to die."

My tears wouldn't be stopped now, so I let them flow. "Jay was only fourteen! And he got killed over a stupid card game." Sniffling, I added, "Because I roped in the wrong man." I swiped at the tears running down my face.

Alejandro held me quietly for a few minutes during which my unfinished tale hung in the air. Finally, he pulled back and stared at me sympathetically. "Obviously, you survived."

I nodded and took a long breath. "He drove out to the desert and stopped. The sun was down by the time he got there, and it was cold. He had driven off road for a long time—I could feel the bumpiness. Out in the middle of nowhere, he opened the trunk, threw me to the ground, and drove away, leaving me there to die."

Alejandro gasped. "How horrible!"

"It was awful. I watched the way the car drove off and found some stars to guide me, then I started walking. I walked all night and half of the next day before I stopped to sleep. Then I woke up that night and continued to drag myself through the desert. I was hungry and thirsty and scared and miserable. By the next night, I wished he'd put a bullet in my head, too." I shivered, remembering the misery.

"I found a road that night and hitched a ride. But nothing was the same after that. I was sick of conning people, and my nerve was shattered. With Jay gone, I was the oldest. But I was only thirteen, and I had no intention of taking over his role. I wanted out."

"Did Bea let you?"

I shook my head. "Not a chance. We never played card games again, but we kept on conning. She barely even mourned Jay's death, just told us to get back out there— that it was the best way forward. It took me four years before I could be free of her. Four more years of running cons with her and Elle."

He cocked his head. "And then?"

I tightened my mouth. "I swindled her. I'd been siphoning money from my cons and had a modest stash.

But I needed more if I was going to live on my own and stop conning. Anyway, the three of us did a con that netted a half million dollars. Since I was the inside man, I got the money first. I took it all and ran to New York City where I did my best to hide from Bea. Also, I put a hundred thousand in a bank account for Elle."

"I'm surprised you didn't split it evenly with her."

I laughed. "That much money was plenty—more than she'd ever had. Bea never let us keep any of the money we conned; she'd search us when we got home, and she even raided our rooms when we were out. The money I left for Elle became her secret stash, and believe me, she was grateful. It helped her get away a few years later."

"Given all this, I'm surprised you're playing con games again. Bea must have some pretty heavy leverage to make you do this."

"She does, because I was stupid and didn't pay attention." I shook my head. "I should have known better. When I got to L.A., she tricked me into handling some drugs she had stolen, then she blackmailed me with the fingerprints on them. Now, if I do anything she doesn't like, she'll frame me with it."

"Wow! That's vicious."

"Yeah, but it taught me a lesson. I've been very careful about what I touch since she did that to me." I pointed a finger at him. "It's something everyone should think about: if you're doing anything illegal, wear gloves!" I laughed sadly, then took a long breath. "Anyway, I'm a con woman again, and I intend to finish this job using all the expertise I once had. I haven't got nerves of steel anymore, but I know how to play the game. If I can keep it together for the next three days, this might just work." I sank back in my chair.

"That's so strange! Your own mother is blackmailing you." His head shook solemnly. "You definitely win the award for having the worst parent."

"I suppose. Anyway, if you want to know what happened to my brother, the answer is that I chose a dangerous mark. Bea always told us to study them carefully, to listen closely and observe them. I screwed up that day, and it got my brother killed."

"You were thirteen, dammit! And your foster mother brought you up thinking that this was the right thing to do. It wasn't your fault."

"Yeah, I've heard that excuse. But it doesn't help much when you have to live with the memory of seeing your brother get killed." I sniffled and wiped my nose, but I refused to let myself cry any more. Jay's death *was* my fault, regardless of what Alejandro or anyone else thought.

Twenty-Three

My night with Alejandro had started off great, but by this point, I was exhausted. After telling him about Jay's death in what seemed like an innocent game of Truth or Dare, I was drained and teary. I needed something upbeat to restore my spirits, so I forced the conversation into acceptable territory. "Enough of this. It's your turn, Mr. Rock Star. Truth or Dare?"

Alejandro stared at me for a few seconds, evidently still taking in my story. Finally, he looked away and took a deep breath. "I'll do a truth."

I needed something light and easy to help me shake off the weight of my sorrow, so I went for something I'd been curious about for years. The usual fan love, but this time I figured I'd get an honest answer. "What's it like, being Alejandro? Is it a dream come true, or is it a living hell with all the paparazzi and fans? And what about women? They seem to throw themselves at you. Have you had sex with thousands of them?" Alejandro's smile was so big that I knew I'd asked a stupid question. "Yeah, I know. You must get asked that a lot. But this time, I want real truth, not media sound bites."

"No, it's a surprisingly interesting question. I was only smiling because I don't hear it much. Nobody ever asks me if my fame is a bad thing, and few women want to know how many others I've bedded. Don't be jealous."

I shook my head. "It's not jealousy. I'm not some delusional fan girl who has fantasies about a life with you.

I'm just trying to figure you out. As close as we've become, both in bed and in this con, I still don't understand you because your fame obscures so much."

"I'm just a man. I put my pants on one leg at a time."

I rolled my eyes upward. "You know what I mean. I bet you've never had to work to get a woman in your bed. You certainly didn't need to with me, and I'm sure that every woman you meet is more than willing. It's probably so easy that you don't even have to try."

He nodded. "It *is* easy for me. Too easy. If I see a woman who I'd like to know better, all I have to do is strike up a conversation. Never fails. Only problem is that when I do that, it gets blasted all over the Internet, so it's rarely worth the cost. And I never promise anything I can't deliver. I always make it clear that we're just having a fling."

"So? I'm sure you don't have an exact count, but perhaps you could round it to the nearest thousand."

Alejandro laughed so hard that he had to hold his stomach. "To the nearest thousand? Then the answer is zero. I'd say closer to two hundred, if you must know. Most of them were during the first year of my fame, when I was impressed by the ease of it, unaware of the media consequences, and too horny to care. I slowed down considerably after that."

I arched an eyebrow. "Slowed down? I don't think so. I've been following you for a decade, and I've seen you with loads of women. Every time I look at the entertainment news, you're there with another glamorous actress or model. And none of them are trying to swindle you."

He darkened. "First of all, the women I date *are* trying to swindle me. Every one of them. Some want my money, and all of them want my fame. Welcome to show business.

But also, just because I'm seen with someone, doesn't mean I've been to bed with her."

"But why wouldn't you want to have sex with these women?"

Alejandro shook his head with a smile. "Okay, Dee. Who do you think I've been to bed with?"

"Well, certainly Quinn Freeling. You two were Hollywood royalty for a while there."

"Sorry, never had sex with her. We were matchmade by our publicity people who thought it would be a good idea. But it wasn't. First time I met her at a fancy media-pumped dinner she was surrounded by dozens of willing boys who kissed her ass. I decided I'd never be one of them, and I told her so that night. Turned out, she couldn't care less. As far as she was concerned, falling in love with someone famous would ruin her. And I can't say I disagree. Once two celebrities start going out, they get judged together, and whatever one person does reflects on the other. Neither of us wanted that, but our publicists insisted. So we agreed to have a one-month media affair, then call it quits. The good news was that we never had to have sex." He gave me a crooked grin.

I frowned. "Still, you can't deny that you're a player. Ivory Doe was practically seducing you during the interview, and she seemed annoyed when I called here earlier."

"Forget Ivory—she doesn't mean a thing to me." I squinted at him, but he merely repeated it. "Not a thing."

I shrugged. "Okay, never mind about the women. Tell me what you think of being the most famous rocker alive today."

He grumbled and shook his head. "At first, it was amazing. People loved me, swarmed me, knew all my songs. Total ego trip. Then it got weird. Too much love, endless swarms, tiresome paparazzi. I'd sold my soul to the devil, and in exchange, I'd lost my own self. Now I can't go anywhere without a bodyguard, nobody tells me what they really think, and I can't trust that anyone I'm with isn't doing it for personal gain. So what's it like being Alejandro? If you'd asked me that question a week ago, I'd have said it's hell."

I stared at him with wide eyes, unwilling to believe his words. He kept making these statements suggesting that my presence had changed something for him, that I was somehow different and better. This was "Truth or Dare" we were playing, but I had a hard time accepting that he spoke the truth. "And now?" My question barely came out as a whisper.

"Since I met you, it's been much more fun to be Alejandro. Almost magical." He closed his eyes briefly and smiled. "Don't you see? I was already impressed after visiting your shop, but when I found your picture, things got even more intense. Suddenly, I was crushing on this cute artist. Made me feel like a helpless teenager. I wanted to find you, but I didn't, because as I've already mentioned, when I call up a woman or drop in on her, things get weird quickly. So I held back, frustrated by my own fame, not knowing what to do. Then you walked in my door a few days later, and I knew I had a charmed life."

Alejandro gave me a heart-melting smile. "Of course, you were using a fake name, and you weren't selling pottery, so I didn't really know how to respond. But as soon as you left, I called my investigators and told them to dig deep, to find out why a New York artist was pretending to be someone else. I told them to work fast, because whoever you were, I refused to let you slip away. The next day, they already had a dossier, and it was amazing. I was blown away. I mean. . ." He shook his hands in front of his face, clearly struggling to express himself. "The beautiful and talented pottery painter was actually a con artist and a forger. I was fascinated! If I'd met you under any other circumstances, we'd never have gotten close. But this!" He grinned broadly. "This has been fun and interesting and so different from my normal life that I can't stop indulging in it. You, Dee, have made being Alejandro fun again."

"But it can't be." I struggled to explain the huge incongruity between us. We had no future that I could see. "We're. . . Nothing." I dropped my head.

"We're not nothing. We're lovers. Which you might think means nothing to me, but you're wrong. I don't take lovers lightly. Most of them don't last because once we make love, they get big ideas. But you don't seem to have any unrealistic notions, and I like that."

He stared at me for a few seconds, then went on. "I don't have any unrealistic notions either. We could indeed end up being nothing—I know that. It's way too soon to say for sure. All I know is that when this con wraps up, we're going to have a serious discussion to see where we stand. I admit I may be ready to move on. You may be, too—that's one of the things I like about you. But in the meantime, believe me when I tell you that you're the most refreshing woman I've met in a long time, possibly ever. So to answer your question: I'm glad I'm Alejandro."

I felt a tingling all over my body. Thrilled that this incredible man wanted me. Sure, I understood that it could all fall to bits. And things were so busy right now that I didn't have the mindshare to dwell on him as much as I'd like. But he was right about one thing: when this con ended, everything would be very different. So I resolved not to overthink it right now.

"Well, I'm glad you're Alejandro, too." I giggled at the absurdity of that statement.

"Good. Now it's your turn—truth or dare?"

Truth didn't work so well for me, so I figured I'd change it up. "I'll try a dare, although I'm sure I'll be sorry I offered." I winced lightly.

He broke out in a wide grin. "Okay, I dare you to accept a side-bet on this con. I bet that on the day of the deal, I'll get George's money before you do."

"Excuse me? You don't even know half of what's happening on the day of the deal."

"I know you're selling George a fake guitar. And I'm fascinated with all your preparations. It makes me want to play again like I did when I was a kid. Also, I really want to take an active role in tricking George. Just a little something to make me feel better about the money he's stolen."

I gave Alejandro a nod. "Okay, I get that. But I already have a plan to get his money. If you mess with it, you could ruin the whole con."

"I'll be careful."

"Yeah, but you can't be careful when you don't know what's going on. You asked me not to tell you things, so I haven't. But you need to know everything if you want a part in the con."

"Oh, come on! All I want to do is take George's money on the day of the deal. I don't need to know more about your details, and you don't need to know more about my plan."

"That's ridiculous. You can't burst in during a deal and just grab the money."

He folded his arms. "I won't interfere with the deal at all."

I arched an eyebrow. "So you'll steal the money from me after the deal?"

He shook his head. "I won't do a thing after the deal, either. All I'll say is that I'll do it on the day of the deal, before it happens. Now, no more questions. I promise I'll be careful."

Just what I needed, another wild card. Alejandro had done a few short cons as a kid, and now he thought he was a pro. I needed to make him understand the gravity of this request.

"You're making trouble for me, Alejandro. This isn't a game."

"But it *is* a game. A 'con game.'"

"Don't be fooled by words. Conning people is dangerous, and George is a dangerous man. If you screw things up, somebody's going to get hurt. And I don't care how much deniability you've got, if you get in my way, I will not be responsible for what happens to you."

"Stop worrying. I won't mess it up for you."

I snorted at him. "You already are messing it up, with this dare."

Alejandro shrugged. "You can refuse the dare if you like. But then you lose the game."

I didn't mind losing this silly game, but something deep inside me told me to go for it. Not because of any pride, but rather because I could handle it if he meddled. I could switch to a different plan.

My current plan was to sell both guitars to George. At the deal, crooked police would arrest us for selling stolen goods, impound it all, and then return it to me. This gave me control of the money, which was important because if I didn't recover Bea's blackmail evidence, I'd need to give her something to keep her happy. If Alejandro took everything before the deal, my safety net would collapse, and Bea might get ugly. Also, I had yet to find any policemen who would cooperate with me on this, so the plan was already doubtful. Now, with this dare, it was useless.

But I had another plan, one that I'd been thinking about for a week now. I hadn't seriously considered it, though, because it was a bit of a gamble and would be very tricky to pull off. But this plan had a number of advantages, including the ability to handle Alejandro's meddling. Suddenly it was much more appealing. In fact, the more I thought about it, the better it got. I still needed Karen, Elle, and Hale. But now I needed them for different jobs. I could make this dare work.

"It's okay, I'll take the dare." Arms akimbo, I stared at him. "Does the winner of your bet get anything besides bragging rights?"

"Hmm. Good idea. How about this? The winner gets a free trip to visit the loser's family."

I squinted at him. "I haven't got much of a family. You certainly don't want to meet Bea, and my sister, Elle, just came here from Oregon, so you'll probably get to meet her soon, no matter how this bet ends."

"I'm not talking about Bea and Elle, I mean your real parents. If I win, we go find them."

I laughed. He'd been egging me to look them up, even more than Elle had, and now he was getting creative. I admit I was growing more curious about them every day, even though things were a little busy right now. But after this con? Sure. I was more willing to meet them now. Imagine how strange it would be to show up at their door with Alejandro next to me. It might even be fun if he won the bet.

"And if I win, we visit your parents?"

"Yes. They're down in Santiago—moved back over a decade ago. All my relatives are there, too. So think of it as a vacation in Chile. We'll spend some time with the family, then go to my beach villa in Zapallar and relax."

"Hmm. That does sound better than a trip to see the people who abandoned me. I think I'll have to win this little bet."

"Says you." He smirked. "Beware, Ms. Kirkland. I'm going to get George's money first." We grinned at each other for a few seconds. Then he leaned in for a tender kiss to seal the deal.

Suddenly the implication of his words sunk in. He wanted to take me on a vacation! Just Alejandro and me on a beach in Chile. That sounded like heaven. A vacation with this man would be an incomparable thrill. I definitely needed to win his bet.

Nevertheless, this game of truth-or-dare was becoming too much work, especially when he took it as an opportunity to mess with my plans. But I'd done two rounds and he'd done only one, so I needed to even things out. "All right, last time—truth or dare?"

"Dare."

Good. I could make this easy for both of us. "I dare you to let me stay here again tomorrow night and the night after, so I have an excuse for avoiding Bea until the con is over. Even if we're not getting hot under the sheets, just let me stay in one of your guest rooms."

Alejandro threw his head back and laughed. "That's hardly a dare—you can do better than that."

"I'm fresh out of dares right now. Let's go back to bed."

"Okay, I owe you one." He stood up from the sofa, flashing his phenomenally built chest. Before I could finish admiring it, he pulled me up and brought me in for a closer view. Yes, it was a great-looking body, and it felt great, too. I hopped on, my arms around his neck and my legs around his waist. Holding me tight and kissing me tighter, he carried us back to the bedroom.

We spent the rest of the night letting our bodies flow, smooth and steady, wild and hungering. The man was so incredibly passionate that I hardly got any rest. But even the scant amount of sleep I got must have been enough, because when I finally woke up, I *did* feel rested and ready for the con to move ahead.

Two Days
Until the Deal

Twenty-Four

Things were suddenly changing fast. As one problem got solved, another became critical. So with the deal coming up in just two days, my head was spinning out of control trying to keep everything from collapsing. And now I couldn't even trust Alejandro, because he planned to meddle with the deal on the last day. Not that I could blame him. But my life was already complicated enough.

I tried not to think about all this as we went for another morning run. Alejandro and I jogged twice around his property in pleasant silence. On the third lap, we turned a corner and saw two women waiting for us, phones snapping away. We stopped where we were, but the women closed the distance, shrieking as they ran. I took a step back and watched.

The women quickly surrounded him, sighing and screaming his name. Alejandro smiled, a gracious host, even to trespassers. "Ladies, I'm glad you like my music, but you have to leave here."

He might as well have been speaking in dolphin. They grabbed his shirt and ripped it from his body, reducing it to fistfuls of scraps which they gathered with deranged glee, as if it were made of gold. In what world was it acceptable to rip someone's shirt from his body? Perhaps they planned to sell these scraps online, pre-owned by Alejandro and soaked in authentic sweat. I had to admit that I didn't really understand the appeal.

Standing there with no shirt, Alejandro snapped at them. "Enough! Now go home!"

But the women were transfixed, staring at something that I hadn't been able to stop looking at, either. His chest. Exposed and gleaming with sweat in the morning light, his entire body flexed with each breath, just like in all my favorite videos. This seemed like the perfect time for his band to start up a song.

While the women stared at him, Alejandro and I made brief eye-rolling contact to share our understanding of the lengths he had to take to keep his fans happy. Then we waited for them to leave.

But instead of leaving, they snapped out of their stupor and lunged at him, grabbing his arms, his shoulders, or any perch they could get to. Alejandro staggered under the attack and shouted at them. Besides leaving trails of kisses, they also clawed at him rather harshly and even took so-called love bites. It was one thing to take the man's shirt, but this was too much. These women were going to leave marks, and that was over the line.

Alejandro might be too much of a public figure to fight this assault, but I could do it. I was a nobody, a mirage, the mystery mousy woman. And part of my con-artist training had included self-defense—an essential skill that could make the difference between getting into trouble and getting out. So I knew what to do. I hoped he didn't mind, but I couldn't stand by while he suffered so much abuse from his fans. Besides, Udo was back at the house, so I was the only one who could help.

I started by crowding in behind the women, as if I wanted a hunk of this man, too. But actually, I was running through their purses. I quickly got their phones, some IDs, cash, and credit cards. Then I wrapped my hand around each of their pinkies and pulled back. Their hands came away easily, and they started screaming at me instead of him. I took a few steps away from Alejandro, pulling the women with me while they struggled to get out of my hold. Finally, I let go and jumped between them and Alejandro, holding up their phones.

"Stop or I destroy these." That caught their attention. They stopped and rummaged through their purses, flashing shocked looks at me.

I set one of the phones facedown across a small branch on the ground. My foot hovered over it threateningly. "If either of you moves one step closer to me or Alejandro, I'll step on this phone and break it in half. Now keep quiet while I erase these pictures." I quickly cleaned up the phone in my hand, then swapped it with the one on the branch, and cleaned that one, too.

I reached into my pocket and fished out the other items I'd taken. Their eyes bugged out as I set one woman's license on the ground next to the other's credit card. Then I took a picture of them with my phone. Finally, I held up all of their belongings.

"I'm going to give these back to you, then you're going to leave. But make no mistake. If you ever come back, I will find you, and I will Kick. Your. Asses." I was having fun, standing up for Alejandro. Taking a page from Vance's playbook, I even scowled at them. "Understand?"

The women nodded, so I gave them their things and sent them on their way, back into the woods. Finally, I turned to look at Alejandro. I hadn't been able to focus on him since I launched my attack, so his look surprised me.

He was still shirtless, and I was still helpless to resist that chest. But he stared, with wide-open eyes *and* mouth, seemingly stunned.

I stepped over to him. "Are you okay? Did they hurt you?"

His stare melted into a huge smile, and he laughed. "I'm great! But how did you do that?" Some of the surprise returned to his eyes.

So he liked what I did. I wasn't sure at first. Now, proud of myself, I stood up straight. "A little pickpocketing and some basic self defense. Two skills that I learned from Aunt Franny."

He shook his head with a huge grin. "I would love to meet this woman."

Now it was my turn to look surprised. He wanted to meet Aunt Franny, the woman who had influenced me so much, the woman who made me into what I was. This was actually more significant than if he'd asked to meet Bea. Yet another sign that he knew me and really cared.

The truth is, women had sometimes cared for me, but men rarely had. The only one I could think of was Uncle Carl. So Alejandro's sensitive side brought out feelings that were alien to me. A sense of how nice it could be to live with such a considerate man, to be able to talk to him freely, to have him listen to me and pay attention to my life.

Oh, how I'd love to find someone this caring, especially one this sensual. Alejandro was almost perfect. Why did he have to be an outrageously popular superstar, someone who could never settle down? Because here he was, stealing my heart just as thoroughly as I'd intended to steal his money.

We quickly finished our morning run, then bathed separately. I had too much to do, and I knew what would happen if we got naked together. Vance was waiting across the road from Alejandro's gate, but nobody cared. Fans probably did that all the time. He snapped to attention when I left and dutifully followed me back to the motel. I nodded at him as I went to my room.

Alone at last, I churned through the backup con, which was now my working plan. Yes, I could do it, but it wouldn't be easy or nice. And if I didn't recover Bea's blackmail evidence, the whole thing would be pointless. I hoped Elle's hacker would come through in time.

In the meantime, I had to move forward with my plan. Elle and Hale were on board, and even Karen was with us—my crew was shaping up. But now I needed someone else—I needed an outsider. Someone that neither Bea nor George knew. I needed Wanda.

The woman was an irresistible force, perfect for this new con. So I called her.

"Dee, honey! How's it going? We miss you, and we need you. It's another record month for sales." Then she started to chant at me, over and over. "We need more pottery. We need more pottery."

"Whoa!" I shouted into the phone. "Take a breath there."

Wanda laughed. "And by the way, guess who's here in the shop?" I heard the sound of hands on the phone, then a new voice came on.

"Hey, pot girl." Only Roman called me that, a joke about my pottery and his pot-smoking.

"Been a while, Roman. I should be back soon. How are you?"

He paused. "You've been gone? Where are you?"

Oh please! It had been almost two weeks since I'd seen him, and he hadn't even noticed that I'd been gone. Some boyfriend. And here I was worried about how he'd feel when I told him I'd had an affair with Alejandro. It occurred to me that I didn't even need to break up with Roman: there was nothing to break up.

I took a long breath, then kept it simple. "I've been in Los Angeles, Roman."

"Cool." He didn't care at all.

I really needed to stop dating this man. His disinterest never bothered me before, but now I needed more. I'd seen firsthand how someone could actually care about me, could *remember* an offhand comment I made about churros and act upon it. Could stop for a second to look at my hair, and notice its natural color. Could ask about my family and listen to my stories. Simple kindnesses like that accentuated the deep flaws in my relationship with Roman. We were over.

This wasn't about leaving him for a new lover. I had no delusions that Alejandro and I would end up together. This was simply how I felt, and I had to tell Roman the truth. After Alejandro had demolished all my lies, I couldn't keep lying about this relationship.

"How long have we been dating, Roman?"

"Dating?" He sounded offended by that word. "How last millennium."

"Okay, Roman. What would you call us?"

"Uh, buddies?"

"Buddies? Like fuck buddies?"

"No need to be crude. We're just buddies. But buddies can have sex."

"We've been together for five years! Don't you think we merit something stronger than 'buddies'?"

"Where are you going with this, Dee? I hope you're not looking for some sort of commitment."

"No, Roman. I know you don't want that."

"Good. So what's this all about?"

"This is about the fact that I think we're done being buddies who have sex."

"Oh. . ." There was a brief silence as he processed this change. "Well, that's okay."

"Really? You don't care?" As much as I knew he wouldn't, it still came as a surprise to hear him say it. And he caved without even asking who the other man was. Not that I would have told him at that point. But I was disappointed that he hadn't gotten even slightly jealous.

"Well, it beats becoming normal. I can't do that, Dee. Getting married and all—it's bullshit. None of those people are happy." He paused, perhaps waiting for me to agree with his stark assessment of men and women. When I didn't respond, he let it drop. "Can we still be friends?"

"Sure. We'll always have that. Put Wanda back on, please."

"Okay, later." I heard him talking to Wanda. "She wants you."

Wanda came back on. "Did you just break up with Roman? Who's the new guy?" Good thing someone in New York paid attention to me.

"You wouldn't believe me if I told you. But yes, there is someone else. Not that it's going to last, but I guess I finally realized that Roman and I need to move on."

"Well, good for you. We can talk about it later, when he's not around. So. . . what's going on?"

"I'm close to wrapping things up out here, but I need your help."

She sucked in an excited breath. "Anything for you, Dee. You know that. Does this mean you're coming back soon?"

"In just a few days, if things work out. But I need a huge favor. You know that big serving bowl that sits by the entrance to the shop—the one that I did in dark greens? Well, if you haven't sold it, I need it out here."

"You call that a huge favor? I'll just overnight it to you. Easy!"

"Yeah, about that. I need more than the bowl—I need you, too. Can you fly out here with it?" Then I added the hard part. "Tomorrow?"

"You need me that badly?" She laughed. "Excellent! What fun. Do I get to meet your new man?"

"If we're still going out. This guy doesn't do relationships any more than Roman does, so I can't promise anything."

"Too bad—you deserve better. Anyway, do I get to beat up Bea for you? You know I want to. That would be *so* great."

I let out a single laugh. "You got it, girl—this *will* be great. And you might even get a chance to work on Bea. Also, I need you to rent a car when you land. I'll pay you back for everything."

"Are you kidding? Going out to L.A. to meet your bizarre family is worth the price of a plane ticket, any day. Don't you ever try to pay me back. This is the most exciting thing that's happened in a long time. In fact, I have to go home right now and pack my best hats. I'll text you when I've got a flight." She hung up.

This was good news. If Wanda was bringing her best hats, then I'd be covered. That woman had more hats than Bartholomew Cubbins, and she never missed a chance to make a statement with them. I couldn't wait to see her in action.

Twenty-Five

I needed more supplies for this new con, so I switched to the black SUV. I also put on the black bob wig—my new look for today that would keep cameras guessing. My outfit was casual: a white blouse with a denim jacket and matching shorts. Bea would have been proud.

Then I shopped. I bought some blank price tags, wrapping paper, and a red marking pen. After that, I went to a camping supply store where I picked up a ski mask and the biggest backpack I could find. I already had a regular-sized one for daily use, but I needed one that could hold two guitar cases at once. The one I found was a large camping backpack that wouldn't enclose both cases: the necks of the guitars would stick out. But at least the bodies would fit neatly inside. Now I'd be able to move about with both guitars on my back and have my hands free.

Loaded with supplies, I returned to the music shop to pick up the fake Dreadnought from Uncle Carl. Before going back to see him, I stopped up front to chat with Franny. "Black hair?" She shook her head with a laugh. She was also in black today, with shiny accents to give it punch. Her black blouse had big slashes of metallic trim at the shoulders, and her matching black glasses had gold highlights. Of course, her lipstick remained bright red. "So, still taking Rawson down?"

"You bet. I'll take those notes you have on him. Also, I need some of those picks." I pointed to the pick bowl by the cash register, still colorfully appealing. Yes, they looked quite nice today.

She narrowed her eyes as she gazed at the bowl. "You're gonna catch that guy with guitar picks? This I gotta see. Go ahead, take what you want."

I pulled out a paper bag and held it open while Franny poured from the pick bowl, filling my bag about a quarter way. Satisfied, I shoved it in my purse. "Very nice. This should be perfect. I'll tell you all about it when the con wraps."

Carl had the fake Dreadnought ready for me. It looked just like the one I'd seen at Alejandro's home. I knew that Peters would spot it as a fake instantly, but I had a plan for handling that.

As I left Carl's shop, my phone rang. "What's up, Hale?"

He sang the birthday song, filling in Elle's name. When he finished, he laughed at his inept performance. "Elle's birthday is tomorrow, so I have a special event planned for her."

"Really? And what would that be?"

"Sorry, it's a secret. Let's just call it a magical wonderland that will be fun for the whole family. If you can spare an hour or two, I know Elle will enjoy it."

I considered his request. Even with the deal happening in two days, I could squeeze this in. "Okay. Let's do it tomorrow, before her party." I'd planned to take my sister out to a birthday celebration dinner, complete with drinks. So we'd do Hale's event just before that. "We'll go in the late afternoon, after you meet Alejandro."

"Seriously? I'm going to meet Alejandro? Hot damn! Looks like I'll get a trip to a magical wonderland, too."

"Magic for everyone tomorrow. But today, details. Gotta go." We hung up.

I moved on to the next of a seemingly endless list of errands: meeting Karen at a nearby coffee shop. Waiting for me in a tiny corner at the back, she was dressed in a full-sleeved white cashmere top over a denim miniskirt and black pointelle tights. She took a sip of her coffee and crossed her black ankle-length booties. "Hi, Dee. Nice hair." We exchanged amused smirks.

Since Alejandro had included her in the con, I had spoken to her about some of the details. So far, she was very helpful. But I needed to get to know her better before I trusted her with the whole plan. I worried that she might have some hidden agendas. Sure, she was friendly and didn't seem to hate me anymore. But I needed more than "friendly" from her—we had to get along in order to work together. Now I was going to find out whether that was possible.

We started off chatting about random things. Karen wanted to know more about me, which made me suspect that she was spying for Alejandro. As much as he claimed to trust me, he obviously trusted her more. He'd known her for years and let her manage his life. So I assumed that part of his insistence on having Karen work on this con was based on his need to find out more about me and evaluate me. Was I a good person or a bad person?

Although I'd been both in my life, I was beyond lying, so I gave Karen some of each. I started with my good side and told her about my pottery career, how lucky I was that my work was popular. I also pointed out that this was honest work, which I admitted was a pleasant change for me. I didn't want to cheat anymore.

She leaned back in her chair with a smile. "But you're conning George now, so you must not hate it that much."

I wondered how much she knew. Did Alejandro tell her everything? "I'm stuck doing this, but that doesn't mean I'm happy about it."

She flattened her lips and nodded. "Well my hat's off to you for it. That shithead needs to be punished."

Her vehemence surprised me. Alejandro had said that Karen disliked George. But I didn't expect her to truly loathe him. "So you know he's been embezzling?"

She laughed. "I'm the one who figured it out. And it's not just the embezzling that makes me hate him. He's always been nasty to me—treats me like dirt, tells people I'm 'Alejandro's slave girl.' He once asked me to fuck some record executive to get a better deal." She rolled her eyes. "I told him he could fuck himself."

Karen shook her head. "He thinks *I'm* incompetent, but I know more about Alejandro's business than he does. So I can't wait to help you take George down."

I started to speak, but she waved her hand and went on. "I know Alejandro's trying to avoid knowing your plan, so I promise not to tell him any of this. But you've *got* to let me be part of George's takedown."

I decided that I liked her. We had a common enemy, and that bound us together. Also, I had already asked her for some favors, which she'd performed perfectly. So I knew I could rely on her to help me and to keep Alejandro out of trouble. She'd be delighted to play a role in George's downfall.

I needed to make sure of one thing. "You don't mind keeping things from Alejandro?"

Karen laughed. "I do that all the time—it's not a problem. He doesn't need to know about every fan letter he gets, every post I make on his social network sites, or every detail about his three houses. He trusts me, which is much more than I can say about George."

I arched an eyebrow. "Three houses? Must be nice."

"They are. His place here in L.A. is pretty awesome, as you know. His hideout in New York is small but quite nice considering the location—a perfect getaway. And his beach villa down in Chile is insanely luxurious with incredible ocean views. I was there once—it's really nice. He goes a few times a year. In fact, I just booked another trip for him." I was glad to see that Alejandro had better places to be than Los Angeles, and although I wondered briefly, I doubted that this had anything to do with his bet. The man simply liked to vacation in Chile, and who could blame him?

Since Karen knew so much, it occurred to me that she might be able to help with something else that I needed. "By the way, do you happen to have access to any of George's accounts? His credit cards, for example?"

Karen shook her head. "Sorry. He keeps his personal finances to himself. Alejandro trusts me with money, but George trusts nobody."

"That's okay. I can manage without it. And your distance from his finances will protect you in the end, so it's just as well." I looked around. We were safe in an isolated nook at the back of the coffee shop. I could talk here. "So, this is what's happening." I scooted closer and explained the details of my latest plan to sell George a "stolen" guitar.

"Aha! That explains what you asked me to do this morning." Karen giggled. "Let's do it."

We went out to my SUV so we could work in private. Hidden in back, I made the needed modifications to the guitar that I'd just picked up from Carl. I'd done my research last night, and I decided that I would sell George prototype number eight. The other two missing D-1 prototypes, numbers one and three, were reputedly in much worse condition, so number eight was my best chance to fool him. First I removed the strings to get into the sound hole, then I managed to stamp the number with the woodworking tools I had bought. A tiny chisel carved out the number while a small wood-burning tool gave it the right aged look. But when I tried to restring the guitar, I was clearly out of my element.

"Let me do that." Karen knew what she was doing and quickly got it back together. She even loosened the strings slightly after she tuned it, so the guitar would appear to have been sitting in an attic for years.

"You really know your stuff."

She grinned. "You pick up a lot when you work for Alejandro. I once had to replace a broken string for him in the middle of a show. His usual roadie was gone, and it was up to me. 'Personal assistant' means basically there's nothing I don't do."

"Do you like the work?"

"I do. And he was right about me—I got too close. Ever since Zenith whacked him last year, he's been depressed and lonely. He hardly goes out with women anymore, maybe two that I can think of. So I had this delusion that I could make him happy, that I could be the one who explodes for him."

I furrowed my brow. "Explodes?"

"Yeah, that's his word for the perfect woman. Someone who's so intense that she leaves everyone and everything in rubble. I figured that as his P.A., I could do that. But I was wrong."

"How did you meet him?"

"I started out as a groupie. My girlfriend and I stalked him after a show one night and ended up in his bedroom.

These were the early days, and he was more available than he is now. When he made love to me, I felt like Cinderella with her prince. I even spent the night with him. But the next day, he made it clear that our time together was over. I understood—I'd gotten more than I'd ever thought possible."

She took a sip of her coffee. "A few years later, when I heard he was looking for an assistant, I applied for the job and got it. He barely remembered me, but we agreed that this was a professional arrangement. And we managed to keep it that way. But let me tell you something. Alejandro is a hard man to work for and not get delusional about." She laughed briefly. "God! He's so gorgeous. I started to indulge in fantasies, even though I knew they were impossible. I got jealous of every woman who showed up—I'm sure I was snotty to you."

"You were fine. It's a difficult job, and he's lucky to have you."

"Thanks. And by the way, thank you for that huge raise I just got. I understand it was your idea."

I grinned. "Glad I could help."

She pointed a finger at me. "You should know, by the way, that Alejandro doesn't do hookups anymore, and he doesn't spend the night with women just because he's horny. I'm not even sure that he slept with any of the women he's been seen with lately. In fact, you may be the first he's been with in nearly a year."

"Oh come on, he was doing Ivory Doe just a few days ago."

Karen furrowed her brow. "All she did was interview him. Then she came back yesterday for a brief visit, but nothing else happened."

"You weren't around during the interview, but I heard Ivory promise to come back at midnight. Those two definitely hooked up."

Karen started to laugh. I didn't think I'd said anything funny, but Karen must have thought it was hysterical because her laughter grew louder and louder, forcing her to cover her mouth. "Sorry," she choked out between belly laughs. "But you're wrong. That 'see you at midnight' line is just Ivory's little flirty thing. She says it all the time, and to everyone, but she doesn't mean it. I've even heard her say it to George, and you *know* she doesn't want him. Also, Alejandro isn't interested. Believe me when I tell you he's never slept with her. Right now, it looks like it's your turn. Just don't get too attached. He may be over you someday, too."

"*May* be? How did I get elevated from someone he will *surely* be over to somebody he *may* get over?"

"I'm telling you, Dee. I haven't seen him go for someone the way he's gone for you. Most women are lucky to spend a single night with him, like I did. You've been with him for two nights in a row, which is rare. Hell, even Zenith lasted only a week, so if you make it past that, you'll set a record."

That caught me by surprise. Sure, he'd insisted that our tryst wasn't typical for him. But he was so famous and alluring that I had a hard time believing it. Now Karen was giving me hope for something that seemed impossible to believe.

"Don't worry. I doubt I'll set any records." I shrugged. "In two days, everything will be over, including Alejandro and me. Just another fling that didn't last a week."

"Are you in love with him?"

I laughed lightly. "Who isn't in love with him? He's the Lord of Rock and Roll. *Super* hot and incredibly sensitive." I shook my head. "That sensitive side really caught me by surprise. I never expected that he could be so caring. And I actually have fun with him, even when we're just talking."

"But he's more fun to be with when you're doing other things." She grinned. "We both know that."

I laughed. "God. You and he *do* talk about everything." I slumped my shoulders. "Yes, he's great in bed. But that doesn't mean I love him. And it certainly doesn't mean he loves me."

"I don't know, Dee. He's pretty taken with you. He likes your art, even your con artistry. He's particularly impressed with your attempt to swindle him."

"An attempt that failed."

She grinned at me. "Peters said that guitar was one of the best fakes he'd ever seen. Anyway, most of the hucksters who try to sell guitars to Alejandro don't do nearly as well."

"In that case, I'm honored." I took a bow, and we both laughed.

We wrapped up our little get-together and went our separate ways. I could tell Karen was going to be a good person to work with.

Twenty-Six

With my black wig firmly in place, I climbed out the bathroom window to my SUV with the Dreadnought waiting in back. Then I drove to George's Bel Air home, only removing the wig when I arrived. This new plan demanded that I hide my movements even more than the old plan, so a wig was essential whenever I went out. Good thing I kept my bleached hair unkempt, because these wigs weren't helping me look any kind of put-together.

George had a very nice three-bedroom house set in suburban splendor. Nothing like Alejandro's incredible estate, but few homes were. I was amused to see that he didn't even have an alarm system, which further explained why he kept his guitars elsewhere.

I knocked at the door, and it opened quickly, as if he'd been waiting anxiously for my arrival. "Hi, George."

He eagerly waved me inside. As we walked through his house, I noticed how his eyes stayed glued to the guitar case. My eyes were also watching carefully, but I was observing his clothes. No bulge in his pants pocket, so that meant he kept his wallet in his jacket. I needed that wallet.

George pointed the way to his living room, and I kept up a steady patter, droning on and on about my mother's amazing attic and all the rare finds that were emerging from it. As I approached the door to the living room, I was so focused on what I was saying that I "accidentally" whacked the end of the guitar case into the doorframe, bouncing back into a collision with George, all flustered and apologetic. While one hand struggled clumsily with the unwieldy guitar, my other hand found its way into his jacket and took his wallet.

George was completely focused on the guitar. He grabbed it and—as an afterthought—reached out to steady me. "Careful with that, Ms. Gleason. It could be a valuable instrument." If he only knew.

When we made it to the living room, he gestured to the bar on the left. "Something to drink?"

"Coffee?"

He nodded and walked off to the kitchen. That gave me the time I needed. I quickly opened his wallet, pulled out a credit card, and snapped a picture of the front and back. Then I returned it to his wallet and tossed it onto the floor outside the living room, right where we'd had our collision. He'd find it later, still intact, and assume he'd lost it in the commotion.

George returned with coffee for me, and I set the guitar case on the table, gesturing to him to have a look. He rubbed his hands together like a praying mantis, then reached out to unlatch the case. Reverentially, his hands roamed over the outside for a few seconds, as if he was fearful of what he would find inside. Finally, he flipped open the case, took one look, then started hooting and fist-pumping. I thought he'd soil himself right there.

"I knew it!" He carefully picked up the guitar, handling it like a holy sacrament. "I've been trying to find this for years. Another Dreadnought D-1." He peered into the sound hole. "Prototype 8! Incredible."

I pointed to the case. "There are some accessories, too. Don't know if they're worth anything."

George set the guitar down gently, then opened the accessory compartment. Inside was a plastic bag filled with the picks I'd taken from the music shop. He smiled as he studied the picks, rolling the bag back and forth in his hands to examine the colorful ones. With a diminutive laugh, he tossed it back in the case. "Cute, but worthless." He turned to me and squared his shoulders. "How much do you want for the guitar?"

I put it back in the case and set it on the floor. Time to get tough. "I know this guitar's value—I looked it up. There are only four D-1 prototypes left, so it's quite rare."

George frowned. "I don't like where this is going. What's the price?"

I stood up straight. "If you want just this guitar, it'll cost you eight hundred grand. If Alejandro wants the Stratocaster too, I'll discount the pair to an even million. But that's my only offer—I'm not negotiating here. And we're doing this deal, along with the Stratocaster, in two days, as scheduled. I've already found another dealer who wants this guitar, so if you can't come up with the money in time, I'll just sell it to him. Doesn't matter to me." I knew I had an offer he'd be unable to refuse.

Indeed, he couldn't resist. "I'll take it. Both of them, for a 'full rock,' know what I mean? A 'meal ticket,' heh heh." He reached into a wooden box on his coffee table and pulled out a cigar. "Fine Cuban habanos. Want one?"

Great! He fancied himself a gangster and was throwing around stupid expressions for a million dollars while flashing cigars. How annoying. I stared at him with a furrowed brow, silently conveying my wish that he drop the street slang and cheap Cagney imitations. But he showed no signs of shame over this, which only fortified my resolve to swindle him.

"No thanks. Enjoy yourself." I waved away his phallic hunk of tobacco.

George cut off the tip of the cigar and lit it with a dramatic strike of a match, stoking it a few times into a cloud of foul gray smoke. I ignored him and looked around his living room, which was more interesting than him or his cigar. This is where the deal would happen, so I needed to understand the space. Soon he realized that he wasn't getting a rise out of me, so he got serious, pointing with the cigar. "This needs to be authenticated, you know."

"Of course. Will you use Mr. Peters again? Does he know about acoustic guitars, too?"

"Yes, Oscar's my man. Knows everything about guitars. I've used him for years."

I wondered whether Alejandro had contacted Peters yet. Would he be able to influence the man? I needed a less thorough examination for this guitar, if possible. In any case, I pretended I wasn't worried. "Well then, I hope he likes this one, too. Why don't you have him come on the day of the deal?"

"No. I want to know about this one beforehand. If I'm going to liquidate that much cash, I need to be sure." He looked at his watch. "Too late to call Peters today. Bring this back here tomorrow morning, say at ten."

"Very well. See you tomorrow."

I indulged in a quiet breath. The deal was on, for a million dollars! Things were falling into place. I even had Wanda flying out here tomorrow—I couldn't wait to see her.

Now all I had to do was take care of two minor details: find Bea's blackmail evidence and get this guitar authenticated. My chest felt tight, just thinking about it.

Twenty-Seven

Alejandro had told me to come over again when I was done for the day, so I left the SUV and the black wig at the motel and got my undisguised self into the brown sedan. Before starting the engine, I sat there and thought about this incredible trip to Los Angeles. Here I was, about to spend another night with the most outrageously gorgeous and sexy man ever. A man who I and millions of others had admired for years. And he wanted *me* in his bed so that we could have the best sex since. . . Hmm.

I'd had a few other lovers in my life, and some of them had been quite good. But even the best of them couldn't compare with Alejandro. In fact, the real man was so incredibly good, he was even better than the fantasies I'd had when I watched his videos. Oh yes, the best part of my day was just getting started.

To dampen my enthusiasm, I also considered the other aspect of this incredible trip to Los Angeles: Bea. After she tricked me into coming here, I sought some closure, a better understanding of her, and possibly a new start as adults. It sure didn't work out that way, though. Truthfully, I did have a better understanding now. One thing I understood was that Bea and I could never make a new start. Also, the closure I was about to get was not something I could ever have predicted. So strange.

I sent a message to Alejandro, telling him I was on my way. This would give him the opportunity to stop me if he had more important things to do. Or at least divert me to a guest bedroom. If that happened, I would understand—the demands on his time had to be enormous. For the next two nights, all that mattered was that the city surveillance cameras thought I was dividing my time between the motel and Alejandro's home. But nowhere else.

His reply came quickly. "Come on over." So I did.

It felt strange to be driving to his estate again. The strangest part was how familiar it was becoming! La-di-da, I think I'll go visit this guy I just met, *the Lord of Rock and Roll*. Oh look! There he is on a billboard, advertising his latest album. His seductive smiles now had new meaning. Farther down the road, amid all the graffiti on the walls of an underpass, his name had been spray-painted in large puffy letters. Alejandro was everywhere, appealing to everyone. They even played his songs at the city's lost-and-found department! So his desire to be with me still had an unreal quality.

I made it there quickly and didn't even notice Vance following me. His dark gray car just seemed like a shadow to me now, and I didn't care anymore. At some point before the deal, we needed to talk. But for now, I let him do his job.

Alejandro had given me the code to his gate, so I drove right up to the house. Karen was gone, leaving the burly bodyguard to open the door. He nodded with a smile. "Good evening."

"Hi, Udo." How strange was this? The man I once feared was now my friend. I even had an urge to give him a hug.

Bodyguards probably didn't do hugs—I imagined that they needed large amounts of personal space in order to do their jobs. When I was a kid pulling cons, I avoided hugs unless I was picking someone's pocket. In fact, it took me a long time after I moved to New York before I'd let anyone near me. Which, when I thought about it, was another reason why I ended up with Roman, a man who avoided physical contact much of the time.

But I liked Udo, and I was feeling pretty happy at the moment, so I thought, "Why not?" Standing next to him, I turned and wrapped my arms around his barrel chest.

He squirmed a little, perhaps unsure how to respond. I didn't want to make him too uncomfortable so I pulled away. "Sorry." I gave him a friendly smile to let him know all was good. "How are you?"

He stepped back and nodded. "I am vell. I hope you are, too."

Udo closed the front door and pointed down the hall. "Alejandro is in zee kitchen." With a tiny smile, he walked away.

I found Alejandro at the counter, chopping vegetables. Over his white tank top, surfer shorts, and sandals, he wore a big apron. This was not exactly my image of the rocker, although he looked great in anything. Who would have guessed that he had a domestic side?

"Hang on. . ." He finished dispatching an onion, then turned to me. I could see the front of his apron for the first time, and I nearly fell on the floor laughing. It had a huge picture of him on it, strumming a guitar. Still laughing, I pointed to the picture, unable to express how strange it was to see him wearing his own paraphernalia. "Hey!" His mouth slowly twisted into a grin. "This is a very popular item."

"I'll take one. But it has to be the one you're wearing, with stains all over it." I touched a dark greasy splotch near his heart. His superb chest pounded under my touch, as his sparkling eyes danced with mine. We gazed comfortably for a few seconds, then I pushed away with a smile. "Yes, I like this apron. It's a work of art."

"Coming from someone as good at art as you, that's quite a compliment." He took it off, folded it up, and handed it to me. "It's yours for a kiss." He opened his arms, so I paid him with a solid hug and a very tasty kiss.

"Hmm. Oregano?"

He grinned and pointed to a saucepan. "I can't resist tasting everything. It's almost ready."

"I didn't expect to find you cooking."

"Hah!" He stood up tall in mock offense. "Shows what you know about me. It's much easier to cook dinner here than to go out among the fans and the paps. And my parents are both great cooks—they taught me all their recipes." He waved at the ingredients on the counter. "Tonight, I'm making a few classic Chilean foods. Asado— Chilean barbecue, with Papas Cocidas—boiled potatoes. I also made a spicy Pebre sauce to go with it. And because I want you to have the full Chilean dinner experience, an appetizer of machas a la parmesana—Chilean clams."

I nodded at all the food he had prepared. "Very impressive. The only recipes I ever learned were how to make stuff with chocolate. We didn't have much else to eat at home. I bet you could make mole with some Nuts To You bars."

"No," he groaned. "You've got it wrong. Mole is Mexican. Don't confuse it with Chilean food. I know you Americans think anyone who speaks Spanish is Mexican, but it's just not true. And don't ever wish me a happy Cinco de Mayo. Mexican Independence day is fine for Mexicans, but it's not my holiday."

"Okay, I get it. Sorry about that." I swiped a finger across a big wooden spoon he had used to stir some sauce. It was delightfully tasty with an amazing range of spicy flavors.

"Mmm. Your parents taught you well! Are you close to them?"

"Sure, but they're living in Chile now."

"I understand you're heading down there soon. Do you visit often?"

"Occasionally, when the mood strikes me. It's been a while, so I figured it was a good time for a visit."

I thought about the stories I'd read about his family. "So why did your parents go back to Chile?"

"They came to the states to escape poverty, but when I was seventeen, the poverty caught up with them again. Dad lost his job in the US downturn, and Chile was doing better. So they moved back."

"This was after you broke up with your first love."

"Yeah, I needed a fresh start at that point, so I was ready for something new. Still, it was hard to leave, because I was in a band and we were starting to do well. We were playing clubs and making a little money here and there. If I'd been more like you, I'd have struck out on my own. But my parents wanted me to come with them, and I'd just been dumped, so a new life in Santiago sounded perfect."

"How did that work out?"

Alejandro laughed sadly. "It was awful. I spoke some Spanish but not enough to fit in. Face it, I'm a US citizen, not Chilean, so I didn't belong there. All the kids shunned me and called me a gringo."

"So you came back."

Alejandro grinned. "Yep. Just two months later. Even my parents agreed that Chile was wrong for me. My bandmates were delighted to see me back here, and they let me sleep on the floor of their loft. I even finished high school, although I don't know why." He squinted at me. "You ran away from home when you were seventeen. Did you finish high school?"

I blurted out a laugh. "Are you kidding? Certainly not. Sure, I was only a few months away from graduation when I ran away. But since I was in hiding, the last thing I was going to do was register with the authorities." I shrugged. "Besides, I made my own way in New York, so a high-school diploma was pointless."

"Well, my diploma was utterly useless. Within a year after I got back to L.A., our band was playing clubs all over the city. I was finally making enough to support myself. Two years later, I had my first hit song, which won a Grammy. So you get no argument from me about the value of a high school diploma."

I watched as he finished the salad, sautéed some clams, and went out to his poolside barbecue to check on the meat. Finally, we sat down to eat.

Alejandro's cooking was spectacular. "Wow, you're good. Do you cook often?"

"Not often enough. I'm usually out at some event or dining with someone politically useful."

"Well, tonight *I'm* politically useful. Let me tell you the latest on my plot to destroy your business manager." I told him how the second guitar had been made, shown to George, and was being tested tomorrow. There were many things that I didn't tell him, though, including the fact that I was selling the first guitar, too. George would have become suspicious if I'd withdrawn it from consideration. So even though some of the money I'd get was from Alejandro, to pay for the guitar he supposedly wanted, I'd simply have to make it up to him after the deal.

Alejandro wrapped me in his arms and gave me a quick but intense kiss. "Thank you for doing this. Good luck tomorrow. And by the way, I called Peters and talked to him about authenticating the Dreadnought."

"Good. Is he going to give it a passing grade?"

"He was very mysterious about it. All he would say was that when he analyzed the guitar, he'd bring a different set of tools and chemicals. Then he said that he didn't like to discuss these things on the phone." Alejandro shrugged. "That's all I got out of him."

"Could his alternate set of tools and chemicals be fake? Might they always come up positive so they pass any guitar?"

"That's what I'm thinking." He nodded. "But I can understand how he wouldn't want to say that over the phone. You never know who is listening these days, and talk like that can come back to bite you."

"Okay, so this could be good. With Peters on my side, the deal will go smoothly." But I was also aware that Peters might *not* be on my side—Alejandro's conversation didn't assure me of anything. I'd know tomorrow. Good thing I had backup plans.

All of our talk about swindling George seemed to excite Alejandro. He pulled me hard against him. "We're going to make a lot of money."

I sighed. "It's not about the money."

"Don't be ridiculous. It's always about the money."

"Okay, but it's not *primarily* about the money. It's about getting my life back so I can leave this city. Happy?"

"Sure, I'm happy. Especially since meeting you. But I'm not too crazy about you leaving L.A."

"Thanks, but I have a life in New York, and I love it. I don't have to trick anyone there, and I don't have to worry about getting killed by George. So I'm going to finish this con, then I'm going back."

Alejandro let out an amused grunt. "You're the first person I've met in years who didn't turn into a money and fame hound after sleeping with me. Do you realize how unique that is?"

I chuckled. "Women all over the world must think I'm nuts."

"Personally, I love it. You know I have a place in New York City—close to your shop in Chelsea. When I'm there next, I'd like to take you out. Can you handle being seen in public with me?"

I squinted at him. "How public?"

"Just the usual. A date. You know, dinner, dancing, stuff like that. Nothing as extreme as that *No Moss* media event. Just you and me and a thousand cell phone cameras recording everything we do." He laughed and shook his head. "That's what women have to endure if they're going to be with me. Can you handle it?"

I must have blushed as I smiled, because I could feel warmth spread across my face. He kept arranging ways to see me after the con ended, first the family visit part of our wager, now a date in Chelsea. Could there really be more to us after the con was over? I would love any time I could get with this stunning man, this sensitive friend, this passionate lover.

Alejandro had powerfully captivated me. What had started as fan lust was now something much deeper, something I really had no experience with. Was this love? I couldn't tell. But one thing was certain, every moment spent with him filled me with more happiness than I'd ever known.

So if he really wanted to see me again, I'd gladly let him take me out in public. Assuming that the con went well. If things went badly, however, then Alejandro would need to establish some distance from me. I tried not to think about that, because I was falling way too hard for him.

Yes, I'd gotten past "Don't fall for the mark," and was now squarely at "Don't expect the mark to fall for me." A skeptical voice reminded me that Alejandro was simply enjoying his latest conquest. These phenomenal nights together would warm me for decades to come, but nothing serious could ever come of it. The voice also warned me not to even think about the possibility of a life with him. That would be delusion on an epic scale.

But I'd still love to have a date with him. "Sure." I shrugged. "After this is over, we can go out in public. If you and I cross paths and we get photographed, I won't mind." At least I hoped that would be true.

We quickly finished eating his unusual and tasty meal. Alejandro leaned back and looked at me. "You've mentioned that you had a boyfriend who wasn't serious. Is it true? Do you really have a lame boyfriend waiting for you in New York?"

That made me laugh. "I did, until this morning. Roman and I were together for five years, and the most I could get out of him was that we were buddies who sometimes had sex."

Alejandro's face twisted into a look of confusion. "What does that even mean?"

"It means that he hates labels, so he never uses words like 'boyfriend' or 'dating' or 'relationship.' Not that I would apply any of those words to you, but after the time we've spent together, I know I can never go back to him."

Alejandro grinned at me. "I've ruined you, eh?"

"Completely. You should be ashamed of yourself."

"With any other woman, I might feel remorse. But not you. I don't know if I can put it into words properly, but I find myself growing more and more drawn to you. So if I caused you to break up with your boyfriend, I'm glad."

"Hey, it wasn't all your doing. I was just killing time with him, and you made me realize it. This whole trip to Los Angeles has been a rediscovery for me. After hiding for the past seven years, I'm finally emerging again. So even though you and I aren't necessarily going anywhere together, I finally understand that Roman and I aren't, either."

"He sounds lame. Tell me more about this man who did so little for you."

"Oh, Roman wasn't that bad. He fit my need to hide and not have to answer any questions. I'll tell you this. . . If I'd met you seven years ago, I'd have run away as fast as possible. You're just about the worst imaginable boyfriend for someone trying to hide!"

He grinned. "You always see the worst in me."

"Wait, hang on to your ego, because it's about to get worse." I giggled. "Roman rejected your music when your fourth album came out to excessive fanfare. As far as he's concerned, you're a sell-out."

Alejandro laughed. "How did you two meet?"

That was an even stranger coincidence. I took a few seconds to appreciate the unusual way the world works, then I explained it to him. "Believe it or not, we met at one of your concerts. Soon after I got to New York City, Wanda and her friends went to your show, and I joined them. Sorry to say, but that was the first time I'd actually paid to see you perform. Before that, I always found a way to sneak in. Anyway, Roman was there and I thought he was cute."

"Let's see him."

"Look at you—jealous!"

"Not even close. Just curious to know what you've been putting up with."

I grabbed my phone and looked through my pictures. "Here he is." This picture was a typical Dee and Roman pose. Our arms were around each other's waists, and I was smiling at him. But he was leaning away from me, staring at the camera, his face blank. Seeing Roman through fresh eyes, I noticed his disinterest.

This made me realize that Roman was right: the most we had been was buddies. He barely seemed to want me, so the sex was only average. And compared with Alejandro, sex with Roman was awful.

Alejandro laughed at the picture. "Did you tell him about us? Is that why you broke up?"

"No way! I haven't told anyone about you—this is none of Roman's business. Besides, what would I say? That we had wild sex while I executed an elaborate con? Not a chance. He doesn't even know I'm a con artist. No, I broke it off because he never even cared, as you can see from this and other pictures." I swiped a few times to show more shots of my former not-boyfriend. There were also pictures of him with Wanda, and he was leaning away from her, too. He even did it with male friends, so I doubted it was a women-only thing. Roman simply didn't connect well with other people.

"And you stuck with this for five years? Wow. You really aren't much for relationships."

I laughed. "Like you are! You haven't been in love since high school."

"Not true. I fell in love just last year, right before my thirtieth birthday. Only the second time it's happened to me. Her name was Zenith." He took a long breath. "Anyway, I thought I was in love. But I was wrong." He fell silent.

I waited for him to go on, but he seemed reluctant. "Sensitive subject? Not your high-point, as her name might suggest?"

He laughed. "Yeah, she should have named herself Nadir." He took a long breath, then went on. "She was a beautiful woman, and she even played guitar. We jammed together a few times. She was in a band—I had drinks with her bandmates one evening. A decent bunch of kids." He paused again, staring into space.

"But. . ." I prompted him.

He looked at me with a sigh. "I fell for her hard, within days. She was one amazing lady, and I was ready to do anything she wanted. I would have recorded her band's next album. I would have invited her on tour with me." He shook his head. "I thought I'd found a winner, but she turned out to be another reporter. Sure, she could play guitar, but she was never in a band. The so-called band members I met were her colleagues at some entertainment blog. They'd faked everything, even their nonexistent band's website. All she wanted to do was get close to me, then sell her story. The shocking tale of how she wheedled herself into my good graces and took advantage of me. George had to pay her off to kill the story."

I swallowed and admitted the potential similarities between me and her. "She conned you."

"Yeah. Happens to me a lot. Everyone thinks that it's easy for the famous Alejandro to find love, but in fact, it's harder for me than for anyone else. I can't trust anyone."

I grimaced at his predicament. "And you definitely can't trust a con artist."

He chuckled. "The funny thing is, I *do* trust you. Given your own exposure in this con, I doubt very much that you'll sell me out when it's over. Still, I've got my eye on you. Since my episode with Zenith, I'm much more careful with anyone who gets close to me."

"So now you run background checks on all of your potential girlfriends?" I grinned. "And here I thought I was special. What else is in that report? How much do you know about me?"

With a laugh, he recited another line from one of his songs. "In one kiss, you'll know all I haven't said." I knew that line, a quote from a Pablo Neruda poem. As a Chilean poet, Neruda's work appeared frequently in Alejandro's songs. He even did an entire album of Neruda's love poems, entitled "Twenty Love Songs for a Brief Affair," a riff on Neruda's own work, "Twenty Love Poems and a Song of Despair."

I smiled at his quote. "You realize that you're more popular than Neruda, even though he won a Nobel Prize. That's why I worry about being with you."

He lowered his head. "I told you it's not easy being me. The fame makes everybody a little crazy occasionally, even my staff. Look at Karen."

That reminded me of something Udo had said earlier. "Speaking of your staff, what's Udo's story? He said something about his wife being gone. Must be hard being your bodyguard."

Alejandro frowned. "It's not his job that's to blame. As my parents found out, coming to America can be difficult. Udo knows that now, too. His wife got thrown out of the country on a technicality and had to move back to Germany."

"That sucks. What did she do?"

"When she and Udo first came here, they had visas. He worked for me, so I helped him get permanent residence. After that, he even got citizenship. But during all that time, she had to keep her visa current. Unfortunately, she missed it one year, by only a week, and it put her on some government list. Now she isn't even allowed to enter the country."

"But Udo's her husband, and he's now a US citizen. Shouldn't he be able to bring her here?"

"You'd think so, wouldn't you? But red tape is very sticky. He's been fighting it for years."

"Wow, I'm sorry to hear that. He should talk to Elle— her crew loves to fix those sorts of things."

Alejandro raised his eyebrows. "Your sister can hack government computers?"

"Let's just say that her crew has done some interesting jobs. I'll talk to her about Udo."

He laughed. "And you wonder why I like you so much. Just look at the things you can do."

I folded my arms. "I can do quite a few things, you know. Let me show you one." I threw myself at him and plundered his mouth for another kiss. He quickly responded and pulled me closer. And just like that, we were done talking.

Con games were dangerous and exciting, but Alejandro was dangerous and much more exciting. We made love two or three times that night—I lost track. Nobody had ever aroused me so fiercely, and I found myself doing things that I'd never done before, wanting things I'd never wanted before, and loving someone like I'd never loved before.

One Day
Until the Deal

Twenty-Eight

In case I didn't have enough to think about today, it was Elle's birthday. Hale was going to take her out for a celebration this afternoon, then we'd have dinner and drinks together. Alejandro needed to visit a new recording studio in the early evening, but he insisted that we reconnect after our respective activities were finished. Naturally, I agreed.

The past three nights had been the most passionate time I'd ever had, but this could be my last night with him since the con would end tomorrow. Sure, we talked about dates and family visits, but they were in the distant future. Any number of things might emerge to change those plans, including the possibility that the con would go bad. And although he kept assuring me that I meant more to him than other women, I still didn't know how to gauge his words, considering they were coming from a man so incredibly famous and desirable. Even he had to admit that his fame got in the way of normal interactions. So I continued to enjoy being with him, one day at a time. Besides, at this point in the con, I wasn't able to focus on anything beyond the next twenty-four hours.

I started my day with the most critical and nerve-wracking step: getting the Dreadnought authenticated. I'd been trying to ignore the bad-con tension that surrounded this, but my body kept reminding me, with irregular heartbeats and sudden urges to run away. The best I could do was to keep myself moving, taking each small step as it came. Anything more, and I might start to disintegrate.

I brought the guitar to George's house in my black SUV —fingers crossed the entire way. Oscar Peters, the guitar authenticator, would be meeting us there at ten, so I arrived early and parked on the street. I needed to talk to him before we went in, because if he wouldn't speak freely over the phone, then this would be my only opportunity.

Peters was not someone I could take lightly. After all, he had spotted Uncle Carl's fake Stratocaster right there during the evaluation, even though Carl had assured us it would pass. I needed to make sure that there wouldn't be any snags today.

A car pulled up to the front of the house, and Peters got out. Rushing over, I stopped him before he could go anywhere. "Good morning, Mr. Peters."

He smiled at me. "Ms. Gleason. How are you?" He seemed to be in a good mood, which gave me hope.

"I'm very sorry about the guitar that I brought to Alejandro last week. I honestly didn't know it was a fake."

He snorted. "No need to apologize, Ms. Gleason. You're not the first person to try to trick Alejandro." He chuckled lightly. "I understand that you're going to try to do that again now."

Great. He had me pegged as a crook. I couldn't blame him, though. First, I'd tried to pass a fake guitar, and then I'd gotten Alejandro to call him up to manipulate the second appraisal. Oh, and another reason I couldn't blame him for thinking I was a thief was that it was true. I needed to do something to make him doubt his preconceived notions.

"Really, Mr. Peters, I'm offended that you think so little of me. My mother's attic is full of junk—I have no idea where any of it came from. And *you* are the one who approved a fake guitar last week. So it's *your* opinion that seems to be for sale." I might be a swindler, but this man was no saint. He'd even told Alejandro that he would bring a different set of testing tools today. That might well indicate that his opinion *could* be bought.

He laughed heartily. "Ms. Gleason, you've got the wrong idea about me. I am scrupulously honest to my clients, and my opinion is not for sale. I'm the best in the business—I will spot every one of your fake guitars. I even know all of the forgers out there. If I'm not mistaken, the Stratocaster you brought in last week was made by Carl Geiger. He's good, but I'm better."

My heart jumped into my throat. The man really did know guitars—he even recognized Uncle Carl's work. Might his boast about honesty be a cover for the fact that Alejandro had influenced him? The possibility was seeming more and more remote. I gave it one last shot, even though I didn't believe it would help. "Someone bought your opinion last week. You lied about that guitar."

"I never lie to my clients. I told Alejandro that the guitar was a fake. But since he was my client, I honored his request that the information be withheld from you. That is why I announced, while you were present, that the guitar was authentic. Too bad for you, Mr. Rawson has not made such a request about my work today."

Okay, this conversation was not helping at all. In fact, it was only making things worse. Peters was acting like he was completely above board and could not be influenced. I had hoped to get some sign from him that he would pass today's guitar. Instead, he was becoming even more stubborn. He made it seem like it would be a struggle just to get a fair appraisal. I hoped that would not be the case.

"Mr. Peters, I think you are being terribly unprofessional. I'd expect someone like you to treat each new guitar with an open attitude. But instead, you've got me pigeonholed as a forger. All I'm doing is bringing guitars from my mother's attic. I'm hoping that this one is authentic, but that will be up to you to decide. Try not to let your obviously negative feelings about me affect your work today." Before he could respond, I turned and carried the guitar up to George's door.

He harrumphed, clearly not placated at all. "Very well, Ms. Gleason." He said nothing more as he followed me up the walkway.

There wasn't much more I could do at that point. I'd failed to restore any of his confidence, so I'd just have to let him look at the guitar with a certainty that it was fake. But I had a contingency plan in place, so I tried not to worry. Besides, I convinced myself that everything was for the best —if he was too friendly with me, it might make George suspicious.

A smiling George greeted us at the door and eagerly invited us in. He seemed to be in good spirits, which encouraged me. But when I got to the living room, I saw two men sitting there. Two big men who looked weathered and tough in their black leather jackets. A cold sweat slithered across my skin.

These men were undoubtedly George's thugs. They stared at me with the ferocity that Roman slaves must have seen when confronted by lions in the Colosseum. They wanted blood.

This was exactly the sort of thing I hated about con games: the fear of being overpowered during a con. I could easily do short cons, forgery, and other miscellaneous crimes. But when the odds were stacked against me and the mark was heavily fortified, it brought back too many bad memories. I set the guitar case on the table and held my arms rigidly against my side, willing myself to keep a cool head.

To cover my nerves, I nodded my chin toward the two thugs. "You have guests." I'm sure my voice wavered under the pressure, after which my teeth ground together with enough force to crush diamonds.

George pointed his thumb at the men. "Don't mind them." Yeah, right. I never minded it when two armed mercenaries wanted to kill me. Just another day in the life of a con artist.

George didn't bother to introduce his goons. Instead, he focused on the guitar. When he flipped open the case, I thought he'd start to cry. He picked up the guitar, hugged it, then strummed it a few times. Way too excited, he jumped around like a kid during school recess. "Oh my God. If this is the real thing, I'll love you for the rest of my life."

I surely had no interest in George's love. All that mattered right now was a reprieve from his violence if this guitar failed authentication. I had no doubt that George's thugs would beat me senseless, given the chance.

With a nod from George, Peters got down to business. I took a seat on the other side of the room from the thugs, acting indifferent and staring out the window. In truth, I was looking toward the backyard, wishing I could go out there and never come back.

This was the moment I'd planned for the past few days, but I never expected it to be fraught with so much tension. I knew that the guitar was not "as advertised," but I still held out hope that it would pass. Peters was the unknown factor here. Professionals like him always made me nervous, and too much was riding on this deal. If he didn't pass the guitar, I'd do my best to pull a quick disappearing act before suffering any of George's retaliation. With any luck, I'd still be able to meet Elle for her birthday. But the party might turn out to be my last appearance in Los Angeles. It might even have to be held at a hospital.

Peters opened up his testing kit and started to pull out his equipment. "I have new gear today, George." He swept his hand over the collection of chemicals, lights, and cameras. "State of the art, even more accurate than my last kit." George nodded absently.

I felt my heart beat even harder as sweat practically poured from my body. Peters' kit was better than before, not worse. Apparently, the man was so scrupulous that Alejandro's call had alarmed him, making him more suspicious. And it certainly didn't help one bit to talk to him before coming inside today. Now, Peters was committed to finding flaws. He would keep testing this guitar, more thoroughly than ever, until he found something wrong. And given his level of expertise, that might not take very long.

When he first looked into the guitar case, he stared for a few seconds, then raised his gaze to me. I met his stare but tried not to focus too hard on it. Good thing he also kept his eyes shuttered and didn't allow any emotions to show. Instead, he started testing. After that, the rush of tension made it hard for me to concentrate on anything else.

Over the loud throbbing in my eardrums, I could hear Peters working on the guitar. So far, he hadn't made any snap judgments, which was good. But the man was a mystery. He might be doing all this work to cover the lie he intended to make. Or, if he was as honest as he claimed, he might be saving his negative evidence, planning to make a single pronouncement when he was done. I had no idea.

He ran the guitar through a long series of tests, explaining each one to George. I forced myself to wait for the verdict, hands folded in my lap to keep them from twitching furiously. At one point, I thought I heard him say, "Kill her best." But when my heartbeat returned to normal, I realized he'd just said, "Filler test." I was a wreck.

I stared at the backyard, just a few feet away from where I sat. Good thing George's place wasn't very secure. No locked doors and a low fence around the yard. I could make it there quickly and jump the fence into a neighbor's yard. From there, it would be a short distance to the street. I couldn't run as fast as Elle, but I could probably beat George's ruffians. It made me realize that I should have arranged to have my sister help with this. As the expert at disappearing and reappearing elsewhere, she could sneak around anything, which made her perfect for rescue jobs. Something I needed right now.

Eyeing the yard desperately, I considered every eventuality, including the possibility that this might be my last few moments alive. God, how I hated con games.

Twenty-Nine

Sitting there facing George's thugs, I wiped the sweat from my brow for the millionth time. Peters had been droning on about each test for so long that one of the thugs had fallen asleep. George, by contrast, was riveted to each word. I stayed awake for entirely different reasons.

Peters was delivering another of his tired lectures, this one about the condition of the fret markers. As he explained this next test to George, he rubbed a special cloth over the little white dots on the neck, pausing, then rubbing another one. After testing the last of the markers, he stood up straight, suddenly silent after what had seemed like an endless diatribe about guitars.

George noticed the silence and jumped in. "A problem?"

"No. Not at all. I've done all the tests I can do right now. But just to be sure, I'd like to take a small sliver of the wood and have it analyzed further. It will only take a few hours—I'll call you with the results later."

George didn't seem happy. "You want to carve this guitar up?"

"Just a tiny piece from inside the sound hole. You'll never notice." He unstrung the guitar and reached in with a knife. Then he pulled out a minuscule slice of wood which he placed in a bag. After that, he packed up his gear, quietly and quickly, showing no emotion at all.

I averted my eyes and avoided any conversation with the man. He must have had an opinion about the guitar by this point, but he wasn't saying anything. Either he knew it was fake, and was holding the information back from me, or he had decided to declare it real, and didn't want me present when he told George.

Either situation was better than the current predicament, with George's thugs ready to act. This way, I could leave safely, which was excellent news. In fact, I was so relieved to be able to walk away from George's house, that my entire body collapsed into a gelatinous heap in the chair. No longer supported by the incredible tension of the situation, fatigue ganged up with gravity to pull me down. I had to take a few calming breaths to inflate myself back to full size.

I avoided any eye contact with George's thugs. They seemed annoyed to have sat there for the past hour, twiddling their beefy thumbs without having the chance to use them on me. I waited for Peters to restring the guitar, then I packed it up, ready to leave.

George turned to the appraiser. "Oscar, as I told you earlier, this one's off the books." He started to peel large denomination bills from a fat fist full of cash. "You never saw this guitar, and you didn't visit me today. Right?"

Peters nodded and pocketed the cash. "Of course." He grinned. "I never saw any of you today." His eyes connected with me briefly. "And I obviously don't know anything about you." He turned and left the room.

It made sense that the authentication of a stolen guitar had to be done in secrecy. This suited me perfectly, since I'd been trying to stay invisible all week. Having Peters agree to hide my presence was a bonus but not completely unexpected. Things often worked this way when people were involved in illegal activities. Although Peters acted like an honest man, he clearly understood how things worked and was more than willing to keep secrets.

When I got back to the motel, I peeled off my sweaty clothes and took a shower. The sweat rinsed off quickly, but my rattled nerves took much longer to wash away. Finally clean and much more calm, I called Elle to check in and wish her a happy birthday. I still didn't have a deal setup for tomorrow, and Bea's blackmail evidence was still at large. But at least I had a sister and some friends. And one of the most incredible lovers in the known universe.

"Happy birthday, Elle. By the way, I just came from the authentication and wow, was it tense! George had two of his thugs there, ready to trash me."

"I warned you about him. Maybe I should keep my eye on your New York friend tomorrow, just in case."

"Yes," I agreed. "Wanda's not a pro, so she could use all the help she can get. Thanks."

"No problem. And by the way, my hacker pulled George's financials last night. Not a pretty picture. The guy has been cheating on taxes for years and has some secret bank accounts down in the Caribbean. I'll send it to you."

"Excellent. I'm going to need this. Also, I'd like you to start following George now. Sorry this has to be on your birthday."

"Not a problem. I'm on it." She hung up.

I went down to the motel's office. Their computer had a printer, which I used to take care of some last-minute details. I printed out Elle's new evidence against George, as well as some contingency items. I also grabbed a few newspapers. This deal still had some unknowns in it, and I had to be ready to jump in any direction on a moment's notice. I'd lost track of whether this contingency was for Plan B, Plan C, or something even more remote. With all the variables piling up, I needed to prepare for each of them, just in case.

When I got back to my room, I was surprised to see Vance waiting for me. He must have sneaked into my room while I was down in the office. I'd hoped he'd leave me alone after I threw him out last time, but the man smelled like a distillery, so his judgment was worse than usual. Dealing with him would require more than simply ignoring his presence. "How did you get in here, Vance?"

"I forced the lock. Don't worry, nobody saw me." He gestured to the bed and wiggled his eyebrows. "What do you say to a little fun?"

Damn this man. I was tired of managing him all the time. Besides the fact that he was telling Bea everything, he was interfering with my plans, and now he was being a lecher. I could handle him, but with things coming to a head so quickly, I didn't have the energy to do it nicely.

My arm shot out to point at the door. "Get out! Now!" I gave him the sort of withering scowl he used to give us.

"Oh, come on, Dee. I'm. . ."

"Out!" I cut him off, then waited as he slowly dropped his head and made his way to the door. Finally gone, I locked the door and engaged the deadbolt.

Pathetic Vance—he needed to stay in his car. After a few deep breaths to purge his annoying energy, I relaxed and was able to rest for an hour.

I must have fallen asleep, because I was awakened by my phone. I picked up quickly. "Howdy, Hale. Are you ready?"

"You bet. Are we really going to meet Alejandro?" The poor boy was only a little anxious to meet his rock idol, and who could blame him?

"Definitely. Are you at the pizza place? I'll come pick you up."

"Yeah, I'm here." He paused. "Uh, does he like pizza?"

I laughed. "Seriously? You think Alejandro needs pizza as a house gift?"

"Sorry, I'm just nervous about meeting him."

"Yeah, I know how you feel. He still makes butterflies dance around in my stomach, too, and I've been hanging out with him all week. But he's really nice—you'll like him. Relax."

I put on the long blonde wig. Then I picked up Hale in the SUV, and we went over to Alejandro's. Although there were some significant issues left to resolve, the minor details were all falling into place. Elle was following George, Wanda was in flight to Los Angeles, and Vance was watching the television flicker in my empty room.

Karen opened the door for us, wearing a black miniskirt suit with white buttons on the jacket and a white scarf. Her black knee-high boots were quite eye-catching—I saw Hale's eyes drawn to them immediately. Karen hugged me while she laughed at my latest disguise. I pulled off the wig and did the introductions. "This is Hale, a grifter from way back. Hale, meet Karen, Alejandro's assistant and an aspiring grifter."

Hale took a step closer to her, staring up and down. "I heard Dee's teaching you to play. She's one of the best, you know."

Karen smiled and closed the distance between them. "Actually, I heard that *you* were one of the best. Maybe you can teach me." She stared at him for a few seconds, while he kept his gaze on her.

Whoa! Was I really seeing this happen? Hale and Karen looked like love-struck teenagers. They stood so close to each other that I could practically see sparks arcing between them. I took a step back, wondering if they would start making out right there in Alejandro's foyer.

But Karen moved away to take control of the situation. "Come on. I'll introduce you to Alejandro." Hale nodded eagerly, but I was no longer sure that his excitement was entirely focused on his favorite performer.

We found Alejandro in his study, playing guitar. He jumped up and shook Hale's hand. "I've heard about you from Dee. Welcome."

"H-Holy shit," Hale stammered. "You *are* Alejandro."

I snorted. "You didn't believe me?"

"I don't believe much anymore. Reality is too easy to manipulate."

I laughed. "Then speaking of manipulating reality, why don't you check out the incredible collection of guitars here?" I cocked my head at Alejandro. "Can you give us a tour? I hope you don't mind, but Hale needs to see this, especially the security around George's collection."

"Certainly." He led Hale through the house, showing off his guitars as well as George's. I was surprised to see Karen following the tour. Usually, she had better things to do than wander around the house. But today, she took an active part in the show-and-tell, reaching out to touch Hale's shoulder as she filled in details that Alejandro omitted.

When we went into the inner vault of stolen guitars, Hale took pictures of everything. He had become noticeably more relaxed by this point, finally over his delirium about meeting the rocker. He took charge and asked detailed questions about the security measures in the room. I was glad to see that even in the presence of the famous musician, Hale remained a thief and a con artist. I knew I could rely on him.

After the tour, Karen led Hale away, ostensibly to offer him some T-shirts and other Alejandro gear. But I suspected other motives. Alejandro had other motives too, as he led me back to his study. His hot mouth fell on mine, and we kissed until we were numb. I couldn't get enough of this man, and his attraction seemed just as strong. Whenever I was in his arms, nothing else mattered, not even this con. I let my mind fly away to a better place, free of fear and deceit and con-game details. Every remaining minute of his attention was a treasured delight.

Unfortunately, my phone interrupted us. I tore myself away from his exquisite lips long enough to glance at the number. Then I pushed back and took the call. This was important.

"Hey, Elle. What's happening?"

"I'm afraid I have bad news. My hacker has been all over Bea's life, and she can't find any mention of a storage locker. She even checked some traffic cameras, but nothing turned up. The old F.M. must be very careful about it."

"Damn. I need that evidence back." Bea still held her power over me, and George hadn't called me about the second guitar. What good were all of my details if the major problems remained unsolved?

"Sorry. But there's good news: George just went to the bank with an attaché case, and when he left, he was noticeably hefting it. I've sent you a picture. I think he's got the money for the deal now." That was encouraging. He hadn't contacted me about the authentication of the Dreadnought, but if he was getting money, then there might still be hope.

"Thanks. Consider yourself off-duty. Hale and I will meet you at the pizza place, and then we'll celebrate your birthday." I hung up.

Alejandro smiled. "Things must be going well if you're partying before the deal."

"Some things are starting to look up, but I'm still not sure." I shook my head. "This is such a mess! And today is my sister's twenty-first birthday, so we have to celebrate. I'm taking her on an outing, then we're going to a bar for her first legal drink."

"Bring her over later. I'll be home by nine." He leaned closer to me. "And I want to see you again."

"Oh, don't worry. You're going to see all of us later. After this outing, we have some business to take care of back here. This isn't just a social call, you know."

"I suspected as much. Does that mean you have to go now?"

"Afraid so." I gave him one last lingering kiss, then turned and left the study.

"Hale?" I called out as Alejandro and I wandered the house. When we heard sounds coming from a room, I opened the door then quickly closed it. Hale and Karen were doing much more than looking for T-shirts.

Alejandro laughed. "Your friend moves fast."

"Hey! Don't lay it all at his feet." I grinned at him. "Karen's doing her part, too."

Hale emerged a few minutes later, and I noticed that the buttons on his shirt were shifted. Karen followed him, fixing her hair and straightening her skirt. Alejandro and I tried not to smile too hard.

I did my best to act professionally. "Elle's done following George. She's meeting us at the pizza place. Let's go."

"Right." Hale extended his hand to Alejandro. "It's been more than a pleasure to meet you. We'll be back later." I felt bad having to drag him away.

Thirty

With my long blonde wig back on, Hale and I drove to the pizza place to meet Elle. She was talking on the phone with one of her crew members. ". . .Looks like we'll have to do a Kansas City Shuffle. Make him think we're trying to steal his car when what we really do is steal the bonds. . ." She noticed us. "Gotta go. Later." She hung up with a grin.

I wrapped her in a hug. "Happy birthday, sis. Are you ready for your present?"

"You got me something? You didn't have to do that, Dee."

"Oh, don't thank me," I shrugged. "Thank Hale. He's the one who arranged this little outing. I don't even know where we're going." A small part of me wished we could go far, far away and never come back.

Hale gave us a group hug. "Don't worry—you'll love it." He reached behind the table and pulled out a few backpacks as well as a large rifle with a sniper scope. At first, I thought it was a real gun, and my heart started to drum. But when I noticed the attached tubes and canisters, I realized it was a fancy paintball gun.

I squinted at him. "You're taking us to a paintball range, Hale? I have to warn you that an evening spent shooting things, even with paint, is not my idea of a good time."

He laughed. "You don't get to shoot this, just me. Now stop asking questions, and let's go. I promise you'll love it." We piled into my SUV and set off, Hale giving me directions.

South of Pasadena, the terrain became much more industrial. We wound through some warehouses that looked like they hadn't held any wares for years, then we pulled to a stop at a poorly lit dead end. Across the street, a chain-link fence had been mangled and ripped from one of its posts. Hale handed us each a backpack, then with the paintball rifle slung over his shoulder, he crawled under a gap in the fence. I shared a shrug with Elle, then we followed behind him.

Elle caught up with Hale. "You call this a birthday outing?"

"Quiet. We're almost there." He turned down a corridor and we emerged at the end of a row of storage lockers. Suddenly, I understood where we were. Hale was taking us to Bea's locker!

"Oh my God," I whispered. "You found it! Why didn't you tell me sooner? I've been worried about this all week."

"Shh," he whispered back. "I only found it yesterday. Come on."

I nearly danced for joy. Suddenly, my life was very much better. I would be safe from Bea, and regardless of whether I would be able to con George tomorrow, at least I had my freedom.

Evening was darkening the sky, which gave the place a post-apocalyptic feel. More and more, I felt bad about bringing my little sister here on her birthday, even though I knew she'd love it when she found out what we were doing. This was one of the seediest storage lockers I'd ever seen. Hale stopped at one point, his hand held up to keep us behind him, then he slowly stepped forward. Rounding a corner, he crouched down and aimed his paintball gun, sighting it carefully and squeezing out a few shots. Then he motioned us forward. As I followed him around the corner,

I noticed that a security camera was now dripping with black paint.

He stopped in front of a locker with a wave of his hand. "Happy Birthday, Elle. Shall I pick the lock, or would you like to do the honors?" He held out gloves and a set of picks.

Elle turned to him with her hands on her hips. "We're robbing a storage locker for my birthday?"

Hale grinned. "Not just any locker. This is Bea's."

Her face lit up like a fireworks finale, and she snatched the picks from his hand. We all put on gloves, and Elle set to work on the lock. She had it open in seconds and burst through the door.

I had to admit, Elle's birthday celebration was indeed stellar. Hale had found the ideal setting for a con artist's birthday, which Elle and I really appreciated. The place made Willy Wonka's chocolate factory seem like a dump.

"This is incredible, Hale. Thank you so much." Elle hopped excitedly as she wandered around the place, her head snapping left and right to take in all the sights. I had a great time, too, but I tried to rein in my enthusiasm. This was Elle's birthday, after all, so I pretended it was just another bonding event between two sisters. But really, it was much more than that.

Everything was in black plastic tubs with notes on the lids. One tub had gems, another had gold and silver, including Alejandro's Grammy award. Four tubs contained cash. One was labeled "Marked Cash," and all the bills in it had either blue ink or consecutive serial numbers. But the other three tubs were stuffed full of perfectly negotiable money. They were labeled "100s," "50s," and "Small Cash." By my quick estimation, Bea had about four million dollars in there. And to think that she couldn't even be bothered to feed her young children, when she'd had enough to treat us to five-star meals every day.

Elle grabbed fistfuls of cash and stuffed it in her backpack. She even handed some bundles to me, which I figured I could use to offset all the fake guitars I'd been buying. But the goods I really had my eye on were sitting in a tub labeled "Evidence." Inside were a dozen large plastic bags, each with random valuables in them and a name written on the outside. Bea had been blackmailing many of her so-called friends. As I'd suspected, I spotted a bag with Carl's name on it. Even worse, another bag had Franny's name on it—my foster mother was shameless.

Near the top, I found a bag with my own name and the purloined cocaine inside. I loaded it into my backpack, along with the rest of the evidence. She could keep her stolen jewelry, but she did not get to blackmail people anymore.

Elle filled her backpack and rummaged through every tub. I watched with fascination as she examined all the amazing items Bea had collected over the years. The "Props" tub had trick cards, trick glasses, trick dice, and every other trick you could think of, many of them triggering nostalgic memories from the good old days of con games. Seeing them now was even more relevant since we were back in the game, up to our necks in deceit.

A tub labeled "Documents" had deeds, wills, and other instruments of dubious legality. We even found a "Miscellaneous" tub that Elle explored with unrestrained glee. She found a number of items that she couldn't resist taking. I nicked some documents, but other than that, I was satisfied with the Grammy, some cash, and Bea's blackmail evidence.

Finally, we decided to get out while we could. I cleaned up the place, removing the now-empty $100s tub, $50s tub, and Evidence tub. I wrote "Free" on the labels and left the tubs at the end of the row of lockers. They'd be gone soon enough.

As we climbed back under the fence, Elle was pouring over a document she'd found. Then, before we got to the car, she stopped me. "Dee, I think you should let Hale drive back. This is something you need to see."

I eyed her and the paper. "What?"

"Give Hale the keys and you'll see it sooner."

That suited me fine, so I yielded the trip home and took the passenger seat. As soon as we got on the road, Elle leaned forward with an envelope in her hand. It had been torn open, and something hard had been stuffed into it. "I found this in the locker."

With such a buildup, my hand shook a little as I took the envelope. I turned it upside down to get at the thing inside, and when it fell into my lap, all the breath rushed from my lungs. It was my toy tiger, the one I'd used to warn my crew when there was trouble in a con. Although I'd had a few of these toy-warning signals when I was a kid, I could tell that this was the one I'd lost the night Jay got killed. It had been stepped on years before, and I recognized its bent neck.

"Oh, God. How did Bea get this?"

Elle pointed to the envelope. "The letter explains everything. It's from the vigilante who killed Jay. He tricked Bea and wrote this letter to boast about how he did it. According to the letter, he met her in a bar one night and chatted her up, trying to get an angle on her operation. He even claims that he got her so drunk that she bragged to him about her con-artist children and told him about your little warning system with the toy tiger. That's how he knew to grab it."

I slowly started to breathe again, still numb from this revelation. "I can't believe it. If this is true, it means that *Bea* is the one who got Jay killed."

"No doubt about it, the guy was after your card game. He followed you and Jay home one night so he could find Bea. Then he targeted her in a bar and got her to spill everything. That's how he knew how to take you two down, how to act like a perfect mark so you'd choose him to play Three Card Monte. I know you've felt guilty about it for years, but this letter makes it clear that you did nothing wrong."

Hale was outraged. "Can we hurt this asshole? There must be something in there we can use to find him."

Elle shook her head. "I doubt it. And the letter is ten years old, so he's certainly moved on. Jay died, and we stopped playing card games after that, so he achieved his goal. He only wrote that letter to make Bea feel bad. No idea why she kept it, though."

I snapped out a bitter laugh. "She probably kept it to remind herself to get him back someday. The woman holds grudges forever. At least now I understand why we stopped playing card games after that. Suited me fine. We never stopped conning, though, and it took me months before I could work again. I remember lying in bed and staring at the ceiling forever, while you and Bea did cons on your own. She could tell I was useless."

The sob came upon me unexpectedly, shaking me hard while copious tears started to pour down my face. I called out Jay's name, over and over, mourning his death. For the very first time, I could do it without any guilt. I could feel the sadness that I'd denied myself for so long, when my mind told me I didn't deserve to mourn him. I cried for Jay like I'd never done before.

Elle shared this moment with me, and we offered apologies to Jay for our foster mother's cruelty. He would have loved to be there with us in the locker today, so we dedicated the day to him and asked him to watch over the deal tomorrow. Somewhere up in con heaven, we knew he would protect us.

Thirty-One

After Elle's birthday outing, we made a quick stop at the motel so I could ditch my backpack full of contraband. Then we went to a gastro pub for dinner. Elle was twenty-one now, and although fake IDs were never a problem for her, there was still a special significance to the fact that she was finally old enough to have a drink without lying.

I know I needed a drink to quell all the excitement in my head. Besides the con wrapping tomorrow, I'd just recovered Bea's blackmail evidence and found out that Jay's death wasn't my fault. Add to that the spectacular nights I'd been spending with Alejandro, and I was ready to launch into orbit. I hadn't heard from George yet, but at this point, I didn't care if the con fell apart. I was with friends, so nothing could touch me now.

I'd invited a number of people to our little gathering, including Wanda, who had flown in that afternoon with my big green bowl. She'd heard plenty of stories about my sister, so she was excited to finally meet her.

When we got to the restaurant, Wanda was waiting there in a classic 1940's sailor's outfit. A fitted dark navy jacket with gold insignia on the sleeves, matching skirt, low-cut white blouse, and a proper sailor's hat. Typical Wanda—a power uniform if ever there was one.

The four of us got a booth in the back and ordered drinks. Much to Elle's dismay, the waiter didn't card her, even though she had a driver's license ready to show him. When we started to chat, Wanda bonded instantly with Elle and Hale as they traded stories about me. Each of them knew only part of my history, so they shared what they knew.

Elle soon told them about our last great con including my surprise disappearing act, seven years ago. "I remember that afternoon." She rolled her eyes at me. "Bea and I were in the park across from the guy's office building. You went in there to pick up the money, then you came out a half hour later, all smiles. We knew it had gone down perfectly." She leaned back in her seat.

"It *had* gone perfectly." I grinned. "But not for Bea."

"Yeah, I should have known. You'd just gotten your driver's license, and you gave us some story about needing to go to the DMV. I realized later that you'd made it up so you'd have your own getaway car and could escape. But back then, we just watched you go around the corner to your car, then we got in ours, planning to meet back home." She leaned toward Wanda and pointed her thumb at me. "But this one never showed up! Bea and I waited for *hours*. First we thought she'd been arrested. Or that the mark had caught her. Her cell phone was off, and the car was parked by the music shop, empty. I'm telling you, she simply vanished from the face of the Earth." Elle laughed, then quickly got serious. "Bea was so pissed. I had to hide from her for over a week. And I had no idea what had happened to you."

"Hey!" I protested. "I got in touch with you a few days later."

"You call that getting in touch? You sent me a text message from a burner phone. All it said was 'Your hundred grand share of the deal,' and then gave a bank account number. No 'I'm fine' or 'How are you?' or anything like that."

Wanda arched an eyebrow. "You gave your sister a hundred thousand dollars? What was your share?"

Elle laughed. "We never did 'shares' when we lived with Bea—she took everything. If we tried to keep any of it, she'd punish us, usually by locking us in a closet. So a hundred grand was very nice."

Wanda hugged me. "God, girl, how sad. I can see why you had to cheat that woman to get free of her. She sounds like a real piece of work."

Our drinks arrived, and we ordered dinner. Then we raised our glasses to Elle in a birthday toast. After taking a sip, she told a story I had never heard. "Check this out. Bea called me a few months ago, pretty drunk, and told me about *her* mother. We may have suffered, but Bea had a pretty nasty childhood, too. Her mother had a one-night stand with some guy and ended up pregnant. So she raised Bea by herself and filled her daughter with a hatred of men. Our foster mother was taught, from an early age, to cheat every man she met."

Wanda frowned. "That's no excuse. She had no right to turn you two into criminals."

Elle shrugged. "Yeah, she's deadly. But Dee outsmarted her. Ran off with a half million dollars in cash."

Wanda whistled. "So you showed up in New York, loaded. No wonder you rented that fancy apartment."

Hale and Elle cocked their heads and raised their eyebrows, silently demanding more from Wanda. Never one to avoid a good story, she dove right in. "You don't know about her place?" Wanda grinned at me, ignoring my frown. "This little bundle of mystery moved in across the hall from me. My place is smaller and unfurnished, so the rent is only scary. But her place is the fanciest on the floor, a corner unit, and fully furnished. I knew the rent had to be astronomical. And she just showed up there without bringing anything more than a suitcase." She grinned at me. "I had to know more about this girl."

I laughed. "Price didn't matter when I had a suitcase full of cash—I really arrived with little else. Besides, I needed a place that was ready to go. By that point, I was happy to ignore Bea's rules about hiding, so I made up my own rules. Why do you think I bleached my hair?" I grinned at them. "Two hours after that deal went down, I was on a plane to New York. I'd found the place online, so I moved in that night."

"Aha, now I get it. I knew you were a trickster, but I didn't realize you were a con artist on the run. No wonder you wouldn't let me use your picture anywhere."

I nodded. "I was hiding from Bea, so getting my picture taken was a bad idea."

Hale chuckled. "So how the hell did you become a popular artist?"

Wanda puffed out her chest. "You can blame me. I got her started."

"She's right. We went to one of those paint-your-own pottery parties, and she liked what I did."

Wanda darkened. "It was only the best pot anyone had seen, including all the people who worked there. They were knocked senseless by your technique." She propped her hands on her hips. "I watched you paint it. You used the tiniest brush and made this gorgeous textured scene with colorful flowers. An incredible impressionist work. Took you almost two hours to finish it, but it blew everything else out of the kiln. The pottery place wanted to buy it and put it on display."

I shrugged at Hale and Elle. "You two know how it used to be. I was Bea's forger so I was used to making throwaway art, disposable fakes. One of the last forgeries I'd done was Renoir's *Two Sisters*, a bright and colorful work. So I painted it on the pot, but I gave it a little twist, just for kicks. I gave the girls baseball caps."

Elle laughed. "You always wanted to do that, didn't you?"

I flashed a grin. "Yeah, I used to complain to you how boring it was to do faithful recreations. Now I had a chance to make it fun."

Wanda laughed. "You called it fun, but I called it amazing. I had to do something about it."

Hale squinted at Wanda. "What did you do?"

She shrugged. "Not much. I'm from New Jersey, and my parents have a big suburban home there. So one night, when they were hosting one of their country-club parties, I visited and put the pot on their living room breakfront."

She grinned at all of us. "The entire snoot-set was there, and the pot turned into a huge sensation. Everyone wanted to know about where it came from and where they could get one. I was on a roll, so I made up a phony story about my up-and-coming artist friend, how she was sweeping the New York art scene, appearing in magazines and galleries." She shrugged. "The usual story. At the time, Dee wasn't the least bit famous, but I knew she could swing it, with a little help. I even got three of my parents' friends to order one that night."

I groaned. "I didn't want to start painting pottery, but Wanda had wangled such a high price for them that I couldn't resist." I turned to her. "What was it, like two thousand each? Kind of stunned me."

Wanda shook her head. "That was just the introductory price for people who wanted one that night. After that, the price went even higher. I made a website and planted stories about you to make your hot new artist persona real. And since you never let me use your picture anywhere, that made you even more mysterious and desirable." She chuckled at me. "You had all the makings of a new phenomenon: interesting art, an unusual medium, an enigmatic artist, and rich patrons. It was a winning formula, and it caught on like a grass fire in a drought."

Hale and Elle stared at me with pride, so I finished the story. "She had me painting another piece every day. Then —get this—she rented a storefront with a kiln in back, started buying unfinished porcelain by the palette load, and hired edgily dressed people to sell my pottery. That's when I knew I was in trouble."

Dinner arrived, and we started to eat. After a few minutes of attention to her meal, Elle smirked at Wanda. "I've known about the pottery business for years, but I always thought it was Dee's little con. It seemed so perfect."

I grinned and shook my head. "It's all Wanda. She's a harsh taskmaster. Now I have to paint for her all the time."

"Oh you poor thing," Wanda condescended. "You paint one pot a day, just a few hours of work, and then you're done. Stop complaining."

My face scrunched up. "I feel guilty that I'm doing so well, especially when I have all that money in the bank, and my friends are struggling."

Wanda pointed her thumb inward. "This friend is doing fine. I take a nice slice, thank you, so don't feel guilty. Besides, people love your art. You've got real talent, Dee. And whatever it is that you're doing out here, I'm happy to help."

"Thanks, Wanda." I filled her in on the task I had in mind for her. My team was growing and now included Wanda, as well as Elle, Hale, and Karen. In fact, I expected

Karen to show up at any moment. She had to work late and told me she'd eat dinner there, but I asked her to join us afterward so we could take care of some last-minute details.

Soon enough, Karen arrived, still in her power mini-suit and fresh from a day of organizing Alejandro's life. She sat down next to Hale and they held hands. But as soon as she and Wanda spotted each other, the two of them stared with narrow eyes. "You're familiar, but I don't know why." Wanda agreed but couldn't explain it, either.

While they were puzzling over this, the waiter came over to take Karen's drink order. When he left, Karen brightened. "I know!" She pointed at Wanda's hat. "You work in Dee's shop in New York."

Wanda slapped the table. "Right! That's it! You bought a small vase a few weeks ago. Were you shopping for Alejandro?"

"Of course. He was there in disguise, then he told me what to buy and left. That's the way he operates, you know."

"Oh my God!" Wanda cried out. "Alejandro was in my shop!"

I patted her on the back to calm her down. "He says he's been to the shop a few times. Turns out he has a place just a few blocks away. Next time you see someone in a hoodie and dark glasses, look more closely."

Karen laughed. "The next time we're in your shop, I'll introduce him properly."

Karen's drink arrived, so she took a sip, then she settled next to Hale and started to snuggle. I gave Elle a nudge with my elbow. "Look at these two. Have you ever seen anything so cute?"

Hale grinned, but Karen blushed. "Look who's talking." She sat up a little straighter. "If you guys want cute, you should see this one with Alejandro. The two of them are inseparable."

Wanda stared at me with huge eyes. "You and Alejandro?" She let out a little shriek. "I can't believe it. Oh my God! Is he the most awesome man, ever?" Wanda started to giggle. "No wonder you dumped Roman. Wow." She shook her head. "You and Alejandro."

I rolled my eyes. "Yeah, me and Alejandro. For one more day."

Karen shrugged. "Who knows? He's not typical boyfriend material, that's for sure."

Elle stared at me. "Alejandro? Definitely not boyfriend material. But still, sis, I'm very impressed! I mean. . ."

She never finished the sentence. Instead, she dropped her head and covered it with a hand. "Cops," she hissed.

Hale and I looked around discretely, then carefully turned our faces away. If there was one thing that five scheming grifters did not need on the night before a big con, it was the police.

Always willing to help out and clearly unaware of our feelings about this, Karen jumped from her seat and ran after the officers while the rest of us cowered in the booth.

Thirty-Two

Hale, Elle, and I tried to hide while Karen ran over to the policemen who had just entered the bar. "Nice girlfriend, Hale," Elle whispered. "But maybe you should explain to her that if she wants to hang out with a con artist, she can't go chasing cops."

Hale squinted at me. "I thought you set this up."

Before I could explain, Karen returned to our table with the two officers in tow. Familiar ones: Lucky and Myles. The same policemen who had come to Alejandro's home the day I tried to sell him the first guitar. Good thing I had pulled off my wig before we went into the restaurant. They'd be suspicious if they saw me in a disguise.

To be fair, I *had* set this up, days ago when I had different plans. Initially, I'd hoped to use Lucky and Myles' dishonest side to trick George. But Karen had called them and asked enough discrete questions to convince herself that this wouldn't be possible. Another reason why I'd switched to a con that no longer needed crooked cops.

Always prepared for surprises, I was still juggling a number of possible plans for the con. Even honest police figured in some of them. I was curious to understand the way they worked, their procedures and responses. So I'd told Karen to keep our meeting with Lucky and Myles. Unfortunately, I'd expected to do it sooner, not here at a pub with my whole crew in attendance. Regrettably, this was the only time the boys in blue were available. Hale and Elle would just have to tough it out.

As the swaggering young officers came up to our table, Myles grinned at me and offered his hand. "I remember you from Alejandro's place. Who are your friends?"

I shook his hand and introduced him to Wanda, Hale, and Elle. What followed was probably the strangest conversation I'd ever had—two policemen chatting idly with five scheming grifters. Karen drove the conversation, asking them all sorts of questions about the crooks they'd encountered. She wanted to know what gang members were like. How did the boys in blue catch arms dealers? Drug dealers? Car thieves? Lucky and Myles had a great time explaining their techniques to us, and the five of us did our best to act like concerned citizens, appreciative of the efforts that these fine officers took to keep us safe.

Our bizarre encounter with law enforcement ended abruptly when the boys got a call and left to respond. We waited until they had gone, then let out a long group sigh. Hale tried to explain the situation to Karen. "You need to know that there are quite a few policemen out there who want to bust me. Next time, don't invite them back to our table."

Karen blushed. "Sorry about that. But this is all part of the con. Right, Dee?"

"Uh, well, maybe. But I think you freaked out Hale and Elle."

Karen slunk down in her seat with a pout. "Sorry about that."

Hale wrapped his arm around her shoulder. "Just give me a heads-up next time the cops are coming to dinner."

Elle giggled and knocked back the rest of her wine. "Good thing we're not in Oregon right now, where the police know me much better. At least they can't bust me for underage drinking."

I looked around the table and noticed that we had all finished dinner. "So are we ready to move this party to Alejandro's place?" Everyone nodded, especially Wanda, who was thrilled beyond measure to be meeting the rocker.

Before we left, I needed to figure out some logistics. I'd told Wanda to rent a car, knowing that we'd need one now. "What kind of car did you get?"

"Oh, it's so cute." Wanda shimmied as she described her car. "One of those tiny ones with no back seat. I love it! In red, too."

Oh no! She'd rented the worst possible car for what we needed. Our next task involved moving some guitars. Vehicles with trunk space were needed at Alejandro's place, not little pods on wheels. Who would have imagined that Wanda would rent something so extreme? Well, okay, I suppose I should have imagined it. She was wonderfully eccentric.

I let out a little laugh. "Well, I'm afraid I'm going to have to upgrade you to a big black SUV. We're switching cars." I handed her my keys.

"A black SUV?" She cocked her head for a few seconds, then nodded. "Just as absurd. You have a deal." She laughed as she gave me her keys. "Does it have those huge tires that are so big they can crush other cars? I'd really like to drive one of those."

I gave her a hug. "You do this for me tomorrow, Wanda, and I'll buy you one of those cars, I promise. Anyway, take Elle in my SUV. Hale can go with Karen." I winked at him. "I'll see all of you there later. I've got some errands to run, first." They nodded and got up to go.

The notion of meeting Alejandro had completely perked up Wanda, even after a long day of travel. She started to belt out her favorite Alejandro song while dancing her way out of the bar. Powerless to resist her charms, I heard Karen, Hale, and Elle singing along as their voices faded into the night.

Alone in the booth, a smile slowly spread across my face. I took a moment to appreciate the love I had from these friends. From every part of my life, they had come together to help me with this delicate plan. They made me feel like I had a real family, something I never felt with Bea.

As I stepped out of the bar, I slipped my long blonde wig back on. Wanda's tiny car was instantly recognizable in the lot, so I drove it to a big box store for some last-minute shopping. Nothing unusual—just a few cleaning supplies that motels don't usually provide. Finally, I returned to the strip mall.

I'd never driven a vehicle as outlandish as this mechanized bug. It felt strange to see people turn their heads as I drove by. But I realized that I liked it—it flew in the face of Bea's rules about hiding. And I was through with Bea. Through! Now that I had her blackmail evidence, I was free. After tomorrow, I didn't ever want to see her again.

Back in my motel room, I emptied the backpack I'd left earlier, removing the various items I'd taken from Bea's locker. Then I spent some time destroying evidence and preparing for tomorrow. Even though I'd be back here in the morning before the deal, I needed some things tonight, while I was at Alejandro's home. It took me a while to get ready and even longer to clean up the bathroom after all the contraband I'd flushed away. Bea seemed to favor drugs as her method of blackmail, and I had to dispose of an awful lot of it. A total mess, I had to scrub down the counter and even the floors when I was done. I also kept a list of people that I would contact later so I could inform them that their evidence had been eliminated.

The television continued to play against the closed curtains of my room as I climbed out the bathroom window to get to Wanda's red pod. I'd normally take the brown sedan to see Alejandro, but tonight I had some late-night activities planned, in addition to my fun with the sexy rocker. My nerves zinged over the thrill of this upcoming con, and they scintillated even more over the excitement of another night with this incredible man. I couldn't wait to see him.

I arrived at Alejandro's home just as my friends were finishing up their tasks there. They had emptied out George's collection of guitars and managed to fit them into Karen's car and my SUV. Whatever happened tomorrow, it was necessary that Alejandro distance himself from his scheming manager's illegal activities. Karen had been spending some time looking through the room full of Alejandro's lesser stuff, and she replaced the stolen guitars with innocent things that had sentimental value, things that could reasonably live in George's secure room. When all was done, it was filled with Alejandro's notebooks, his first guitar, his less important Grammy awards, a few trophies, and some miscellaneous memorabilia. The perfect inner sanctum.

Hale hacked into the security system to make sure that the cameras hadn't captured their activity. He also overwrote the old video so it now showed the current contents of the room. If anyone tried to say that Alejandro had a collection of stolen guitars, there would be no evidence to support that. The four of them also wore gloves when they handled things so that a fingerprint sweep wouldn't identify them. Finally, Hale, Karen, Elle, and Wanda drove off with a baker's dozen of hot guitars. Alejandro and I stood by the door and watched them go.

Before they departed, Elle winked at me. "Have fun, Dummy."

I laughed and shot it right back at her. "Happy Birthday, Loser." Then they were gone. Alejandro must have heard our interchange, because he arched an eyebrow.

"An old nickname and a long story." I left the rest as a mystery. Besides, we were alone at last, so I had other things on my mind besides childhood nicknames.

Thirty-Three

Standing with me outside of his house, Alejandro squinted at my little red car. "You're driving that now? It's the third car I've seen you in this week."

With a huge grin, I shrugged at him. "I like to mix it up. Another thing you don't want to know."

"You're right, I don't want to know. You must be juggling all sorts of details right now. I'm impressed. What time is the deal tomorrow?"

"I wish I knew. So far, George hasn't set up anything. Peters wouldn't give him his answer at the authentication this morning. Said he needed to do further tests."

He frowned. "That's unusual. Oscar generally spots fakes instantly."

"Well, this wasn't a normal authentication, because you called him about it. Still, I know George went to the bank to get money, so hopefully, it went well. Let me find out."

I pulled out my phone and called George. He was supposed to know about the results by now, so I figured I could check in. He picked up quickly. "Ms. Gleason. I'm glad you called. Oscar got back to me a few hours ago—sorry I didn't call you, but I was busy."

"And. . ." I was safe, here with Alejandro, so even if the guitar was revealed to be a fake, he couldn't do much. I had Bea's blackmail evidence, so nothing could touch me.

"Your guitar is the real thing! I can't tell you how excited I am to get it."

All the air blew from my lungs in a loud rush. I had done it! The deal was in the bag. I sighed and gave Alejandro a thumbs-up and he nodded happily. "So," I continued with George. "We have a deal?"

"Absolutely. Tomorrow at noon, right here. Bring both guitars. I already have the cash."

"Wonderful." I hated to challenge him when everything was going so well for me, but I needed one more concession from him. "I have a request. Don't bring those guys who were there today. This is between the two of us, and I don't like any outside factors."

"But. . ."

I cut him off promptly. "No buts. If I see them—in your house or anywhere outside—the deal's off. Is that clear?"

George grunted, then acquiesced. "That's fine. Just you and me."

"Good. See you tomorrow." I hung up.

That was a huge relief. I'd been juggling two possible outcomes for this deal, but now that the guitar had passed authentication, the main plan was back in force. Half of me was delighted, but the other half was now facing a very complex con tomorrow. Good thing everything was in place.

I smiled at Alejandro. "We're on for tomorrow at noon. If this works as planned, George is headed for a fall."

"About time." Alejandro gave me a big hug.

I pulled back and stared at him. "Don't you feel even a little bad about taking him down? He made you famous, after all."

"No, I don't. He went way over the line with me, stealing millions. Also, it's not like he made me famous all by himself. He just knew who to call. I had music teachers, a trainer to get me in shape, even a publicist who got me to drop my last name. The guy thought that Alejandro was sufficiently exotic, but Muñoz-Perez was just too ethnic. Then George brought in an agent who took me around to all the record execs. Hey, I was even in the running to be the lead singer of the Fiery Boys, but the record companies wanted me to be a solo act. So to answer your question, George didn't do that much for me himself, and he took way too much money for it. He deserves whatever you can dish up."

Alejandro reached out to take my hand, pulling me closer and combing his fingers through my hair. We fell easily into each other's embrace. After a long day, there was no better way to cap it off than to be held in his powerful arms, feeling his irresistible need. His sexy lips slanted across mine, and we kissed desperately, from light to deep, from playful to soulful.

We didn't even make it to the bedroom, just fell to the nearest sofa in a tangle of limbs, pausing only to remove our clothes then continuing to tangle some more. On our fourth night together, he was every bit as passionate, if not more so. Perhaps he felt as I did, that this might be our last time together, that everything would be different tomorrow. We needed to cherish each loving gesture, given and received. He took me to an orgasmic peak that I would never forget.

After it was over, we rested together for a long time without speaking. Finally, Alejandro couldn't resist. "So, why does your sister call you Dummy?" He propped his head on one hand while the other played with my spiky white hair.

I started by telling him how we had been given names that sounded like single letters so we could play cons more safely. "Then, since all of us kept choosing names that started with J, D, or L, we chose silly nicknames, just among ourselves. I was Dummy, Elle was Loser, and Jay was Jerk." I shrugged. "We liked to tease each other."

"Band members like to tease each other, too. There are jokes for every instrument."

I kissed the gorgeous guitarist. "Tell me some band jokes."

Alejandro thought for a few seconds, then launched in. "Okay, here are the classic knocking-on-your-door jokes. How do you know when a drummer is knocking on your door?"

I shook my head, so he delivered the punch line. "The knocking speeds up." I must not have reacted sufficiently, because he went on to explain it. "It's funny because bad drummers can't seem to keep the beat and usually speed up." I rolled my eyes—it still wasn't that funny.

With a shrug, he moved on to the next joke. "How do you know when a bass player is knocking on your door?" He didn't bother to wait for my answer. "He can't find the key."

I chuckled. "Easy for you to poke fun at drummers and bass players, but what about the singer and the guitarist? Let's hear some jokes I can use on you."

"Okay, how do you know when a singer is knocking on your door? Answer: He doesn't know when to come in." He paused, then explained it. "You know, when to start singing." I rolled my eyes again. "Wait, here's the best one. How do you know when a guitarist is at your door?" This time, he waited for me to answer.

"Uh, he smells like cloves?"

"Close. The answer is: he's delivering your pizza."

Finally, I laughed. "So if you weren't the most famous musician in the world, your guitar skills would only qualify you for pizza delivery?"

He grinned. "Thank God I'm famous. Otherwise, I'd never have a chance with you." He took my hands in his, pulling me close.

"Oh, Alejandro. This is the most fun I've had in years, but we're nearing the end of the con. Karen told me that no woman has lasted for more than a week with you, and this is already our fourth night together. So I still have to wonder if my shelf-life is about to expire." I gave him a self-deprecating grin.

Alejandro gave me a tight hug, then pulled me up to sit next to him on the sofa. "Want to know why no other woman has lasted more than a week? It's because none of them were the kind of woman I was looking for." He took a long breath. "I've been pretty miserable since last year, when Zenith messed with me. I get lonely, especially now that I'm thirty. But I can't get motivated for a random hookup because they always turn into a media circus. My fame is a wall that keeps me in and keeps good women out. Also, I've been drinking too much, although now that I think about it, I haven't been doing as much this past week."

He pulled me tighter. "I know this sounds like a line, but I think you may be what I'm looking for. You, Dee." He kissed me lightly. "You explode. You burst with dazzling colors, so intense that it blows me away." He inhaled deeply and stared at me. "No one explodes like you, Dee."

His words took my breath away, exciting me with the possibilities. Could it be that Alejandro was falling for me, a woman about as different from his usual lovers as possible? Not that the world-famous sex symbol was my usual type, either.

I laughed at the idea of exploding for him. "I've never seen myself as the least bit incendiary."

He grinned and stole another kiss. "Oh, but you are! When you tried to swindle me, boom! Blew me away. When I found out that your artistic talent went way beyond painting pottery, boom! I was scattered all over the pavement. Your con skills bowl me over—I get hot just watching you make plans, pick pockets, and talk about safe cracking. Ka-pow!" He spread his hands out and let them float down like fireworks.

I'd always fantasized a life with someone who found my criminal skills intriguing. Could it be Alejandro? I wondered. But honestly, I just couldn't imagine the world-famous rocker settling down with anyone. He was right about his fame: it locked him away. Regardless of our attraction, being with him for a long period of time seemed nearly impossible.

Still, I grinned at him as I whispered in his ear, "Boom."

Alejandro laughed and caressed my face. "And that's another area where you explode for me—your looks. I can't seem to take my eyes off of you."

"But I'm the mystery mousy woman. How do my looks explode for you?"

"Let me tell you something. Most of the women who I encounter are over-the-top sexy. They've been plumped and trimmed and shaved and plastered over, then draped in as little clothing as possible. But when I get to know them, the veneer peels away and I can see the ugliness underneath. They're shallow and uninspiring, which ruins their physical appearance. After a decade of this, I can spot them quickly. They're everywhere."

He pulled me tight against him. "Now you are completely different. The more I get to know you, the more intrigued I get. You start off by being an eye-catching beauty, then when I look underneath, I see a solid core of competence and independence. An artist who I respect, and a clever woman who understands the world. It makes you even more beautiful. Don't let Ivory twist your head with words like mousy. You're very good-looking, Dee, and combined with what I see underneath, you're spectacularly beautiful."

He crushed an intense kiss to my lips that burned right through me with its need, its heat, and its combustible energy. His kiss! Oh how I loved his kisses. An intoxicating duet of gliding lips and dancing tongues that lingered for a long, long time.

We pulled apart, our foreheads touching, his gaze locked on mine. "Look, I have no idea what's going to happen tomorrow, but I want you to know that I've had the best time watching you plan it. I'm expecting a huge explosion, and I can't wait."

I pulled back and sighed. "Easy for you to say. You're insulated from it all. I'm the one who's exposed here."

"I know, and I appreciate it. Another reason why I'm having so much fun—I'm safe. But don't worry. If things get ugly, I'll do what I can to get you out of it. I'm on your side, and I won't let you down."

This was not the Alejandro I'd ever imagined. A caring man who needed someone to trust. A lonely man, locked away by his fame. An incredible man, who surprised me all the time. I kissed him gently, silently thanking him for his support during the most amazing week of my life.

The kiss started off slowly, but it didn't stay that way. We fell to the sofa and began to roll around, our hands caressing and playing. In the middle of all this groping, something fell over on the coffee table. That stopped us, and we sat up to make sure we hadn't destroyed the entire living room.

"Let's get out of here." Alejandro stood up from the sofa, naked and aroused, standing over me with his hands extended like a dream scene from one of his videos. Then, continuing the dream, he reached down and picked me up, scooping my legs and shoulders so he could cradle me to his magnificent chest. I wrapped my arms around his neck, and we kissed as he carried me to the bedroom.

This could well be my last chance to experience his carnal devotion, so I let myself get lost in the whirlwind of his heat. I had a dizzying rise to an incredible peak, followed by a slow, comforting descent in his capable arms. Such an incredible lover, he continued to worship my body as much as I worshipped his. He thought *I* was explosive? Hah! His energy level was in the megaton range.

Mildly hungry after all the physical activity, we got out of bed and wandered to the kitchen for a bedtime snack. I needed my sleep tonight and was suddenly fatigued from all the activity of the day. As we passed his study, I noticed an attaché case that looked very familiar. Brushed aluminum, with black corners, it looked like the one I'd seen in the photo Elle had sent me this afternoon. The photo of George with his case full of money.

I smiled at Alejandro's obvious plan. This case was full of fake cash, probably the same three-dollar bills and Monopoly money that he'd offered to me. He would switch it with George's before the deal tomorrow in an attempt to get to the money before I did. I wasn't surprised that he knew the kind of luggage his manager had. Also, people only have so many tricks that they use over and over. He was obviously trying the same trick on George that he'd tried on me.

I had already considered that he would do something like this and had prepared for it. I believe it was backup

Plan B. Alejandro's con-artist aspirations were so charming, that it made me smile. Oh, how I loved this man. We snuggled in the kitchen nook, kissing while we snacked on strawberries and chocolate. The perfect relaxation after our intense outbursts of lust.

In the middle of licking the chocolate from each other's lips, his phone buzzed. He looked at it with a frown, then spent a few minutes scrolling through a long message, grumbling every once in a while. I watched as his face slowly collapsed in annoyance. Finally, he set the phone down. "Damn her."

"What's wrong?" I prayed that this wasn't another hitch in the deal.

"Ivory. She sent me a draft of her article for *No Moss*. Not very complimentary. Claims that after ten years, I've finally lost my mojo. And she blames the 'mystery mousy woman' for it."

I stared at him in shock. Some people said that his songs weren't as good anymore, but I still loved them, and so did most of his fans. Sure, they did have a similar sound —each artist has their own style. I found it impressive that he managed to mix things up as much as he did. But blaming me for any of this was totally ridiculous. "Great! In Ivory's mind, I've single-handedly caused your decline. Now you know why I don't like her."

Alejandro shrugged. "That's show business."

I leaned closer to him with a sly smile. "You know what? I'm going to call in my dare from the other night. I believe you owe me one."

"Okay." Alejandro chuckled. "What's your dare?"

"I dare you to get all references to me out of that article."

"This article won't appear until the con is over. And you agreed that we could be seen and written about then. So why bother?"

"I guess I'm still not ready to be Alejandro's next big thing. Or perhaps I just don't believe it. Also, if this con goes wrong, you won't want me to be associated with you. You keep saying that we'll spend some time together after this con, but right now, I'm trying to keep myself from thinking about everything that will mean."

He nodded for a few seconds, then he called her up. "Ivory, honey. Love the article." He listened for a second then jumped back in. "No, no, don't apologize. You're absolutely right about my music, and your article is fabulously strident, as always. Never change, babe!"

Alejandro's voice lowered. "But I need a favor. Take out that crap about the mystery mousy woman." He pulled the phone away from his head, wincing as he tried to attenuate Ivory's response.

"Of course you're allowed to print anything you want. But listen. . . No, just listen! I'll make a deal with you. If you pull her from this article, I'll give you an exclusive on her if anything takes off. And I'm hoping it will. What do you say?"

He smiled at her response. "Thanks, Ivory. You're a goddess." He ended the call.

I looked at him timidly. "Thank you so much."

"It was the right thing to do. Besides, that article was the wrong way to introduce you to the world. It was rude. Ivory sometimes tramples on people she thinks are beneath her. But when she gets that exclusive, we'll be able to better control how you're portrayed."

I laughed. "*When*? Pretty sure of us, aren't you? You even told Ivory that you wanted this to work." I shook my head. "I still don't believe that it's possible. But I want you to know that I would love nothing more. I'm. . ." I paused, afraid that I was about to make a fool of myself. "I'm sure you hear this all the time, so forgive me for being trite. But I'm really falling hard for you and not just as a fan of your music. You're so easy to be with, so different than I expected. But when you talk about us as if we're something that Ivory Doe needs to write about, it really messes with my mind. I don't usually let myself have such foolish hopes." I shook my head some more, not knowing what else to say.

Alejandro pulled me into a hug. "It's not foolish, Dee, because I feel it, too. Right now, I have many hopes. I hope everything goes well in the con tomorrow. I hope you're still with me tomorrow night. And as I told Ivory, I hope that I *do* end up giving her that exclusive interview about us. But as I've warned you, when that happens, you're going to be very famous."

My heart thumped like a kettledrum. Alejandro wanted this as much as I did, which brought a tear to my eye. I rubbed my face to hide my feelings, then I gave him a quick kiss. "Thank you, but I can't even think about that right now. Let's go to sleep." We wandered back to the bedroom, got washed, and crashed in his bed, our bodies resting against each other as we drifted off.

My phone woke me at two in the morning, rousing me from a satisfying chunk of sleep. Bursting with con energy, I quickly got up and climbed out of bed. Alejandro stirred, then fell back asleep. I hated to leave his bed like this, but I had work to do, and nighttime was the perfect time for it.

With my small backpack already prepared, I drove to George's place and parked two blocks away. Dressed in black, I wore a ski mask over my face and gloves on my hands. I quickly picked the lock on his back door. Worst security I'd ever seen. It actually took me less time to pick that lock than it did to put on the gloves! Then I slipped inside.

As expected, the attaché case in George's living room was identical to the one in Alejandro's study. I silently laughed over my famous lover's obvious plan to swap the cases and steal the money. I just hoped that he didn't screw up the whole con when he came here tomorrow to do it.

So much depended on tomorrow's deal that I needed eyes and ears in George's living room. I attached Hale's spy camera to the wall, hidden next to a painting. It pointed directly at the table and would help me keep track of that case full of money.

Just as I finished planting the camera, I heard noise from down the hall. George was awake. In a panic, I quickly surveyed the room. I'd have preferred to leave his house, but I couldn't chance making noise and alerting him. So I decided to hide behind the sofa. I'd be safe there, and could move to another hiding place if he came close.

George wandered into the living room and walked directly to his briefcase of money. He squatted down and stared at the side of the case, running his fingers along the edge. Then he straightened up and wandered to the kitchen. I waited patiently while he rummaged around. After a few minutes, he wandered back through the living room on his way back to bed.

I waited another fifteen minutes before I left my hiding place. Finally, I stood up and went to examine the briefcase. What had George been looking at? The side of the case seemed normal to me, so I pulled out a small pen light and examined it more closely.

That's when I saw it. A small piece of clear tape bridging the gap between the lid and the bottom of the case. George had put it there as an extra security measure, so he'd know if anyone opened his case. Thank goodness I'd been here to see this, because otherwise when Alejandro went to swap the cases, George would know immediately.

I had a few other things left to do in George's living room to prepare for tomorrow. I started by helping myself to a fistful of his cigars. It's not that I wanted to start smoking those foul tobacco sticks, but his precious Cuban habanos were taking up too much space in the humidor. Sitting next to the case full of money, his cigar box seemed like an obvious place for some items that would be needed in the deal tomorrow. So I tossed the cigars in my backpack and pulled out the replacement items that would now fit there. One item was from Aunt Franny, a notebook with all of George's nefarious contacts, including the people who sell drugs for him and the people who supply them. I also left a printout of the financial misdeeds that Elle's team had uncovered, as well as Karen's notes on George's embezzling. And if those things didn't cool him out, I left another little gift that would certainly do the trick.

With a long breath, I looked around the room one last time. Everything was in place for tomorrow's deal, so I went back to Alejandro's. Before returning to the bedroom, I added a piece of tape to the side of his case, exactly where George had marked his. Then, I slipped back into bed and finally let myself sleep through the night.

The Day
of the Deal

Thirty-Four

On the morning of the deal, I headed back to my motel to get everything ready. This was the day when everything would come together, one way or another.

I was less fearful this morning than I usually was for con games, thanks to another wonderful night with Alejandro. Also, I had plenty of last-minute details to do, so much to think about that it kept me distracted. Still, I found myself nervously tapping the steering wheel at every red light. "Please please please," I whispered to myself. "Let this all go well."

Back in my room, I dug into the supplies I had bought a few days ago and put on gloves again. Then I took two price tags and wrote "$39.95" on each, a very low price for a guitar. I taped the tags to the backs of the two fake guitars, grinning at how this would be received. Finally, I wiped down the guitars and the guitar cases and stuffed both of them into the oversized backpack I had bought.

Props ready, I dressed for the con. Today's Deborah Gleason outfit was a sleeveless black pantsuit over a white roll-neck blouse. For Bea's approval, I completed the look with a stylish black beret that hid my bleached hair. Ready as I'd ever be, I carried the big backpack down to my plain sedan.

I was about to leave when Vance knocked on my window. I rolled it down and cocked my head to the side. "What's up, Vance?"

"Where were you last night?" Now, this was interesting —Vance seemed to know something about my whereabouts. I didn't expect him to notice I was gone, but now he was suspicious. My non-stop television playing had finally become too much, even for him.

I went for denial. "I was here."

"Watching television all night?"

"I mute the sound, but I like the TV. Reminds me of the busyness of New York." What a lie! Would he buy it?

Apparently not. "I don't think so. I sneaked up to your room and broke in. You weren't there." He gave me a grin of superiority.

"You going to tell Bea about this?"

He shrugged. "Depends."

I offered the truth, hoping to defuse the situation. "I was with Alejandro. Sneaked out when you weren't looking."

"But your car was here all night."

Vance was acting much sharper than I'd expected. This would require a fresh layer of lies. "Sneaking past you does me no good if I move my car. So I took a cab."

Vance frowned. "But you couldn't have sneaked past me to get back in your room. I've been watching carefully since I noticed you were gone." He drummed his fingers on the car door, fidgeting as if he wasn't sure what to do next. For Vance, this was difficult work. "Maybe I'll just go there and tell Bea everything—let her figure it out."

Great. Now Bea would be even angrier. She already knew that I'd been spending time with Alejandro, but when she found out that I'd been tricking Vance, too, she'd be livid. I knew he would complicate things, but I didn't expect this to happen on the morning of the deal.

As much as Vance annoyed me, a part of me felt sorry for him. He'd been following me all week, day and night, without any noticeable breaks. So even though he'd been a troublemaker, I wanted to do something for the poor man.

"Can I ask you something, Vance? Why did you do this for her? Don't you have a family waiting for you at home? You've spent so many days doing nothing but watch me."

"Sure, but we need the money, and this job was easy."

"Has she paid you yet?"

Vance frowned. "No, she said she'd pay me when this was done."

"Well, it ends today, and I'm going there now. When we get there, go in and get paid. You've done great surveillance work this week; don't let her cheat you." I'd feel bad if Bea swindled him, too.

I got in my car and drove to see the woman who had taught me so many dishonest tricks. Vance's information would complicate things, but I wasn't too worried about how Bea would react. Another lecture about romancing the mark? Yawn. Anger at me for evading the world's worst surveillance? She'd have to be kidding. Besides, I now had *two* guitars and a bigger promise of money. That sort of action eclipsed minor mistakes.

But I'd be a fool to think she wouldn't be angry. Also, I knew she'd be upset about the additional guitar. Just because she planned each con with plenty of options, didn't mean she liked to have a new one sprung on her. And she'd be even more upset to have a change like this show up at the very last minute. Still, I couldn't tell her about it until I had the second guitar. Only after it passed Peters' authentication did I believe the con would include it.

Another reason I waited until now to tell her anything was that I needed to find the cocaine first. Now that I'd removed her blackmail evidence, I could tell her things like this with less concern for her displeasure. She would simply have to deal with the change.

Vance and I arrived together at Bea's house. I left the big backpack with both guitars on her back porch, then I followed him inside.

Vance began by telling her how he'd caught me sneaking out of the motel room. Bea said nothing as he gave his report, but she shot me a look of veiled displeasure. She clearly didn't want to give me her full reaction in front of Vance. When he was done, she thanked him and told him he could leave.

Vance hesitated. "Is this job done?" He knew it was—this was just a segue for him to ask for payment.

Bea's frustration was evident. "Yes, Vance. Now get out!"

But Victory Vance needed his final victory. "You owe me for this. We had a deal." I winked at him, a silent thumbs-up for facing down Bea.

She stared at him for a few seconds with lidded eyes. Finally, she relented. "Okay." She reached into her purse and pulled out a roll of cash. "Three hundred dollars, right?" She peeled off three hundred-dollar bills and slapped them on the table. Vance smiled and grabbed the cash.

I was shocked. The man had been living at my motel for more than a week, never leaving his post. Sure, he sucked at surveillance, but he'd put in way too much effort for a mere three hundred dollars. It wasn't right.

Before I could control my reaction, I spoke up for the poor guy. "Three hundred dollars? Is that all?"

Bea arched an eyebrow. "You think he deserves more?"

"Damn straight I do. You can't treat Vance that way."

"I can't? Okay, then. Since we're partners in this little scam, why don't you give him a bonus?"

I couldn't resist. Elle and I had found huge piles of money in Bea's storage locker, and I happened to have some of it. So I reached into my purse and pulled out my own pile of hundred-dollar bills.

"You did nice work this week, Vance. So I'm giving you an extra thousand." His eyes widened as I peeled off ten bills. "But in case my *partner* hasn't already told you, this whole deal is a secret, right?"

Vance nodded. "I know. If anyone asks, I didn't do this job for Bea."

"And you never saw me either, right?" I pulled out two more hundred-dollar bills and waved them in front of his face to make sure he was paying attention.

With a nod, he quickly took them from my hand. "I never saw you either, Dee."

"You're a good man, Vance. Thanks. You can go now." Vance didn't need to be told twice. He raised his arms in the air, just like he'd done years ago when he'd scored another video game victory. Then he bolted out the door.

That left me and my dear foster mother. "Total waste of money," she grumbled. "You really have a lot to learn." Then she launched into yet another lecture about the ill-advised practice of romancing the mark. The lesson was becoming tiresome, but I understood that she needed to vent. So I stood there calmly, taking it all in and letting it pass through me. There were plenty of things to worry about today, but her conning lessons were no worry at all, especially now that she couldn't blackmail me.

When her venting had wound down, I decided to introduce the second guitar. "By the way, I've sweetened the deal. Wait till you see what I've got." I went to the door and brought in the oversized backpack that held both guitars.

Sitting it on her kitchen table, I opened it and lifted it by the bottom to let the two cases slip out.

Her brow creased as she stared at them. "*Two* guitars?"

I nodded. "Alejandro has a collection but so does George. And the centerpiece of George's collection is a rare prototype that has only three others like it. I had Carl make another one of them."

I pointed to the Dreadnought case, and she flipped it open. "This is supposed to be a rare guitar?" Her eyes were barely slits as she regarded it.

"Yep. It's from my *mother's* attic. You're not going to believe it, but this particular gem brings the price from four hundred grand to a full million. George can't wait to do this deal." I elbowed the case closed and winked at her. "It's almost time. The deal is happening at George's home."

She rubbed her chin. "Where does he live?" Her voice was too light, artificially so. I doubted this was idle chat. Still, she didn't seem too upset by this, which was probably due to the extra money she'd be getting. I smiled and tried to remain calm.

"In Bel Air. Nice place." I had the card George had given me with his home address on the back, so I tossed it on the table and flipped it over. "That's his address."

She picked up the card and studied it for a few seconds, her mind doubtlessly churning through this new information. Suddenly, a dark cloud drifted over her face, and a different woman emerged. I'd seen this woman too many times when I was young—she still scared me. So even though I knew Bea wasn't about to hit me or lock me in a closet, I took an instinctive step back.

She closed the distance in no time at all. "You scheming, ungrateful brat! You've really pissed me off this week." I could see that—she practically had steam coming from her ears.

I tried the obvious defense. "Hey, we're getting even more money. I thought you'd be happy."

"I get happy when my team talks to me and tells me what's going on. When they run around behind my back, I get *unhappy*. And you!" She pointed a shaking finger at me. "Have made me *unhappy*."

"But Bea, this deal is going great. In fact. . ." I checked my watch. "I have to go there now. I'll be right back with a huge pile of cash." I picked up the big backpack and opened it all the way so I could stuff the two guitar cases back in.

But Bea stepped between me and the guitars. "Not so fast, little girl. If you can change plans, then so can I. Now *I'm* doing the deal."

"But. . ."

She held up her hand to silence me. "Trust me on this: you don't want to go to George's place to do this deal."

"I don't?" To be honest, she was right. I didn't want to go there to do the deal. I hated doing deals, although I doubted that was her reason for taking it away from me.

She spoke with grim determination. "If you do this deal, I promise you'll get busted for drug trafficking."

Her trump card again. She didn't know that I'd taken that card away, but I wasn't about to correct her now. Let her do the deal—fine by me. I sighed and slumped my shoulders, then stepped away from her. "Okay. You do it."

She gave me a tight smile and went into her bedroom briefly, emerging with the old-lady wig she'd worn when we'd first roped in George. Then, with her Bonnie Gleason persona in place, she bent down to pick up the guitars, her eyes locked on me the whole time. "See what happens when you think you're the boss? I'm the boss! You're just a

washed-up con artist who can't be relied on for anything."
She curled her lip and growled at me. "Stay here and keep
the hell out of trouble." She walked out, threw the guitars in
her trunk, and drove away.

Bea's change of plans wasn't completely unexpected. I
knew she'd be upset, that she'd do something to interfere.
And besides, the last time she let me do a deal, seven years
ago, I'd run off with all of the money. So I'd anticipated this
switch.

Truthfully, I was pleased to let her do the final deal. My
part was over—the con would take place without me. A
huge relief. Soon, I could return to my normal life. As
strange as it sounded, I longed for the peace and quiet of
New York City.

Now, with less fear in my heart, I found myself curious
about the fate of this deal. After all my planning, a small
part of me still wanted to be there, or at least nearby. I
wanted to watch it all go down. Sure, deals made me
nervous, but they were unquestionably exciting. Let Bea do
the deal—I just wanted to watch.

And I could. My phone was able to connect to the
camera I'd left in George's home last night. I'd put it there
for emergencies, to keep a watch on George and his money.
This sure seemed like an emergency to me.

In no time, I was looking at live video from George's
empty living room. The case of money that I'd seen last
night still sat on the table, next to the cigar humidor.
Unless, that is, Alejandro had already made the switch.
Regardless, I found myself engrossed with the scene.

After watching this unchanging vista for a minute, I
needed more. I needed to be closer to the action. Not *in* the
house—I had no intention of getting involved in this deal.
But I *could* park a few blocks away and watch. After all this

planning, how could I sit in Bea's kitchen and spin my wheels? Besides, what if someone needed my assistance during the deal? A good con artist is always prepared, just in case.

I left a piece of paper on her kitchen table with the address of her storage locker as well as the locker number. When she saw this, she'd realize that her leverage over me was gone. Then I got into my brown sedan, put on the curly brown wig, and headed over to George's house.

Thirty-Five

As I drove to George's house, I kept one eye on my phone. So far, his living room was empty. But even this period of quiet made me tense, considering what was about to happen soon. I was so glad I was safe in my car.

Soon, George appeared on my tiny screen. He came into the living room and started to pace back and forth, humming and occasionally muttering to himself. It was early, but he was visibly anxious. I wondered how he'd react when Bea showed up instead of me. Would he still want to buy the guitars?

The doorbell rang, much sooner than I expected. Bea had left before me, but she couldn't possibly be at George's place yet. I eyed my phone very carefully while I kept on driving.

A man came into the room, and I recognized him immediately: Alejandro. He was wearing a hoodie and sunglasses, but I could tell it was him. That trim and muscular body was unmistakable. Damn! I knew he was going to switch the cases of money, but did he have to do it this close to the deal? I wanted to shout a warning to him. Get out! Bea is on her way! I prayed that he'd be quick about it.

The two men talked for a minute, then George wandered off to the kitchen. This was Alejandro's chance, and I held my breath as he headed back toward the front door with George's case. I heard the door open, then Alejandro reappeared with the identical-looking case that

I'd seen at his place last night. He deftly set it down on George's desk, then he wandered around the room, trying to appear casual. I made a note to give him a few tips on acting casual, if we ever got a chance to talk about this again. When George finally returned, Alejandro made some excuse and quickly left. My breathing returned to normal.

I had to hand it to him; he did that well. He even wore a glove when he brought in the fake case, so he wouldn't leave his fingerprints anywhere. Of course, I wished he'd done this earlier, not minutes before the deal. But Bea wasn't there yet, so he seemed to have made it out the door in time. Now the case sitting on George's table was full of fake cash.

I knew that Bea wouldn't fall for this trick any more than I would. Things at George's place needed to slow down, so I made a call. Elle picked up instantly. "What's the plan?"

"Bea's coming. Once she goes in, get Wanda in position and wait for my signal."

"Got it. She wants to talk to you." The phone got handed off.

Wanda started right in, very excited. "Oh, oh, oh! This is so much fun! We're outside the guy's place. Someone just paid him a visit."

I chuckled. "Yeah, that was Alejandro. He's gone now, right?"

"That was Alejandro? Heavens! Why didn't you tell me? I forgot to get his autograph last night, and my niece. . ."

"Wanda!" I cut her off. "We haven't got time for this. When you see a gray-haired woman show up with two guitars, that's Bea. You and Elle go to the front door, but wait for my signal before you knock. When you leave, look for Elle and follow her. She'll keep you safe. Good luck."

"Got it, boss! I'm going to beat her up."

I snorted. "I know you want to do that, Wanda, but punching her is not an option. Stick to the plan."

"Okay, okay! I'm on it."

After hanging up, I floored the car, racing it down the freeway. On the way, I churned through the possible scenarios that were about to play out.

When I was a few blocks away from George's house, his doorbell rang again. I quickly pulled over and parked—this was close enough. Bea had arrived, and now everything was in motion. Sparks were about to fly.

George went to get the door, and his voice did not sound happy. "Mrs. Gleason! What are *you* doing here?"

Bea's voice oozed with con-woman warmth. "Oh, hello, George. Deborah couldn't make it, so she sent me instead. And look what I brought!" The two of them appeared in the living room, where Bea set both guitar cases on the table next to the fake cash. She opened them up with a proud smile.

George smiled, too, when he saw the guitars. "Well, I guess that's okay. Those are certainly the guitars I wanted." He reached for one of them but Bea quickly closed the cases.

"Now show me yours." She grinned and nodded toward the case of money.

This was it. Bea was about to examine the money, and I needed her to stop. I picked up the phone, whispered, "Go, Wanda," then disconnected the call.

Back in the living room, the doorbell rang before Bea could open the case. George and Bea frowned at each other for a second. Then with his mouth tight, he went to the door. I could hear the conversation unfold off camera.

"Can I help you?"

"Good day, sir." I giggled at the sound of Wanda's voice, and I sat back to enjoy this part of the show. The woman could talk and talk, which is exactly why I'd brought her out here. She let loose with a full blast before George could say a word. "I'm going door to door, collecting for the fireman's fund. The boys are hoping they can count on you this year. They risk their lives every day. . ."

"I'm very busy right now." George tried to interrupt her, but he had no idea who he was up against.

Ever cheerful, Wanda went right on. "That's quite all right. This will only take a few minutes. Let me just. . ." I heard a shuffling off-camera as she powered into his house.

"You can't come in here, miss." George attempted to stop her again, but he was too late.

Wanda appeared in the living room and continued her patter. She wore a fitted red dress with a calf-length pencil skirt. Rather modest, although her bizarre hat did give me a start. Was that a giant spider perched on the side of her head? Leave it to Wanda to make another statement with her choice of millinery.

She rushed to the living room table. "Oh, guitars! Did you know that the firemen are having a campfire at their fundraiser this year? They play music and sing songs all night long. And since they're firemen, you can be certain that there's no chance of the campfire getting out of control! Why, last year, the fund raised. . ."

"No!" Bea tried her hand at stopping Wanda. "What made you think you could just barge in here and bother us? Get out and leave us alone. Right now!"

"There's no need to be nasty." Wanda knew she was talking to my foster mother, someone she'd heard me talk about for years. Her dander was up, so she went in for the kill. "Firemen risk their lives! *Their lives!* And all you can do is stand there all smug and safe. Just last year, three of our boys died from smoke inhalation. It's a tragedy!" Wanda advanced on Bea, arms waving in the air. I'd seen her in action before so I knew that even Bea was powerless to stop the onslaught. She stepped back to get out of the way.

Wanda continued her tirade, a nonstop stream of words and gestures and bluster. God, how I loved that woman. In a battle of words between Bea and her, my money was on Wanda every time. I watched for a few minutes as she kept up a steady harangue, dominating the room and freezing out Bea and George's deal.

I was enjoying this scene right up to the moment that a police cruiser passed my car, heading down the street toward George's place. Suddenly, I had other concerns. As I slumped down in my seat, my gut rumbled and my heart thumped like a fifty-piece drum corps.

Trouble was here, and I needed to act fast. Bea and George could rot in jail, for all I cared, but Wanda needed to get out of there. I sent her and Elle a simple text message: "Cops. Out now."

Back on the video feed, I saw Wanda pause in mid sentence and pull out her phone. She glanced at it, then smiled at Bea and George. "You know what? I can tell you're busy today, so I'll come back tomorrow." She turned and ran from the room.

I exhaled my relief when I heard the door close. Wanda had done her part perfectly. Elle would be hiding, waiting to quickly escort her away through the neighbor's yard. That way, the police wouldn't notice them as they approached the house. In Elle's capable hands, Wanda would be safe.

But safety was elusive, and the time for celebration was not yet at hand. Seconds later, I jumped at the sound of the police, banging on George's front door. Before George could even answer, two policemen came barging in with guns drawn. Not just any policemen, either. Today's representatives of L.A.'s finest were the same swaggering kids I'd met a few times already: Lucky and Myles. Those boys seemed to show up every time I looked around.

"Nobody move!" Myles shouted. "We have a search warrant." Yes indeed, I was glad to be here in my car.

Then, as if there weren't enough things happening at once, the door to my car opened and Alejandro slipped into the passenger seat, still holding George's attaché case. I looked around in panic, but nobody had noticed him—the hoodie was pulled tight over his sunglass-covered face. Thank goodness he knew how to avoid attention. But what was he doing here now?

"Miss me?" He grinned and gave me a quick kiss.

He was having fun, but I was on the edge of sanity here, worrying about how this was going to play out. "Do you mind? I'm busy."

He looked at my phone and noticed what I was watching. "So you bugged the place." He let out a big laugh.

I scowled and pulled the phone away from him, holding it to my chest. "Troublemaker. I saw you in there earlier."

"Aww, how cute. You're angry." He sat back in his seat. "Come on. Don't hog the video. Let me watch, too. Who knows, maybe those policemen will arrest George. I can dream, can't I?"

I lowered the phone, and we leaned in to watch together. "Incredible!" Alejandro chuckled. "I may not know what's going on here, but I do know one thing. Right now, there's a big ball of shit that's only inches away from some shiny new fan blades."

Thirty-Six

Alejandro leaned over to give me a kiss on the neck. I wanted to kiss him hard, to push his seat all the way back and throw myself on him. And at any other time, I would.

But right now, I had different things on my mind. Like the fact that the police had just arrived as the deal was about to happen. Bea and George stood there, staring at each other with hard eyes. Lucky and Myles brandished their weapons and tried to act mature. Young and thin, they seemed more like a comedy duo than police partners. But what did I expect in Los Angeles?

Things could go in any number of directions now, so this wasn't the best time to get lost in Alejandro's kisses. "Stop distracting me. I'm trying to watch." I gave him a playful smack on the arm.

He turned so he could watch the screen. "I know those two. They were the ones who came to my place when Karen called the cops on you."

"Yep. And she just called them again." I grinned at him. "Karen really hates it when people try to sell fake guitars."

"Wait! You *want* the cops to be there?"

"Shh! This isn't over yet—let me watch. I'll tell you all about it later." We turned our attention to the police action going on in George's home.

Bea and George had their hands in the air as Lucky and Myles explored the room. She seemed very upset but spoke calmly. "Why are these policemen here?"

"Good question." George straightened up to his full height and turned to Lucky. "What are you doing here, officer?"

"We're following up on a lead. What's all this?" He pointed to the cases on the table.

George shrugged, clearly unconcerned. "Just a business transaction, completely legal. Mrs. Gleason here is selling me two guitars. That's my payment." He pointed to the case that I knew had fake cash. "I would appreciate it if you would let us finish this deal, because I really want those guitars." George had once boasted that he could purchase a stolen guitar even while the police watched, so I knew he would go forward with the deal.

Lucky turned to Bea. "Is that correct? Are those your guitars?"

Bea stiffened. "Yes. They're rare musical instruments." She pointed to the cases. "I can show you." Lucky nodded, so she opened up the guitar cases. "See? Guitars." George came closer. Even through Hale's spy camera, I could see his eyes glimmer with undisguised enthusiasm as he peered into the cases. But Bea quickly closed them up. "Now since we're not doing anything illegal, how about you two step aside and let us finish this?"

Myles nodded at Lucky as they put their guns away, stood back, and folded their arms.

George looked around the room with a smug grin, perhaps remembering his own boast and proud to be able to live up to it. Then he handed the case with the money to Bea.

I inhaled sharply and held my breath.

Bea flipped open the case and stared at the piles of hundred dollar bills. Myles leaned over and looked in the case, too. "Hoo wee! That's a lot of cash. How much you got in there?" He reached out toward the case.

She quickly slammed it shut. "It's enough, and it's none of your business."

I exhaled.

The worst was over, and the deal was still on. I silently thanked Lucky and Myles for running interference. A special thanks went to Wanda for holding things off until my two favorite policemen could arrive. Otherwise, the fake cash would have been a problem.

Bea slid the two guitars toward George. "Thank you." She turned to the young policemen. "Now, gentlemen, if you'll excuse me, I have places to be."

Myles held out his hands. "Not so fast. Let's see those guitars."

George let his shoulders drop. "They're very valuable. Please be careful." He opened the cases again.

Lucky and Myles put gloves on their hands and examined the guitars. Myles examined the Stratocaster while Lucky checked out the Dreadnought. As soon as they picked up the guitars, they spotted the price tags I'd attached to them earlier. They looked at the tags and gave each other a snort. "Yes, I can see how valuable these are."

Lucky patted the Dreadnought, then strummed it and looked inside the sound hole. Myles examined the Stratocaster as well but could find nothing suspicious. Turning their attention to the guitar cases, they felt the lining and checked every surface. Lucky pulled open the accessory compartment door and stopped, his entire body suddenly rigid. I wondered if the video had frozen. But then I heard a quiet whistle. "Myles, look at this," he muttered.

Instead of a few strings and picks, the compartment was stuffed with something big and white, all wrapped in plastic. Myles opened the accessory compartment of his case and found it was also filled with a big white bag. The two of them traded looks, then Lucky pulled his bag out and set it on the table.

Myles got serious and reached for his gun again, keeping Bea and George covered while Lucky carefully sliced into the bag. He sniffed the powder, then nodded his head.

"Well guess what, folks?" Myles leered at Bea and George. "You two are under arrest for drug trafficking." Lucky drew his gun as well.

"Wait a minute." George's face was red. He turned to Bea. "You framed me!"

Bea scowled. "This is Dee's doing." She brought a hand to her forehead. "Sorry, I mean Deborah."

George shook his head. "I don't think so. She showed me real guitars, not cheap imitations. You're the one who cheated." He faced the officers. "This is a huge mistake. I don't do drugs."

Myles chuckled. "You just purchased forty-dollar guitars filled with cocaine using a case full of hundred dollar bills. We call this drug trafficking."

George's angry face looked like it was about to explode. But Bea waved her hand to shut him up. "Don't say anything more in front of the cops." The two of them remained silent while Myles read them their rights.

When they were finished, the boys decided to look around George's place some more. It didn't take them very long to open the humidor on the living room table and find the little presents I'd left there last night. Myles held up a smaller bag of white powder. "You don't do drugs? Then what might this be?" George remained silent, but his face now looked like an overinflated red balloon.

Lucky reached farther into the humidor to pull out Aunt Franny's notebook, Elle's notes about George's financial misdeeds, and Karen's notes about the embezzlement. He leafed through Franny's notebook, stopping at one particular page. "Get a load of this." He handed the notebook to Myles.

Myles read it for a few seconds and chuckled. "So you're the one who's been financing those guys." He pointed to one of the names in the book. "Recognize this one, Lucky?"

His partner nodded and pointed elsewhere on the page. "This guy, too. The detectives are going to love this."

Myles turned to George and Bea. "Are you folks going to come along politely, or do we need to handcuff you?" Dejected and beyond any ability to fight, they let themselves be silently escorted away.

Thirty-Seven

Alejandro and I slunk down in our seats as the police cruiser with Bea and George drove past us. Giddy from the tension, I launched myself at him, kissing him with a desperate release from days of pent-up nervousness. I could grope that fabulous body now—everything had gone perfectly!

Alejandro pulled away from me with a grin. "Very impressive! I didn't see that coming. You got rid of George and Bea in one go. I'm amazed." He stroked my hair and kissed me again, his incredible mouth clouding my mind. Then, still focused on the con, he pulled away with a laugh. "Pretty rough, though, sending them off to jail like that. Did you plant those drugs in George's humidor?"

"Oh, don't tell me you're suddenly feeling sorry for them. I'm not. Bea was going to bust me for drugs—I just beat her to the punch. And yes, I planted those drugs in George's humidor. He's done worse to plenty of people, so he had it coming."

Alejandro held up his hands in surrender. "Hey, I'm not complaining. But what will happen when they don't find any fingerprints on those drugs? George never touched that bag."

I struggled to hide my smile for as long as I could, but finally gave up and grinned full out. "Actually, he *did* touch that bag. All over. When I first brought the Dreadnought to show him, that bag was in the accessory compartment filled with colorful guitar picks. George examined it quite closely and rolled it around in his hands as he studied the picks. So as a matter of fact, the only fingerprints they'll find on that bag are George's."

"Nasty! I'm blown away, Dee. Do the bags in the guitar cases have Bea's fingerprints on them? I saw some writing on them but it was too tiny to read."

I couldn't stop grinning. "One bag says Nuts To You and the other says Low-Hanging Fruit. She loves those crappy candy bars even more than you do and buys them by the bag. I fished those bags out of her trash one night and filled them with cocaine. So yeah, they're crawling with her fingerprints, and nobody else's. In fact, I've had to be very careful about my own fingerprints. I even put the two guitars together in a big backpack so I wouldn't have to touch the cases."

He shook his head slowly, smiling with obvious approval. "And, if I may ask, where did you get so much cocaine?"

I smiled innocently. "Those drugs belong to Bea. I just borrowed them."

He cocked his head and stared at me, probably waiting for me to explain my use of the word "borrow." I continued my story of the cocaine's history.

"When I first arrived in Los Angeles, Bea stole a pile of goods from the police evidence locker, including two bags of cocaine. I told you how she tricked me into touching them, then stashed them in her secret storage locker and blackmailed me into conning you. Well, thanks to Hale, I found the locker and now I had some cocaine on my hands."

"Wow. Repackaging all those drugs must have been a mess."

"It sure was. And I couldn't just throw away the original plastic bags, so I had to rinse them out carefully. The coke got everywhere and I ended up scrubbing down the entire motel bathroom. Took me half an hour yesterday evening."

Alejandro nodded and was about to say something when a car stopped next to mine. The door opened, and Udo stepped out. "Your ride is here." I pointed with my chin.

He held out a hand. "Your ride, too. This isn't over yet." I liked that idea, so I followed him to the limo. Alejandro brought the attaché case he'd taken from George earlier, and I brought my backpack. As the limousine rolled away from the scene of the crime, we snuggled in the back seat and kissed.

But Alejandro couldn't focus on his lust right now. He was too excited that the con was finally over, and he wanted to hear everything. "So. . ." He pulled his mouth from mine and spoke as he nibbled an earlobe. "How did you find her secret locker?"

I let him nibble for a while before I answered. "Remember when you gave me that Grammy award? Well, I gave it to her, knowing full well that she'd stash it in her locker. But before that, I put a tracking device in it, courtesy of Hale."

"Good man, Hale. Seemed to know my security system cold. And Karen's nuts about him."

"They make a good couple, don't they? Anyway, that birthday party Hale threw for Elle yesterday was really a visit to Bea's locker. It had all sorts of skeletons in it." I instantly sat up straight, much more excited. "Get this! Elle found an incredible revelation about Jay. Turns out his death wasn't my fault after all." I explained the letter from the vigilante who had killed my brother.

Alejandro was shocked at the story. "That's terrible! But at least you don't have to blame yourself anymore."

"I know. It's a huge relief. And by the way. . ." I reached into my backpack and retrieved the Grammy. "You can have it back, now."

He took the award and turned it over to reveal the small, nearly invisible device wedged into the base. His face burst into a huge grin. "You sure? I'd say you've earned it after what you just did."

I chuckled. "Why don't you take it for now. It would only cause suspicion if people found your Grammy sitting on my shelf."

He nodded and set the award on the floor of the limo. Then he sat for a few seconds in thought. "So now I know why you insisted on getting George's guitars out of my house."

"Yeah. When the cops talk to him, he's likely to rat you out. I not only had to get them out of there, but I had to make it look like they'd never been there. That's why Karen redecorated the room with your other memorabilia, and Hale wiped out the security video."

"Karen told me she's made a shrine to me in there. I'm afraid to look." He laughed and shook his head. "So what did you do with the guitars? Did you put them in Bea's locker to frame her even more?"

"Well, first of all, Bea's locker still has incriminating things in it. Elle and I raided it yesterday, but we didn't empty it. She took the usable cash, but we left the jewelry and plenty of marked bills. Too hard to fence that stuff anyway, and all that incriminating evidence will sink her case even worse when the cops find it.

"But secondly, there's no need to complicate the case more by having George's guitars show up there. I wanted this to look like a deal between two relative strangers. If she was holding guitars with his fingerprints on them, it would only confuse things. Third of all, those guitars are quite valuable, and you wanted to recover some of the money he embezzled from you. If we'd put them in Bea's locker, they'd get impounded along with everything else in there when the police find it."

"So where are they?"

"We rented two other lockers and put the guitars there."

"George didn't have that many guitars. Why would you need two lockers?"

I chuckled. "One of the lockers was rented using George's credit card, which I borrowed from him. We put three of his stolen guitars there, so when the police go looking, they'll find even more illegal activities on his part."

"But the other storage locker is under Hale's name, and it has the bulk of George's guitars. He's going to sell them, and you'll be getting most of that money."

"Incredible!" He kissed me even harder, and we rolled around in the back seat for a few minutes, steaming everything up. We didn't even notice when the limousine came to a stop in front of Alejandro's mansion. Udo opened the door then stood back to give us some privacy.

Slowly, we disengaged and emerged from the back seat, each of us carrying our items. As we walked to the front door, Alejandro continued his questions. "What else did you take from Bea's locker?"

"I took only what I needed. I got the Grammy back, and I took the drugs she was using to blackmail people." But then I realized that I'd found something else of value in her "Documents" tub. "Oh, oh! I just remembered. I did find something else." I couldn't wait to tell everyone.

Udo was standing in the front hall, waiting for us to walk by. But I was so excited I needed to give him another hug. He didn't seem to mind it much the last time I did that, so I wrapped my arms around him and gave him a little squeeze. "I've got something for you, Udo. A way to get your wife into the country." I stepped back so I could speak to both of them. "Bea had all sorts of interesting documents in her locker, including three blank passport books. Passports are nearly impossible to forge—too many security features in them. But if you have a blank one, they're not too hard to fill-in. Elle has someone on her team who can do it. And get this!" I bounced on my toes. "She says her hacker can wipe your wife's record clean, too, and get her a passport in a few days. All she needs is a blank passport book and a picture."

With an ear-to-ear grin, I raised my hand and held up Udo's wallet. Then I started to look through it until I found a woman's picture. "Is this her?"

Alarm spread over Udo's face as he patted his pockets. "Hey! How did you get my vallet?"

Alejandro started to laugh. "She does that all the time. Must have gotten it from you when she hugged you just now." He looked at the picture and nodded. "Yep, that's her."

With a shy grin, I handed the wallet back to Udo. "Sorry about that. I couldn't resist. Can I keep this picture?"

Udo seemed much happier as he put his wallet back in his pocket. "Sure. Is zis for real? Are you honestly going to get my vife into zee country?"

"Yes!" I grinned. "I'm going to do that. But let's not call it 'honestly.'" We all laughed.

"I cannot zank you enough, Dee." He turned to Alejandro. "You really should keep zis one." Then he wandered away with a smile on his face.

I was amused by Udo's suggestion, but Alejandro took the advice with tight lips. He went to his study and sat down on the sofa. I joined him there, and we kissed briefly. Then he must have thought of something because he leaned back with a smile. "Good thing you had me on your side to call up Peters. Getting him to pass the second guitar made it a slam-dunk for you."

I grunted a laugh. "Is that what you think happened?"

"Sure. How else could he have passed that second guitar? I knew when he said he would bring his alternate testing kit along that he would do the right thing. Now I know it's a fake one that he uses when he wants to lie about the results."

"Uh, no." I shook my head. "In fact, Peters refused to lie about that guitar. His alternate testing kit is a brand new one with improved accuracy." I twisted my mouth. "Unfortunately, your call alarmed him and made him take extra precautions."

Alejandro shot me a confused look. "But he passed it."

"That's because I was prepared. I asked Karen to get the real Dreadnought for me. She sneaked it out of George's vault and brought it to the coffee shop when we met. Then I doctored it so the '6' prototype number became an '8.' That's the guitar that I showed to George and let Peters authenticate, and it *is* real. I stamped a '6' on the fake guitar I had made and gave it to Karen to put in George's vault. Having a cheap fake there was sufficient, because as long as it looked right, he'd be satisfied. He wouldn't study it too carefully."

"If the guitar that Peters authenticated was real, then why did you need me to call Peters at all?"

I shrugged. "When I asked you to call Peters, I thought I was going to try and pass a forgery. But I couldn't get a decent fake made in time, so I went with modifying the real guitar. Still, I worried when he examined it. The guy was so sure I was cheating that I knew he'd study it thoroughly.

What if he noticed the fresh stamping around that '6'? That would have been trouble."

"I see. So then you swapped the guitars back after Peters authenticated it."

"Yep. But when I swapped them back, I had to change the fake guitar's prototype number to an '8.' Then I could give it to Bea to sell to George." I laughed briefly. "We couldn't have the police impounding a *real* guitar."

"I loved the cheap price tags on the two guitars. Nice touch."

"That was for Lucky and Myles. I needed them to realize that the deal was not about rare and expensive guitars. Then they'd keep looking for the true value, which was in the accessory compartments."

Alejandro grinned. "Nice."

I furrowed my brow and propped my fists on my hips. "'Nice'?" I smirked. "I plan a con that gets your thieving manager and my swindling foster mother out of the way, while netting you millions of dollars, and all you can say is, 'Nice'?" I gave him a teasing grin.

Alejandro let out a deep laugh. "Okay, it was spectacular! I can't ever remember having so much fun. But wait a minute. Weren't you supposed to be the one doing the deal? How did you get Bea there instead?"

"You know, confidence games go both ways. Usually, it's about building *up* the mark's confidence in you. But in Bea's case, I had to build up a *lack* of confidence. I had to mess with her just enough that she'd cut me out of the deal at the last minute. In the end, Vance helped me when he figured out that I'd been sneaking around and avoiding him. He tried to make trouble about it with Bea, but instead, it worked to my advantage. Also, spending nights with you helped quite a bit—thanks for letting me come over."

"Okay, it's time for you to stop this."

I frowned. "Stop what?"

"This *lack* of confidence you have in yourself. This attitude that I'm not interested in you and that I was just doing you a favor by spending time with you. You're good at reading people; can't you tell how incredibly much I want you? How happy I am when you're with me? The con's over, Dee, so I have no more excuses for being with you other than the fact that I want you." He laughed at himself. "I feel like a kid again, chasing women and hoping they'll like me back. Why can't you see this?"

"I'm good at reading normal people. But you're pure celebrity, Alejandro. I haven't got a handle on that. And I've been too busy lately to think deeply about whatever it is that we've been doing."

"Well, I've had plenty of time to think about this. So trust me when I say that we're not done yet."

"Trust you? After you meddled with the deal?" I wagged a finger at him. "I saw you switch the case of money."

"Hey, as you said, we couldn't have the police impounding anything real. And a case with a million dollars in it is seriously real. Besides. . ." He puffed up and smiled at me. "Didn't we make a little wager on who would get to the money first? I believe I won that bet."

Alejandro pulled George's attaché case up into his lap so he could show me. But when he flipped open the case, his face went blank. "What the fuck!" He stared at the contents.

Instead of money, the case was stuffed with the newspapers I'd taken from the motel office. The topmost page had a fake headline on it that read, "Rocker Taken by Con Artist." I'd printed that on the motel's printer, just so I'd be able to tease him. He turned to me with a twinkle in his eye. "How the hell did you do that?"

"You're good, Alejandro, but not that good. I had Elle following George, and she sent me a picture of him with his money. So I knew what kind of attaché case he had, and I noticed the duplicate case at your place last night. It was obvious to me that you'd do a case swap, especially given our wager. So, after you fell asleep, I went over to George's place, setup the camera, planted the cocaine, and swapped the money in his case for those newspapers. Sorry, but it looks like you lost the bet."

Alejandro tried to frown at me, but his grin gave it all away. "You're too much. But don't forget some of that money was really mine, for the Stratocaster you sold."

"Yes, I know you didn't want me to sell it, but I had to. Otherwise, George would have been suspicious." I reached into my backpack and handed him a gift-wrapped box. "So I got you this little gift by way of apology. I think you'll like it."

He hefted the box. "Heavy and solid. Hmm." He attacked the wrapping paper and soon dispatched it.

Alejandro's face burst wide open when he saw what was in the box. He lifted up my big green bowl that Wanda had brought when she came out to Los Angeles. I'd filled it with cash. "There's your four hundred thousand dollars." I gave him a modest smile. "Happy now?"

He hugged the bowl of cash to his chest. "Thank you. I remember this piece—I almost bought it when I was in your shop." He picked up a bundle of cash and fanned the hundred dollar bills. "Love what you've done with it." We both laughed.

I wagged a finger at him. "Still, *I* won the bet. I'll get the rest of the money to you after I deduct my expenses. But don't worry. You'll make plenty more money when Hale sells George's guitars. Also, one of the things I put in the humidor was evidence of his tax fraud and his offshore accounts that Elle's team found. From a quick look at it, it seems to me that you've got nearly ten million dollars hiding in foreign banks. The police will be dealing with that, but you should, too, because George will be out on bail soon. That gives you a narrow window of opportunity to get control back." I handed him the papers that Elle had sent to me. "Get your lawyers on this."

Alejandro's eyes grew large as he studied the papers. Then he slammed the case shut and gave me a mock frown. "That did it! You have gone too far, Ms. Kirkland."

I laughed. "And?"

His frown dissolved into a big smile. "And I'm ridiculously in love with you. I think I'll take Udo's advice." He pulled out an envelope from his pocket and handed it to me. "You won the bet, so you're going to meet my family. I'll just have to find some other way of tricking you into calling up your birth parents."

I opened the envelope and found two first-class tickets to Santiago, leaving in five hours. I knew he was planning this trip, but I'd doubted it was connected with our bet. It surprised me that he'd actually anticipated my victory. "Do you also have tickets to Ohio to see my parents?"

"No. I knew you'd win. I gave it my best, but I bow to your skills. Also, I think you should keep the other six hundred thousand. You've earned it, and you've recovered more money from George than I'd ever thought possible."

"Wow! Thanks. But how did you know I'd win?"

"I had *confidence* in you. And I have confidence that this vacation will be one of many we take. Better get packed."

Oh, yes. That sounded like fun. And as it turned out, I was already packed.

Epilogue

Karen and I sat in the shade by Alejandro's pool, watching the men swim. She turned to me with a big smile. "Like my new sunglasses?"

I'd seen better ones—these looked pretty standard to me. "They're cute," I offered.

She shrugged, not put off in the least by my lack of enthusiasm. "Can I show you a card trick?" She reached for a deck. I thought we were talking about her sunglasses, but now she had shifted to doing card tricks. I chuckled at her love of games.

"Sure, show me a trick." Karen was always trying to fool me. I had to give her credit for honing her skills—Hale had taught her to shuffle cards with one hand, and she could deal from the bottom of the deck. But she hadn't been able to pull one over on me yet.

"This is a new one, Dee. Hale says he just learned it, so I bet I can trick you." She shuffled the cards smoothly, then she asked me to pick a card.

I pulled a card, looked at it, then pushed it back into the deck. With a grin, she asked me to shuffle the cards, so I did my best to mix them up.

Karen took the deck back and started to look through it. I'd seen quite a few card tricks in my day, but one thing I hadn't seen is someone who could do tricks with sunglasses on. It made me suspicious.

"Hang on there." I reached out to take off her sunglasses.

She smiled. "They've got full UV protection." She let out a little chuckle that had a nervous edge.

Hale may have taught her card tricks, but he hadn't taught her to deceive. I immediately knew that this trick involved the glasses. I should have guessed earlier, when she introduced the trick right after putting them on. Now I felt certain. When I looked through the glasses at the deck, I knew I was right. The backs of the cards were marked with ink that only the glasses revealed.

I laughed. "Trick glasses and marked cards. Nice try." I tossed the glasses back to her. "Next time, take off the glasses before you start to find my card. You already know which one I pulled by that point, so you don't need them anymore. Then, you won't arouse as much suspicion."

She blew out a long breath. "You're too hard to trick."

"Sorry. I've been learning tricks since I was old enough to talk. I'm told that my first words were 'Take a card.'"

Hale came out of the pool and stood there dripping on the deck. He saw the cards and the glasses and arched an eyebrow. "Did she fall for it?" He gave her a little kiss.

"No," Karen grumbled. "She figured it out before I'd even told her what card she'd picked."

He started to laugh. "I warned you."

Karen flopped back in the deck chair. "One day I'm going to fool you, Dee, just like you fooled me."

I sat up straight and slapped a hand to my chest. "I never fooled you, Karen. I haven't conned anyone in a year."

"Yeah, but you married Alejandro last month. *That* sure fooled me."

My husband came out of the pool at that moment and ducked down to plant a hot kiss on my lips. The drops of water falling from his hair seemed to sizzle and evaporate on my skin. He pulled back and grinned at us. "She fooled me, too." He chuckled. "I never imagined I could be this happy." He reached up and ran his fingers through my new hair. The bleached part finally got cut off, just before the wedding, leaving me with blonde hair reaching almost to my shoulders. For the first time in my life, I didn't feel the need to hide it.

I gave Karen a grin. "Well, you married Hale—I didn't see that coming. So I'd say we're even on that score."

Honestly, many things had fooled me over the past year. I didn't expect to start conning again when I came to Los Angeles. I didn't expect to meet Alejandro, let alone find out that he knew who I was. And never in my wildest dreams did I expect us to fall so deeply in love that we'd marry. Even when we were working together that fateful week, I doubted that his feelings were so strong. It wasn't until later that I finally understood.

It all started simply enough. After the con, we went down to Chile for some much-needed vacation. I met his family, then we hid at his beach villa in Zapallar. Without the tension of a con to keep us busy, I expected that he'd quickly lose interest in me. But instead, the two of us got along beautifully. We spent our days relaxing by the Pacific, talking about life, and making incredible love. We even took time to work on our art: he wrote some songs while I painted the stunning ocean vistas. Through it all, we did our best to ignore the news, which would surely be about him.

When we returned to Los Angeles, the media descended on us with a vengeance. The gossip rags were ablaze over the arrest of his manager and our subsequent romantic jaunt. They'd also noticed that Bea was my foster mother, and they'd uncovered the truth about my childhood.

The good news was that Ivory Doe got her exclusive while we were in Chile, which let her beat everyone else to the announcement of Alejandro's new love. Her article had a generous tone, which helped me survive the media frenzy. In it, I was seen as an unfortunate child who had been abused by a manipulative foster mother and had no involvement in the recent drug scandal. First of all, my foster mother had committed the crime, not me. Secondly, Bea's claim about my involvement was different than George's, which made both of them seem like liars. Thirdly, they were the only two who even mentioned my name—Vance and Oscar Peters held fast. Even Alejandro, who gave a press conference about the incident, did an impressive job of appearing shocked by it all and emphasized that I may have had a shady past, but I hadn't committed any crimes since turning eighteen. So all was magically forgiven. Besides, nobody wanted to believe that Alejandro was dating a criminal.

With the drug scandal behind us, I still had to face daily microscopic examinations by the media, who searched desperately for cracks in our relationship. At first, they were certain we wouldn't last. Every story about us—and there were hundreds of them—insisted that the rocker was merely having a fling. They never even used my name, just some sound bite to describe me: "Alejandro Kisses Pottery Girl," "Alejandro Dates Juvenile Delinquent," "Alejandro Falls for Con Artist." My name didn't seem to matter because I'd be gone soon enough.

But I kept showing up with the man, regardless of their predictions, which only served to make them more and more crazed. Stories about us became increasingly outlandish every day.

Under pressure from Alejandro, as well as from Wanda and Elle, I looked up my birth mother in Ohio. She was delighted to see me but refused to name my father. The two of them had only dated for a few weeks, then they had split up. He never even knew she was pregnant, and she didn't want to have to tell him now. Also, my mother was married and had two teenage kids, so she had enough trouble trying to explain me to her husband. The last thing she needed was an old flame to enter the picture.

Of course, her concerns about me were greatly ameliorated by the fact that I showed up at her door with Alejandro standing next to me. His presence knocked the entire family off their feet, making all of them more than happy to hear my story. Her children were intense fans, and the parents were nearly faint with excitement.

Mom looked just like me, with a delicate nose and a small mouth. I could tell she knew who I was from the moment she opened the door. As soon as she saw me, her eyes shot open and she had to hold onto the doorframe to steady herself. Then she noticed Alejandro standing next to me and had to grip the frame with both hands. We made quite an entrance.

Elle was right—meeting my mother helped me deal with my childhood. She told me how she prayed for me daily and always hoped we could meet some day. Her words were exactly what I needed to get past a lifelong feeling of not being loved. I forgave her and spent a few days getting to know her better. Then Alejandro and I went back to Los Angeles. I didn't see her again until the wedding.

Los Angeles was a circus by that point. The press wouldn't let us alone, and who could blame them? I was dating one of the most famous performers in the world! He had warned me about this, but it still came as a shock. I was the subject of every talk show and blog, was part of every comedian's monologue, and appeared on the front page of nearly every supermarket tabloid. They chased us and camped by his estate, waiting for a chance to snap a picture or ask a question. In a few short weeks, the woman who'd hidden herself for twenty-four years was suddenly a monster celebrity. I had no idea how to cope.

I was desperately in love with Alejandro, but after a few intense weeks, I couldn't stay at his estate any more. Besides, I had work to do back in New York. Udo helped me sneak off to the airport, and I made my way home without generating any front-page news.

Unfortunately, the paparazzi quickly spotted me and started camping outside my New York building. I needed to think about this all by myself, especially after everything that had happened to me. So I stayed inside and kept away from the windows. I didn't let any friends come over, and I stopped answering my phone. Too many reporters wanted to talk to me, but I had no interest in any of them.

In fact, I didn't even let Alejandro call me during that period. I loved him fiercely, but I needed a break from him and his fame. He understood, and he didn't try to call me too often. I knew he wanted more, but he was decent enough that he didn't push me too hard.

Only Wanda was allowed to visit, which she did every night, along with groceries and take-out food. She'd knock with a special beat from an old Alejandro song, so I'd know it was her. Then we'd eat and catch up with our days. She understood that I needed some space, so she always left me soon after dinner. It had been a grueling time in Los Angeles—I slept late every day.

After a week, I went to my studio to do some painting. It seemed like a good distraction, and it really was the reason

I'd come back. But where I'd once found solace in painting pottery, I felt nothing but emptiness. The pictures I'd painted in Chile made me feel wonderful, but the pottery left me drained. I gave up and went back to my apartment.

That night, wallowing in self-pity and day-old take-out containers of Chinese food, I heard Wanda's knock. I wasn't in the mood for a visit, but I let her in anyway. This time, she had two other people with her: Karen and Hale. They burst in with hugs all around and pried me out of my stupor. Seeing them again really helped raise my spirits.

Alejandro needed me back, they insisted. He'd orchestrated this intervention and flown them out to get me. Even Wanda joined in, demanding that I get up off my ass and get on the plane. They wouldn't take "no" for an answer, and insisted that I had to do it now.

How could I refuse? I missed Alejandro terribly and craved his company. So I agreed to go with them. What else was I doing?

I wrapped myself in a hoodie and dark glasses so I could make it through the sea of paparazzi camped outside my building. Karen had a limousine waiting, which took us to the airport. From there, we boarded a charter flight directly to Los Angeles. As soon as we landed, Udo ushered me into a waiting limousine, with Alejandro inside.

The two of us hugged with the desperation of shipwrecked sailors who'd found land. We were so hungry for each other that we made love during the limousine ride home. After that, we talked and caught up easily, once again comfortable with each other.

Alejandro proposed to me that night, down on one knee in the traditional style. He told me that he loved me and needed me, that he hadn't been able to sleep since I'd left. I felt very much the same and told him so. I'd never loved anyone more deeply, and I hadn't been able to sleep without him, either.

I was stunned. I'd been inhaling those Internet fumes so much that I expected him to move on while I was in New York. But Alejandro proved them wrong.

To top things off, my engagement ring was enormous, an immense diamond, set with smaller ones all around. I felt a little embarrassed wearing it, but Alejandro pointed out that something like this was expected of him. When the world's most eligible bachelor got engaged, the ring needed to be world-class, too.

Naturally, the media went ballistic. Ivory, now a good friend, came over every day to help me plan a wedding that would be worthy of this world-famous man. I'd become the envy of every woman on Earth, so I owed them a spectacular event. Ivory seemed to enjoy helping me navigate through the world of celebrity. Although I really didn't want any of it, I definitely did need her help, and she loved playing wedding planner for the musician she'd helped make famous.

Curiously, after getting engaged to Alejandro, the media became much nicer to me. I'd worried that we'd get inundated with even more trashy attention, but our engagement had the opposite effect. I was now honored as the woman who had conquered Alejandro, a never-before-accomplished feat. Suddenly, most of the stories about me were positive. Still, whenever we needed some laughs, Karen could always find a tabloid story or two claiming that I was pregnant with Alejandro's three-headed alien love child.

With George out of the picture, Alejandro needed a new business manager, and he wondered if I wanted the job. But I was already going to spend my life with him, at home and on the road. I didn't want to work for him, too. Besides, I vastly preferred painting to accounting. So I turned that particular offer down.

Interestingly, Hale asked for the job. He and Karen were already deeply involved, so he saw it as an opportunity to spend more time with the woman he loved. It also gave him the chance to go straight, or as Bea would have put it, to pack in the racket. He was ready for that, too. Alejandro agreed to let him have the job, especially since he knew Hale could never do anything illegal while I was watching. Apparently, Alejandro was starting to grow fond of con artists, especially those who were on his side.

So Hale and Karen eloped in Las Vegas, and Alejandro and I got married six months later. I moved into his amazing estate and settled right in. Life with him was an endless string of parties and tours, and we enjoyed every minute. Women still swarmed him continuously, but he never treated them as anything more than excited fans, and he resisted all of their attempts to muscle me out of the way. Sure, I had to fight them off occasionally, but I now had my own bodyguard, who helped me with those chores. And these women's smarmy comments didn't bother me, either —Alejandro was mine and I was his. We made that clear every day.

Wanda finally moved out to Los Angeles, too, just last week. She opened a new branch of her shop. I already had an amazing studio at Alejandro's place, so it was easy to keep her supplied. She also started selling my paintings. In what could be called an even more impressive con game, my art had become surprisingly valuable. As Alejandro's wife, I could command enormous sums. At least according to Wanda.

So my life settled down to a routine of painting, ignoring paparazzi, and having entirely too much fun with Alejandro, night and day.

I guess Los Angeles isn't such a bad place, after all.

About the Author

After completing my *Westerley* trilogy, I didn't have to think very hard about what to write about next: rock and roll! It was an obvious choice, because I was once the lead singer of a California garage band. Of course, the things that happen in my books never happened to me, but it was fun to pretend.

After a lifetime of reading general fiction, I discovered romance at age 59 and fell in love with it. Now I fill my time reading and writing romance novels.

Life in Northern California is full of surprises, including my novels. I have been happily married for over thirty years, and we have raised two wonderful children. I honestly wouldn't trade places with anyone else, living or dead, real or imagined.

—Sage